# The Puppet Master

### By
### Abigail Osborne

First published in 2016 by Abigail Osborne Publishing.

Re Published in 2017 by Bloodhound Books.

www.bloodhoundbooks.com


Print ISBN: 978-1-912175-75-8

*For my Aunty Gillian*

# Part One

# Chapter One
## Present Day – 2018
### Billie

Billie stole down the street avoiding all eye contact and people. Once a week, on Sunday, she braved the world to visit the bookstore not far from her flat. Once Upon a Time had thousands of books and a quaint little cafe; it was her haven.

"Same as usual, love?" asked the elderly lady at the till.

"Err … yes, please," whispered Billie, blushing bright red. She focused on her tray, the same hot chocolate and sandwich she had each time. She didn't really like the sandwich but she felt silly just buying a drink.

"That's five pounds fifty then please, love." Avoiding her gaze, Billie handed over the money she had already got out in preparation.

"Thank you," Billie said, and scuttled off to the same table by the window that she always had. She liked this table because she could look out of the window at people hurrying down their way through their lives no one stopped or took their time any more. But if she didn't fancy that, she could people watch in the cafe. It was a small, intimate place with a few tables and lots of quirky signs dotted around. Her favourite was 'Do not meddle in the affairs of dragons, for you are crunchy and good with ketchup'.

Today, she watched two women through the gaps in her long red hair, shielding her gaze. They were at the table next to her, chattering about the possible affair that one of their husbands may or may not be having. She enjoyed these little snippets of society.

Some days she felt a pang of loneliness. No one would ever sit at this table with her. But mostly that was a relief.

It wasn't safe. People were dangerous.

She looked over at the lady who had served her. Her face was wrinkly with laughter lines, her smile wide and welcoming. White hair bounced cheerfully on her head as she moved. But Billie knew that appearances were deceiving. Nearly everyone wore a mask. No one was themselves any more, too afraid at being judged. Everyone had to fit in with what was 'normal'.

Billie could just make out the lady's name badge. Martha could easily be hiding something. She could be stealing children and cooking them just like the witch in *Hansel and Gretel*.

She shook her head trying to dislodge the feeling. It was no good thinking like this. It would only trigger memories of her past.

She went back to eating her food, surreptitiously watching the people around her. She could live through their lives. People watching was much safer than making actual connections.

At another table, a mother was helping her son with a jigsaw. She watched them and allowed herself to become absorbed in their lives. She wondered what the woman did. She was dressed haphazardly and appeared to be a full-time mum. The boy looked happy and content. Billie hoped his mum would keep him safe. That she wouldn't abandon him when things got tough. That she wouldn't put herself first.

She was distracted from her thoughts by a man who had entered the cafe. She watched as he made the rookie mistake of ordering his food without checking to see if there was a table free. For a moment, his black-clad body stiffened as he realised his mistake. But then, instead of putting his head down and scurrying away as she would have, he moved over to her table. Billie wanted to look away as he stared down at her with his unusual pale-green eyes, which were in perfect symmetry to his mouth. His stance exuded a sense of restless energy.

For the first time she could remember, she wasn't scared. He stood there, devilishly handsome, and she was captivated.

A lock of his wavy blond hair fell casually on his forehead as he spoke.

"Can I sit here?" Billie knew words weren't going to come, so she just nodded.

He was calm, as if sitting next to strangers was normal. She couldn't stop fidgeting, her eyes not knowing where to look.

*Why was he sitting here?*

He sat down and looked at her intently; his eyes were pale and unreadable. But then, as if she had passed some test, a smile broke across his face.

"So, how are you?" he said.

She didn't reply straightaway, thrown by his familiar tone as if they knew each other.

"Err … Fine … Do I know you?" Blushing from head to toe she wracked her brain, trying to remember if he worked with her. She made a point of not talking to anyone outside work, and just kept her head down.

"Nope, never seen you before, just thought it would be rude not to talk," he said. His smile widened and his face changed; a light came into his eyes and her pounding heartbeat lowered. She realised she was staring and quickly lowered her head.

"Okay," she murmured into her shaking hands. She focused on them to calm herself. She'd always had fat fingers, but her fingernails were nice. Now she was grateful she'd managed to kick the habit of biting them.

"Are you texting someone for help? Is that why you keep looking down?" he said.

She looked up instantly, her face feeling redder still.

"I'm going to have to work on my image. I thought I'd mastered looking sweet and innocent but, from your reaction, I don't think it's working." Despite herself, she smiled. Her stomach was fluttering.

"I don't have a mobile."

"How curious, are you also one of those loons that doesn't have a television?" He visibly shuddered. "I'd rather sit on the floor if that's the case. I don't trust people who don't watch TV; it's unhealthy."

She chuckled quietly, still unable to look him in the eye. "I have a TV."

"Is it black and white?"

"No, it's a regular TV."

"Phew, that's a relief, you had me worried then."

She laughed as he flopped back in his chair in exaggerated relief.

It was strange. Although she was wary and uncomfortable, it wasn't as bad as it usually was.

She remembered her first week at her current job. She was staring out of the window, grateful to have a window seat, when one of her male colleagues came over to her.

"Hi, I'm Andy, you must be Billie?" His hand reached out to shake hers and she froze. She stared at it. The hand loomed over her and began to magnify. She could see every hair on it. His hand was massive and all she could think about was how easily it could crush hers.

Instead of shaking it, she got up and ran to the ladies' bathroom. She went in a stall and was sick. From then on she never spoke to anyone unless she absolutely had to and no one spoke to her. She heard the muttered rumours that people said about her, but she didn't listen to them. The only people she talked to regularly were customers on the phone, and they were only perfunctory conversations.

With the shock of this man's arrival at her table wearing off, she was surprised how little she felt intimidated by him. Alarm bells had begun to ring in her head as soon as he had started talking to her but his relaxed manner and humour had put her at ease. She couldn't remember the last time she had laughed with someone, let alone spoken comfortably.

Life had kicked Billie down. The only way she could exist safely in this world was to close herself off from the rest of humanity.

People were dangerous.

She had lived alone, with this mantra, for the last five years since leaving university. She had thought that she no longer felt loneliness, but this stranger was stirring feelings she didn't know still existed.

"Although we still need to discuss the phone thing ... I've never met someone who doesn't have a phone. How do people get in touch with you?"

"I have no one that needs to get in touch with me."

"No one? I don't believe that. What about your parents?"

She sucked in a painful breath and was reminded why she didn't like to talk. People were nosey. They walked around quizzing people about their personal lives, believing they had the right to ask whatever they wanted. Life felt like one big interview and Billie hated it.

"I don't have any, and before you ask, no siblings or any other relations; just me." She hoped her sharp tone would make it clear that she did not want to talk about this anymore.

"Aw. Do you want to talk about it?"

She shook her head and added, "No."

He was quiet for a moment, brow furrowed. Then his face brightened.

"What about work? They have to be able to contact you ...?"

"I have a neighbour; she has a phone that my work can call."

"You know you could just get a phone, don't you?"

"I don't want one."

"Why?"

She floundered. How could she explain that such a simple question would require her life history to answer?

This was the most she'd spoken with anyone for a long time. His light tone and handsome smile had her mesmerized. She was considering telling him everything. She'd never told anyone the whole story and, until now, she hadn't known she wanted to.

She realised she hadn't answered him and she panicked. He must have seen it on her face because he changed the subject.

"So, can I know your name, or would you prefer crazy, beautiful, anti-phone lady?" The word beautiful echoed in her head. She felt sick. He was just like the rest. She got up quickly, sloshing his coffee on the table.

"I need to go, sorry." She ran to the door and out of the cafe. Trying hard to beat down the memory of the last time someone had called her beautiful.

# Adam

Adam rushed into the bookshop at breakneck speed. He hadn't finished the article for his fortnightly column: 'Bizarre things to do in the West Midlands'.

The bookshop was his last hope of making the deadline. He hoped he would find some inspiration for content as this week he hadn't felt like leaving his flat. His father had informed him that Uncle Eric had lost yet another job, and couldn't afford to continue living in an apartment in Windermere, his pension just wouldn't stretch. His uncle had recently moved to Bromsgrove to be closer to Adam and his father but he was struggling. Adam knew his father would not dream of helping out his older brother so he was worried.

He looked around the shop, shaking the negative thoughts from his head; he needed to get this story in. There was a vacancy coming up at the paper and he was desperate to get into hardcore journalism instead of being a columnist.

He had enjoyed doing the column at first because it gave him the opportunity to do things he was never allowed while growing up.

After his mother died, his father lost his will to live. Adam's life centred around navigating his father's moods and taking care of him. The column had made up for that. But now he was ready to take the next step. His column was a step on the ladder of an over-saturated, cut-throat industry, but he had no intention of staying there.

Having found a book that contained enough details for Adam to use and make it sound authentic, he decided to go to the cafe in the bookshop.

Hunger was gnawing at his stomach. The cafe was a bit expensive but the waitresses were hot, and they did a great BLT. He was busy staring at the sizable assets of one of the waitresses when he realised he'd not checked if there was anywhere for him to sit. Luckily, he spotted a small redhead sitting alone at a table for two. He was about to walk over when her familiar face stopped him in his tracks. He knew this girl. Hers was a face he would never forget. She was a liar and a homewrecker.

As he walked towards her, a plan formulated in his mind. His instinct for a story was awakened and he knew he had the opportunity of a lifetime. This could be his ticket to a better career and, more importantly, he could get justice.

As he got to her table, and as soon as she realised his intention to join her, a flush spread across her cheeks. She looked at him with wariness in her emerald eyes, framed by ruby red hair that contrasted with her porcelain skin. She looked ethereal, fragile.

He took in the black dress that defined her shapely curves and sat down. He knew she was uncomfortable with his presence by the stilted answers she gave to his questions and the fact she barely looked at him. His editor, John, was always saying that Adam was going to make it some day because he had a way with people. He could sense enough about a person to know how to work them. With her, he sensed that she had perfected the appropriate rebuffs so she wouldn't have to interact with anyone. So, he made sure to wrong-foot her.

He did not expect to find that behind her faint smile was a touch of sadness. He would not be swayed by this, though. He knew that the air of fragility and loneliness was a mask. She was a girl who could and already had destroyed lives. No, he would not squander this chance.

He felt anger burning inside him as he thought about what she had done. But he knew he needed to harness that anger and turn it into determination.

Taking a deep breath, he turned his charm-dial up and decided to take advantage of this opportunity. He knew this girl had wrecked lives, and he was going to get her story. He just needed for her to trust him enough to tell it. That meant getting through the barriers she had expertly constructed around herself.

He felt sick with every smile he flashed her. She had caused untold damage, and yet she was here, sitting in a cafe, living with none of the repercussions her victims had to endure. Adam decided it was time that changed.

# Chapter Two

## Diary Entry

I watch her as she walks from the street into the estate full of corporate offices. I am parked in the car park I made sure I woke early so I could get this exact spot. It gives me the best view of her. She is a creature of habit. I'd wager that her foot lands in the exact same part of each paving slab every day. While I wait for her to turn up, I am entertained by the parking wars going on around me. I don't mind waiting. I enjoy the anticipation. Today she is wearing the same black trousers, which are far too big for her, with a matching, over-sized black top that sticks out from her black raincoat. On a dark night she would be invisible.

Her head is down; I sometimes wonder if it is stuck like that. She never makes eye contact with anyone and I wonder if it is the weight of her shame that makes her hang her head and keeps her body hunched. I stare at her so intently it is a wonder she can't feel the heat from my gaze. I assess every part of her. She's no open book and my eyes bore into her, longing to penetrate her skin, trying to see a flicker of what she might be feeling. All I can tell is what everyone else would see if they bothered to study her. She is unhappy; trying to blend into the background wherever she goes. She is timid and purposefully keeps everyone at arm's-length. I cannot contain the joy I feel at having this knowledge. I feed off it. It rejuvenates me knowing that she is suffering after all the damage she has done. Now I will get justice.

Each floor of the building is visible through the large windows that cover one side. It seems to be a modern preference now, opening buildings to the world. There is no privacy any more. I can just make out her moving form.

I couldn't believe my luck when I realised that I could see part of her cubicle from the car park. I wait until I see her sit down, back facing the window, then I drive off. She's made it so easy for me.

Her flat is a five-minute drive from here and I leisurely pull up in front of it. As I unlock the door to her home, I snigger at how someone so fearful could live somewhere with such pitiful security. A cup of tea, a well spun lie and a smile to the friendly landlady who lives in the first floor flat, and I was given a spare key.

I walk into the studio apartment and sit in the solitary black armchair. I see a cat dart under the bed. I feel angry as I look around and see how cosy and tidy the flat is. She, who has ruined so many lives, has a warm and comfortable place to live. It isn't right; she should suffer for what she has done. She has ruined everything.

I breathe in deeply, forcing my righteous anger down. I will make her pay. She will feel the pain that she has caused me. I get up from the chair and explore; my mind filling with possible ways to make her suffer the most.

# Billie

Billie sat on her worn, black armchair, tapping her foot constantly against the small coffee table. It was her only other piece of furniture, apart from her bed in the corner of the room and her mismatched bookcases sagging under the product of her obsession with reading.

When she had returned home yesterday, Mrs Kaye had popped over to see if the cooker had been fixed. Billie hadn't really been listening because something was nagging in the back of her mind. She felt like something wasn't right, or that she'd forgotten to do something. But she tried to ignore it and concentrate on what Mrs Kaye was saying.

"He was such a lovely gentleman," she said.

"What are you talking about, Mrs Kaye?" Billie asked.

"The electrician, dear. Keep up." Sending her a sharp irritated look.

"I didn't need an electrician. He was in this flat?" As soon as she said it, it clicked. The tea towel was folded up in a perfect square on the draining board. And Bobby's food dish was on the other side of the front door. The more she looked, she noticed lots of things had been moved from where they should have been.

"Mrs Kaye, why on earth did you let him in the flat without my permission?"

"Well, you don't have a phone, dear. And as I was telling you, he was such a lovely gentleman."

"But I didn't need an electrician. Why was this man in my flat? Who was he?" She was starting to panic now.

*Who the hell had come into her flat and messed about with her stuff?*

14

"Calm down, dear, there must have been a misunderstanding. Stop acting like someone burgled you. If you'd met Jim you would know that. Wouldn't even let me make him a drink, he insisted on making me one. Hark at that," Mrs Kaye said, as if that settled the matter.

"But he's moved things around in the flat. Look," Billie pointed at the tea towel, "that wasn't there this morning, I keep it in the drawer."

Mrs Kaye gave Billie a pointed look.

"I'm sure you've just forgotten that you put it there. What on earth would Jim want with *your* tea towel?" She left the flat, grumbling to herself.

Billie felt stuck, in a flat that was now unsafe. She was filled with fear and felt violated. This was her space. Normally she loved her little flat. When she looked around it she saw safety.

There had been a stage in her life when she thought she wouldn't make it to her twenty-first birthday. Yet somehow, she had, and now here she was in her own private space that she shared only with her beautiful cat, Bobby. He was under the coffee table and he kept taking a swipe at her foot his way of telling her to leave his table alone.

She couldn't help fidgeting. She wanted to leave; go outside and clear her head. But the only place she felt safe was the cafe and she didn't want to risk another encounter with the man she had met earlier.

The bookshop had become part of her routine. It was somewhere to go when her flat became too confined, and it broke up the monotony of her life. She would go to the bookcases and choose whose life she was going to live vicariously through that week.

With no family to surround herself with, the silence and loneliness seeped into her very bones. Ironically, she searched for books that would give her a substitute family, an improved version of what she had had. But being fictional, they were distanced enough from her to prevent her from feeling the truly devastating pain that only families can inflict. Books were the best form of therapy according to her neighbour, Mrs Kaye.

Mrs Kaye lived in the flat across from Billie's on the first floor. Billie was unable to get rid of her, no matter how hard she tried. When Billie had moved into the flat no one had warned her about the crazy old lady across the hall. Billie remembered the first time she had answered the door to her. Mrs Kaye had walked in, leaning heavily on her stick, her straw-like hair in erratic wisps around her face. She had looked fragile and frail but, once sat with a cup of tea in her hand, she'd dictated to Billie where everything should go.

"I really don't think your bookcases should go there. Be a dear and move them over to the other side."

Since that day Mrs Kaye had decided that they would be friends. Billie was trying to stay away from people and, at first, she was worried that Mrs Kaye had an ulterior motive. But one night a while later, she realised that maybe Mrs Kaye wasn't so bad.

It was a Tuesday night; Billie had woken up sweating and crying. Her dream had been so vivid. She couldn't stop shaking and was on the floor, beside her bed, terrified. A knock at the door stole all the breath from her lungs. It rang out through the flat, interrupting the silence that only darkness can bring. She thought she might die from fear until she heard Mrs Kaye's muffled voice.

"Let me in, dear," said Mrs Kaye.

For a minute Billie was convinced she was going to hurt her. The dreams, fresh in her mind, warped what she knew about Mrs Kaye. "I'm not leaving until you let me in, dear." Without options Billie hesitantly opened the door. Mrs Kaye's hazel eyes softened as she looked at Billie's tear-stained face.

"Is everything okay, dear?" she asked in a gentle voice.

"I'm fine."

"Well, forgive me for saying so, but you don't look it. I heard you screaming." She took Billie's arm and led her to her bed. "Why don't we just sit here for a minute until you feel better?"

she said. In the quiet, Billie could hear her ragged breathing, the grip of her nightmare still clinging to her. Mrs Kaye had sensed this and rubbed her back in soothing circles. Her first touch made Billie's body lock, but the repetitive movement and the calming presence of the elderly lady relaxed her.

They sat there for a while in silence before Mrs Kaye got up and made Billie a 'nice cup of tea'.

"Feeling better now, dear?"

When Billie nodded, Mrs Kaye got up and left reminding Billie that she was only across the hall. Since then Billie had hesitantly returned Mrs Kaye's friendship.

Reminding herself of that night and the nightmares she had gone through, she knew she was stronger than this. She'd lived through the past and come out fighting.

The bookshop nearby was the only place she felt comfortable. She'd tried to go to a bookshop in the city centre and it had ended up with her in hospital.

She was walking down the street when someone had accidently knocked her into a man. She would have fallen to the floor but he had gripped her arms tightly and righted them both. The feel of his grasp on her arm triggered her panic. Her lungs had closed tight and she'd had to force herself to breathe. People's voices had surrounded her, clogging her brain, when what she'd needed to do was concentrate on breathing. Hands touched her, pulling one way and another. Blackness closed in. That is the last thing she remembered.

She woke up in a hospital bed. When they discharged her, she'd had to find her own way home. Never again had she ventured further than a couple of streets away from the flat.

When she left the Lake District to go to university, she promised herself that she would never hide again, and she would be free to live her life as she chose. But it hadn't been as easy as she had thought it would be.

She spent most of her time seeing danger around every corner. But she couldn't stay inside; she needed to get out. After university, she stayed in Worcester. It began to feel like home to her she knew it well enough to feel safe. Well, as safe as she ever could.

Mind made up, Billie walked down the road from her block of flats. She had said a curt hello to Mrs Kaye, still furious with her, as she had left the building.

It was a crisp day, but the sun was shining, which thawed the chill from the air. She liked days like this. The air felt fresh, and the sun accentuated the green in the park that she passed to get to the high street.

The high street was just one road with shops, cafes and restaurants on either side. The cobbled road between the shops was different shades of grey, some of which sparkled in the sunlight. More significantly, there were very few people. This suited Billie.

She kept her head down, only looking up when she passed the green expanse of the park she couldn't resist the beauty of it.

Billie had spent a lot of time walking in that park. The oval shaped lake was flanked all the way around by a pathway that diverted every now and then through the trees. She was tempted to take another long walk around it today. There was nothing like seeing delicate flowers, diverse shades of green and hearing the chirping of birds. They put everything into perspective. They reminded her that the world was much bigger than her and the trauma she had experienced. She went there whenever she felt the darkness of her past overwhelming her She hoped its beauty and serene setting would drive out the darkness. But it was just that bit too cold today, and she knew she would only be going there to avoid the bookshop and the man who might be there.

Bravely walking past the green she approached the bookshop. She was tempted to remain in the doorway; the heating from the air conditioning was blasting down and warming her from head to toe. The idea was disturbed by an elderly lady with a walking stick who whacked the back of her legs and told her to get out of the way.

She scooted towards the cafe, so scared that she would see him she didn't dare look up; she navigated by the flooring and only looked up when she arrived at the counter.

Picking up a tray, she made herself a Hot Chocolate at the machine before spending a minute or so assessing which was the biggest piece of chocolate cake.

Finding her usual table free, Billie looked around the room from her seat in the corner and breathed a sigh of relief. Her routine was back in play.

She sometimes wished that she didn't feel this terrified about forming relationships. But it was better this way. She was content with her life. Other people only brought her pain or trouble, or both. She enjoyed watching everyone in the cafe for half an hour and then went in search of her next literary journey.

Billie decided to go in the park on her way back from the bookshop. She felt happy and rather proud of herself. Her uneventful time had bolstered her confidence.

She had a bag with two new books in it which she switched to her left hand as she opened the gate to the park. She breathed in the cool breeze as it swept towards her, enveloping her in a greeting.

As she walked around the lake, along the small brown path, she tried to locate the birds she could hear merrily chirping in the trees, but green leaves camouflaged them. She rounded the top of the lake and began on the path that would take her round the other side, revelling in thinking only about her surroundings. It wasn't the biggest lake, but it was still lovely watching the ducks swim on it, speaking their own secret language and doing whatever ducks do. This snapshot of nature invigorated her, and her consciousness got swept away as she became absorbed in the magic of nature.

Noises up ahead disrupted her revelry. She could see three teenagers further along the path, blocking it. They were talking to each other; one was on a bike. She thought about going back the way she had come but it was too late, all three of them had swivelled their heads and were looking at her. They are just boys, she told herself as she began to walk towards them. The one with the bike was blocking the path and there was no way past him. She took a deep breath and put on her best 'I'm irritated' face, and asked the boys to move.

"Can I get through, please?"

"Don't you wanna talk? We love talkin' to pretty girls," said the boy on the bike. He looked around at his friends, seeking assurance that he had said something funny. The other two laughed on command as he returned to leering at her.

Billie felt sick inside but she was trying to hold herself together. She was nervous. The matching baseball caps on backwards combined with chavy tracksuits, which shouted their need to be cool, made them look like children. However, there was no doubt the three of them could quite easily overpower her. She tried not to overreact; they were probably all talk. Refusing to cower, she drew herself up straight.

"No, thanks. Now get out of the way before I call the police." Thankfully, her voice didn't shake the way her body did. The boy nearest to her began to laugh.

"Feisty one, you are," he said.

She gave up reasoning with them and edged around the boy closest to her until she was in front of the one with the bike. She'd been through so much more; it was frustrating that she was allowing these boys to scare her.

One of them spoke from behind her. "I think she likes you, Marv."

He must have closed the gap between them as he felt closer now. She could feel his breath on her neck.

The boy in front of her smirked. Thoroughly enjoying himself.

"Oh darling, I'd take you right here if you asked," he said.

Hands came from behind her, grabbing her arms, immobilising her. His fingers dug in so hard that she wanted to cry out in pain. She was on the verge of having a full-blown panic attack. It was getting harder to breathe, as if someone was clutching her by the throat as well as her arms. As her throat tightened it became increasingly difficult to draw breath. The pounding of her heart was so loud in her ears she wondered momentarily if it had moved into her head. She could hear herself wheezing and tried to force air into her lungs. Her panic seemed to be encouraging them.

"She's pantin' with need, Marv. Put her out of her misery," said one of the boys.

Billie was thrown to the floor by someone behind her and she berated her body for being so weak.

The threats and the aggression were triggering memories she'd never revisited. Her lips tingled and black splotches clouded her vision.

"Stop!" roared a voice from somewhere behind her. It was too deep to belong to one of the boys. She didn't have any energy to turn and observe her rescuer. Without looking up, she felt the boys turn around. The looming shadows had moved away from her. She took the chance to curl into a ball and focus on her breathing. That became nearly impossible as Marv, on the bike, rode over her while trying to get to his friends. Unfortunately for them both, she was on the ground and had become lodged between his front and back tyres. She heard pounding footsteps getting closer.

In his desperation, Marv got back on his bike and forced the tyre over her body. It dragged her a short distance until it gained enough momentum to drive over her. She cried out in agony. The shock jump-started her lungs as her mind focused on the waves of agony coursing through her. She closed her eyes and waited for the next attack.

Maybe she was better off dead. Her body had felt too much pain. She tried to sink into the brown dirt of the path, wanting to disappear, to escape from the world and the pulses of pain that her body was suffering.

Soft hands took hold of her face but she cringed away. She couldn't stand to be touched; she just wanted to be left alone. Her body was shaking with the fear of what was to come next. She didn't dare open her eyes in case one of the boys had come back to finish what they'd started.

"Are you okay?" a male voice asked as she began to hyperventilate. "Hey, calm down, I won't hurt you. I promise." The softness of his voice and the gentleness of his hands on her face calmed her enough that she cautiously opened her eyes. They widened in shock when she saw it was the man from the bookshop. Of course it was. She wasn't lucky enough to have a stranger rescue her.

# Adam

When Billie ran out on him he could have kicked himself. He had pushed too hard. As soon as he had called her beautiful, a voice in his head spoke up: *well that was stupid*. It was like ice had come crashing down from the sky, reinforcing her defences, and he knew that he'd lost his opportunity. He had sat there, trying to ignore the old ladies at the next table who were giving him their very best 'how could you?' frown. He wouldn't give up, though. When he first noticed her she had been lost in thought, her head tilted to the sky, shoulders relaxed. Familiarity making her comfortable. He figured she would end up returning to the bookshop.

On what felt like the seventieth day of hanging around the bookshop to no avail, he was politely cornered by the manager to ask if there was a problem, as a member of staff had reported his constant appearances. He hurriedly left the bookshop, red-faced, and looked around as if to find some inspiration for his next move. Then he spotted the back of her head as she was walking towards the park across the road. He blinked repeatedly to make sure it wasn't a mirage.

Before he knew what he was doing, he was jogging to catch up with her. He slowed his pace as he got nearer, realising he needed to compose himself. Each time he saw her, his anger flared. It took every ounce of self-control to be nice to her. Her small stature belied the evil nature that hid inside. He needed to quash feelings like that if he was going to get her story. He made the mistake of going in too strong with her last time, he needed to be careful. Work out how to get past the walls of steel she had built around herself. He knew she wouldn't give anything away easily. Those with something to hide rarely do.

Taking deep breaths, mentally trying to visualise his anger and expel it like he'd read somewhere, he continued to follow her around the lake in the park. His eyes rested on a family of ducks. Smiling, he let their innocence fill his mind. He envied their simple lives with only basic needs. Nature had always made him feel less alone throughout his life. He'd love to be a duck, then his parents wouldn't go off getting drunk.

As he rounded the corner he heard taunting laughter. In the distance he saw a young lad, track-suited, standing on a push bike, flanked by two others who were similarly dressed. The three youths were bearing down on Billie. Even from this distance he could see she was shaking and terrified. She had no escape and they looked like all their Christmases had come at once. For a moment, Adam felt a flicker of delight that she was going to suffer. But when one of the goons stepped forward and roughly grabbed her by the arms, he ran towards them without making a conscious decision. He yelled out, hoping to scare them off. He saw Billie being thrown to the ground; effortlessly, like she was a ragdoll. At the same time, the one on the bike moved towards her as if to run her over with his bike. It was all happening so fast and he knew he wasn't going to get to her in time. In a moment of crazed desperation Adam took off his shoe and threw it towards the boy, hoping to distract him. It didn't work. He ran faster and finally reached her. It turns out that hoping for someone to suffer, and then actually seeing it realised, was not something he could handle.

# Billie

"Can you get up?" he asked. She wasn't sure. Agony reverberated through her body. With his help, she carefully eased herself up to a sitting position. As he kneeled next to her she noticed his dark blue jeans were covered in dirt from the path. She tried to focus on that instead of the pain.

"Are you hurt? Should I call an ambulance? I saw that idiot drive over you on his bike."

"I don't know … everything hurts." She moved to get up, but after a few seconds her legs gave away. Strong hands caught her around her waist, gently lowering her back down to the ground.

"Woah! Slow down."

"I'm fine. I just want to go home."

"Okay, that's fine. Just let me help you."

"No!" she shouted at him. The shock and pain didn't stop her from realising that it would be a terrible mistake. What was he even doing here? Of all the people to be in this park, and just at the time she needed someone. It was too much of a coincidence. "I don't need your help. I will be okay. Thank you, but you've done enough."

His pale-green eyes stared earnestly into hers. "I won't hurt you," he said. The sincerity was evident in his eyes and his voice, but she must have looked dubious as he continued, "You need to call the police. We should do it here but you might be more comfortable doing it from home? If you don't want me to help you back, I will call the police myself and they can take you. Or is there someone else I can call? Either way, I'm not leaving you alone. I'm sure those yobs are long gone, but it's not worth the risk."

His tone was stubborn and she knew resistance was futile. The mention of police stopped her heart. She didn't trust them. Just the thought of them threatened to unlock a door to memories that were scarier than the thought of this strange man taking her home. She just needed to get home and then convince him that she was okay. That way she could shut the world out again.

"Don't call the police yet. I just want to go home."

"Will you let me help you?"

"Yes." Only one word, but it was the hardest answer to give. Letting someone into her home was a terrifying prospect.

His warm body, as he wrapped his arms around her to raise her to her feet, reminded her that she was cold and she shivered violently. He went to carry her but she drew the line there. Instead, she hobbled next to him. Wincing as she felt her jeans rub against the myriad of scratches hidden beneath them. She had her arm on his, using him for support. Muscles rippled in his arm as he supported her weight. She blushed at the intimacy. It had been a long time since she had last voluntarily touched a man touched anyone for that matter. He was so careful with her, his attentive gaze caught every wince like it was a signal that she needed to stop and catch her breath. She was lucky he was there, really, as it would have taken hours to get home alone. However, she needed to find out if this was the world's biggest coincidence or not. Instinct said it was not. These thoughts made her angry that she was letting him help her. She didn't know the first thing about him.

"I don't know your name," she said. She had stopped walking.

"Adam." He didn't look like an Adam. "Am I allowed to know yours? I don't think you're in a state to run off this time." He smiled as she blushed. Recalling her embarrassing attempt to leave when he had asked her last time.

"Sorry about that. It's Billie," she admitted reluctantly.

"Hmm … I prefer crazy non-phone lady, but I'm sure there will be lots of people with that name, so you're right, Billie is better." Despite her concerns she chuckled at his attempt at humour.

He said the strangest things. She noted that he had dropped the word 'beautiful' from his nickname for her. Very perceptive. She didn't know how that made her feel. She was about to ask him what he was doing in the park, but a bright-red sock with footballs on it caught her attention.

"Where's your shoe?" she asked. He looked down and sighed.

"Oh yeah. I threw it at those chavs. I don't know what I was thinking. I thought it might scare them away but I have lousy aim and it went straight into the lake." He didn't look remotely abashed to be walking around wearing one shoe, or that he had tried to throw it at someone. He merely smiled at her. She bit down the laughter trying to escape. He stopped at a crossroads and waited patiently for her to tell him which way to go. She cringed when the grubby, grey block of flats came into view. Irrationally, she wanted to apologise for living in such a dump. She had to lean on him heavily as they took the steps to her flat. She was shivering badly from the cold. The side of her body that was pressed against him was leeching his body heat, but it wasn't enough. The shock was wearing off and she was becoming painfully aware of her injuries. Her hand held her side underneath her clothes, though it did nothing to ease the pain.

She motioned for him to stop at her door. A brass number ten was the only feature of the scuffed, dark-green door. She gasped. It had just occurred to her that she didn't have her bags. As if reading her mind, Adam passed her the handbag he had been holding on his wrist. She could see the white bag of books as well. It made her feel strange. She'd forgotten what it was like to be able to rely on someone other than herself. Conflicting emotions jumbled around her mind, exhausting her. She was so ready for tomorrow to start. This day needed to end.

She swayed slightly as she rummaged in her handbag and his arm moved from her shoulder to around her waist to hold her up. His touch caused her heart to thump so loud it was like elephants trampling in her ears. She was wary of him, but she also felt safe with him. How dangerous could a man wearing one shoe be?

Maybe when she'd been thrown to the ground she'd hit her head and lost her common sense. She found her keys, opened the door and they both went inside. Although Billie was relieved that she was a relatively tidy person, she still felt embarrassed as he took in the studio flat. Her whole world was this room. It was her safety net. She had never let anyone in this space before except Mrs Kaye, but she wasn't given a choice in that. It rankled that Adam was here. Adam. He really didn't look like an Adam.

Her cat looked around from his position, swinging like George out of *George of the Jungle* from her curtains. Deciding he'd greet them, he abseiled down with his claws. She inwardly cringed as he gauged new holes in the cream curtains. When Adam didn't comment on the fact her entire house was in one room, apart from the bathroom, she moved over to the bed. She thought about the armchair but she was so exhausted from the events of the day that only her bed would do.

"Have you got a medical kit?"

"I don't think I need one." She lay down on the bed and closed her eyes. "I just need to sleep. I feel like I've been hit by a bus."

Adam went red and fidgeted but eventually voiced what it was that he wanted to say.

"We need to be one hundred per cent sure. I don't want to have wasted a perfectly good shoe." She didn't have the strength to argue and maybe, after all this time, she wanted to be looked after. He took her silence as an agreement and moved over to her; kneeling in front of her. She didn't stop him as he slowly lifted her top until he got to the large, nasty looking red mark that the bike wheel had left on her side. Already it was beginning to swell and bruise. Trickles of blood leaked out of a few cuts where the wheel had twisted her skin. As she looked at him, she saw a fury burning in his eyes that brought a tear to her eye. He barely knew her but he had shown more care for her than any of her family ever had. She could feel the protective ice around her heart melting from the heat of his compassion. She knew more than anyone that men could make you feel like the centre of their universe then throw you away once they had got what they wanted. The logical part of her brain was insisting that this was Adam's agenda, that he was no different, but at that moment she simply couldn't believe it.

"I don't think you've broken anything." He got up to go to the bathroom and came back with a wet flannel. He gently washed her side with a tenderness that she didn't know men were capable of. Once finished, he lowered her top and sat back on his knees. "Can I get you some painkillers or something?"

"I can't have any." He shot her a surprised look and she added, "I'll be okay."

"Why can't you? Allergies?" He had answered his own question so she just agreed and then lay back on the bed. It was tiring trying to mask the extent of the pain she felt. She knew that she would need to clean up her legs too, but there was no way that she was doing that in front of him.

Adam took his phone out of his pocket and passed it to her. "You need to call the police." She couldn't face sitting up so she reached out to take the phone even though she had no intention of using it. While she weighed up what she could say to convince him, she couldn't help but notice how the locks of unruly blonde hair that had fallen on to his forehead augmented his handsome features. Why did someone like him even care what happened to someone like her? She was a nobody. Maybe it wasn't even about her. Maybe he was just one of those good people that she had read about but had yet to meet. Maybe she was reading too much into things. She just needed to get him out of there, and her life could go back to normal.

"I don't want to call the police. Nothing happened, you stopped it. I can't even remember what they looked like. There's nothing that they would be able to do. I just need to be more careful and sensible in future. Thank you for all your help, but I just need to rest now." Breathless, she closed her eyes, praying that he would take the hint. She attempted to regulate her breathing so it looked like she was going to sleep. There was no noise or movement from Adam. Her skin prickled at the thought of being watched, but she wasn't brave enough to ask him to leave again. She didn't want to anger or upset him, not when he had been so kind. She couldn't turn and face the other way as the pain radiating from her side was worsening. So she lay there, trying not to contemplate the ridiculousness of the past few hours.

After an age she heard Adam get to his feet. She felt his breath before his lips brushed across her forehead. The gesture both warmed and terrified her. Finally, the front door closed and her lungs began to work again.

She slowly got undressed and assessed the damage done to her whole body. There were a few nasty scrapes on her legs too. Written over her body was proof that the world outside her flat was dangerous, especially the people in it. Isolation was the key to her future. This was a stark reminder of the importance of her limited routine outside. She focused on cleaning up her legs with some antiseptic and not on how much she felt Adam's absence. Reminding herself that although she was grateful to him for helping her, she still hadn't asked him what he was doing in the park in the first place. She needed to make sure she didn't see him again. After all, it was her first meeting with him that had set off this disastrous chain of events. Grimacing with pain she tried to remain reminiscent of the fact that she'd been through worse pain, and seen her body in a worse condition, and had survived.

# Diary Entry

My fury at her has intensified. I can barely contain it when I am near her. When I'm not near her, her image is woven into everything I look at. The girls I pass in the street all look like her. Every laugh that floats on the wind is her laugh. She is causing me to lose control. I can't have it. My need to cause her pain escalated when I saw the spring in her step as she walked from a bookshop. The evil in me reared at the sight of her sheer brazenness. *She is a liar! She needs to pay!* Before I knew what I was doing, I had headed over to three teenagers. Sneers dropped from their faces when they caught sight of the money I had in my hand. I followed stealthily behind them and watched with pleasure as the bitch was stopped by them. They were enjoying it so much I wondered if they'd have done it for free. I breathed in the intoxicating sight of her fear. I watched with pleasure as her face paled and her body began to tremble. That's more like it. I wished it could be me doing it, but there is plenty of time for that. I'm not done making her suffer yet. This will have to do for now. When it is my turn, it will be the end. Her end. As she was flung to the ground, I turned and walked away. There was a spring in my step now.

# Chapter Three

## Adam

Adam stood outside the door of Billie's flat. His eyes bored into the brass number ten; as if it could tell him all he needed to know. It was just male hormones that had kicked in and forced him to protect Billie. He was sure that if it had been any other vulnerable girl he would have felt the same fury. When he'd reached her she was on the ground, weak and broken, and it was horrible to see. His preconceptions about her fled at the unadulterated terror in her eyes. As he had picked her up off the ground he was furious with those kids for taking advantage of a defenceless girl. But he was also angry with her for ruining his straightforward plan. He hated to admit it, but he was worried that he might end up caring for her. Whilst helping her home he had tried hard to remember who she was, and what she had done, but her body had felt so fragile against his. Was it part of her act? He didn't want to admit it, but she confused him. He couldn't correlate the woman who had destroyed lives, with this meek and mild girl. Her strength was surprising, she'd been all but trampled by those lads and she'd stood up and walked home with barely a sound. Nothing he'd seen of her matched what he knew.

He rubbed his temple; the confusion was giving him a headache. He had gone to a shop after he had settled Billie in, and bought a phone. It was nothing special, but it was a way for him to keep in touch with her. He was aware he was crossing a line. A risk. It could scare her off. But he just needed to get her story. In his head he had told himself that he needed to capitalise on her vulnerability before she had time to recover her mental defences towards him. What woman could resist a knight in shining armour? He vaguely remembered his uncle saying something along those lines. He placed the phone in front of Billie's door. He had clumsily wrapped it in some brown paper left over from a delivery. He walked away from the door, repeating over and over again: *she's a home-wrecker, a liar, and evil. Do not be fooled!*

# Billie

Billie dragged herself out of bed, groaning at the pain lancing down her side. She gingerly dragged her black uniform polo top over her head; she had to stop several times to catch her breath.

After the agony of putting on her shoes, she had opened the door to leave and tripped almost landing head first. She caught herself from falling and let out a grunt of agony. She turned to look at what had tried to kill her and saw a box wrapped in brown paper. She stopped for a moment, scared to approach it. She never received any post apart from bills. No one knew where she lived.

She crept towards the parcel slowly; irrational fear making her heart pound in her ears as if she was stood next to a marching band. She picked it up and checked the label. She hoped it had been put there by accident. Her name was scrawled on it, along with a message in the same untidy, slanted handwriting. She wanted to throw it away as her intuition was telling her that nothing good would come of this. But her common sense was overpowered by her curiosity. She tore off the paper and found a box with a mobile phone inside. The screen was lit up inside the box, it had already been opened. Still curious, she opened the box and pulled out the phone. It was unlocked and on the message screen; she read the text:

*Billie, don't freak out, please have this phone – it was my old one. Just keep it on you for emergencies, or when you decide to go walking in the park. Adam.*

She didn't know what to think, once again she was torn. Her fear told her to toss the phone, move away and start over somewhere else, safe and away from people. But a small kernel within her wanted to smile at how caring this gesture was. He didn't know her, but he cared about her safety. However, she had been given presents and gifts and fallen for the 'I care about you' line before. It had nearly cost her her life. She took the phone back into the flat and pushed it under her bed. Out of sight, out of mind. She would throw it out later as she was now late for work. She hurried as fast as her carpet of cuts and bruises would permit. It was only a fifteen-minute walk, but she felt every single second of it.

Nearly eight hours later, Billie was hunched up at her desk in the overcrowded call centre. The desk was so small that her phone was wedged under one elbow, and the computer mouse was under the other. It took a certain amount of dexterity to answer the phone and use the computer simultaneously. The company was too cheap to upgrade to actual headsets instead of clunky handsets. Not that the phone rang that often. She stared into space pretending that, instead of this monotonous day job, she was a singer. She'd be in a studio letting all her emotions out through song and losing herself in the music. She jumped when her phone rang, momentarily confused at the sound. She took a customer's order for what she thought was a boiler, and slumped back in her broken black chair that only had one armrest. She tried to remind herself that she was free and safe, and this boring, menial job was the cost of that.

When she escaped from her old life to university, she was convinced that she would have the world at her feet, but she was ruled by her fear. To live the life she really wanted, deep down, would make it easy for her to be found. No one would look for her in a call centre on the outskirts of a city. She had thought about leaving the country, but it was too scary a thought to seriously entertain. She had long ago accepted that she was a coward.

So, here she was, selling boilers and other things she couldn't remember, because it was the only way she knew how to stay safe. After all, everything bad that had happened to her was her fault, she deserved to live this life, Except her rather round physique that was entirely the fault of whoever made chocolate. This was her lot in life and, compared to what her life had been, she knew she should be grateful. She shuddered and forced her thoughts back into the box they belonged, using her honed compartmentalising skills.

The clock struck five, and in a surprising surge of dexterity she detached herself from the cables and wires, and was out of her cubicle and on the street, ready for her fifteen-minute trek home. The pain from her injuries flared with each movement after so much time sitting down. She was about to cross the road when she stopped dead. The hairs on the back of her neck prickled with fear and her heart beat furiously. She was being watched. It was like she was sixteen all over again. The fear threatened to encompass her; she wanted to run away screaming. Her legs threatened to buckle. She took deep breaths and forced herself to look around her. She felt marginally relieved when she saw no one, but she knew someone was watching her through bitter experience. She counted to ten in her head to compose herself. It was working until she was elbowed hard in the side by an impatient elderly gentleman who wanted to cross the road. She almost crumpled to the floor in pain. Convincing her shaky legs to move, she set off home. Shoulders in, head down, navigating by the pavement.

Billie was just dropping off to sleep when she heard a buzzing noise that vibrated her bed. She shot up, ripped from a dark dream of murder and torture. She looked around, trying to work out where the murderer was hiding. When the noise vibrated the bed again, she realised it wasn't someone breaking in, the sound was coming from under her bed. As her brain struggled to catch up, she practically fell to the floor, cursing at the pain radiating from her side. She reached around blindly under the bed trying to locate the source of the noise. She realised it was coming from the phone box. She had been so worn out from struggling through work and the pain, that she had forgotten to throw out the phone. She pulled the phone out of its box and saw several messages. She was shocked to see it was only 9.30pm she'd been sleeping so deeply.

She didn't normally get to sleep before then as the pesky books she loved kept her up all night; she couldn't put them down. She knew that she shouldn't, but she opened the messages on the phone. The logic and reason she normally had, had apparently given up functioning for the night.

Adam: Hey, I hope u havn't thrown the phone away.

Adam: R u ok?

Adam: Stupid qu.

Adam: Plz txt bk.

Adam: At least just tell me u've got the phone and u'll keep it 4 emergencies.

Billie: I've got the phone, you didn't have to. Thank you.

Adam: I wanted to, I've been worried about u after yesterday. U OK?

Billie: I'm okay thanks, don't worry I'll be fine.

Adam: So how was ur day?

Billie stared at the phone. She knew that replying would be a game changer. It would be asking for trouble, being alone was the only way to stay safe. It would be removing a brick from her painstakingly-built barrier against the world. She sat on the floor, leaning against the bed. Her head was thumping in pain, protesting at the internal war going on in her brain. Before she had met Adam, the people she shared the world with were inconsequential to her: just an obstacle to avoid. She had mastered keeping the world at arm's-length. That's what came from being bruised and battered for numerous years. She feared people and entering the world outside her flat and her job. But as hard as she tried, she wasn't afraid of Adam.

She knew she ought to be, he was a man after all. Men only wanted one thing. But she had seen the anger in his eyes at the thought of those boys hurting her, and she had experienced his gentle touch. She just couldn't detect anything evil or duplicitous in him. If she were honest with herself, she ached to trust him. Even after everything she had been through, she couldn't contain her urge to be normal. Wanting to be cared about was a powerful drug to her. It's what started her nightmare last time. Purposefully ignoring the flash of memories her brain tried to throw at her, she pressed reply. Every fibre of her being prayed that she was making the right decision. She didn't think she could rebuild herself a second time around.

# Adam

Adam had always been good at reading people. He could sense after a few minutes what they needed. It was a necessary skill he had acquired as he learnt how to survive living alone with his father, who had a propensity for drunken rages. Too many times he had asked his father an innocent question like, 'please can you sign my permission slip', only to realise that his father was blind drunk. Adam was lucky to get away with a clip around the head so he quickly developed his perception skills. From the little time he'd spent with Billie, he sensed that the only way to make her want to spend time with him, let alone trust him, was to wrong-foot her and take advantage of this vulnerable persona she was presenting. He needed to be as calculating as she was had to be to do the atrocious things she'd done. He had to be spontaneous and persistent if he was going to bypass the pre-programmed rejections she had ready. Anyone could see that she felt uncomfortable being around people. But he recognised a desolation within her that only loneliness could bring. It spoke to the loneliness he had been grappling with since he was a boy. He knew that deep down she wanted to say yes, but something was stopping her. Maybe she wouldn't be able to keep up her façade if she spent more time with him. But she seemed so genuinely afraid. Afraid of getting caught? God, his head hurt.

Her acceptance of the phone was a relief. As soon as she had texted back he knew he had climbed over the first of the protective walls she had around her. He just had to keep going until she trusted him enough to tell him what he needed to know. The truth would straighten out the quagmire of thoughts and feelings he was having. He was quite surprised how much she had revealed about herself when they were texting. He thought it was amusing how she spelt out every word in text instead of reverting to 'text speak' like he did. It was progress though, as he couldn't imagine her opening up this way in person, not yet, anyway. She loved to read, and to his surprise they had read a lot of the same books. They had so much in common and she was engaging and interesting. He had to remind himself he was playing a role; trying to get past the mask she had on to get to the truth.

# Chapter Four

## Billie

They had messaged all through the night and the next day. Billie didn't leave her bed, her whole body bemoaned the events of the past few days. Her head was full of Adam, he had become tangible and intriguing. He was twenty-seven and he had his own column for a local newspaper. He preferred dogs, was allergic to strawberries and had a phobia of aeroplanes. She'd asked him standard questions but he didn't ask her obvious questions. Instead, he asked her things like: what was the last thing to make you laugh hysterically? What would you grab if your flat was on fire? What animal would you be if you could choose? Do you believe in the supernatural? All night he had bombarded her with strange and amusing questions. He had elicited laughter from her when she had thought she'd never laugh again. Her smile grew with each message. Her flat seemed warmer and cosier and, for a while, the fear and sadness that had consumed her for so long had dissipated. During her time at university she had found a way of anticipating what people wanted to know about her and she had pre-prepared lies ready. But it was like Adam sensed that about her. It intrigued her, and it also made her reveal more than she would have. For so long she had been hiding away, and it was nice to have an actual conversation. Her one-sided chats with Bobby weren't enough, it seemed. After a while, she felt brave enough to ask him why he had been in the park, and she was surprised by the honesty of his reply.

Adam: I wonderd wen u would ask me that. I went to Once Upon a Time evry day since we met, hoping to bump into u. I saw u leaving as I was walking 2 the shop and I followed trying 2 catch u up and say hi.

His response caused conflicting responses within her: suspicion and flattery. After everything she had been through she knew she was being a fool. But despite the injuries she had, she couldn't remember ever feeling so positive.

In one of their many text conversations, he had asked her what were her favourite things to do. She deeply regretted admitting her love of nature, as a minute later he was organising a trip to his favourite place. She tried to turn him down but he was persistent, so now here she was, a week later, tramping up a hill trying desperately to hide her gasping breath. She would stop and try to catch it every time he wasn't looking at her. Luckily, she was short and could blame her slow pace on that. She was nervous. It was a long time since she'd spent time with another person. She was worried she would not remember the intricacies of social interaction.

Once again she wished she'd had the strength to turn him down, but she had never been very assertive and he had easily brushed aside her protests. The worst part was that he knew exactly what he was doing and made no apologies for it. He must have been aware that she wasn't comfortable with him, and she had said that she wasn't looking for a relationship. But he just carried on, unwilling to take no for an answer. Deep down, she knew the reason she was such a pushover was because she enjoyed his company. Her common sense was trying to tell her that she was repeating past mistakes, that letting people in is dangerous. But Adam was different, she was sure of it. Although, after her run-in with those kids she was sure that any sane person would be warier of Adam.

They reached the top of the hill, topped with glowing green grass blowing gaily in the wind. It was the kind of beauty that made up for the leg-aching climb. Adam sat down and rummaged around in his bag.

"Well, this is embarrassing." He looked up at her, shielding his eyes. His cheeks were red from either embarrassment or exertion.

"What's wrong?" Billie was curious what could embarrass this confident man that had waltzed into her life.

"I packed a picnic for us, but I grabbed the wrong bag. So, all we've got is half a bag of Minstrels and an empty Lucozade bottle." He pulled them from the bag as he spoke. She chuckled, warmed by the fact that this apparently perfect guy had messed up. It made her feel better to know he wasn't perfect.

"I've been craving Minstrels all day." His relief was palpable.

"I totally knew that," he laughed and lay back on the grass, taking in the view around them.

She sat next to him on his coat that he had spread out for her. "Ow," she cried, as something small and hard jabbed into her thigh. Standing up she picked up his coat and found the offending object. "What's this?"

"Ah, that is my trusty Dictaphone. Don't go anywhere without it. Never know when I might happen upon a story or need to remember something." He snatched it from her rather possessively, then lay back down.

"It makes a lousy cushion." He laughed and then changed the subject. "It's so lovely to be out in the fresh air." She nodded in reply. "We can look down at all the boring people staying at home and feel smug."

"Perhaps they have a good reason to stay inside. Some might say it's safer inside." She had spoken without thinking. He looked up at her with a questioning look.

"One day, you're going to tell me what happened. Not yet, but one day."

"What are you talking about? What do you think happened?" She was startled once again at how perceptive he was but she tried to laugh it off.

"Didn't I tell you I'm a mind reader? Seriously, you can trust me."

She was speechless. At face value he was carefree, confident and fun to be around, but she was beginning to see more depth to him; he was intuitive and hyperaware of the people around him. It felt like he could penetrate a person's front and see right inside to who they really were. Is that what he was doing with her?

Was she a puzzle to get to the bottom of? She stayed away from everyone because she had no faith in humanity. She knew that she would never trust Adam the way he wanted her to. It was just too dangerous.

# Adam

Adam had bombarded Billie with invitations. He was crafty with his build up to asking her, making sure she couldn't refuse him. Their first trip to the Malvern Hills was perfectly planned. He had the picnic, he was going to take her to his favourite spot, the perfect setting for getting close to someone. He'd reminded himself about all the things she had done, which meant it was going to be hard for him to spend so much time with her when the knowledge of her behaviour hung around him like a bad smell. But he needed to use that and concentrate on gaining her trust. After all, what else is there to do on a picnic but talk and eat? He didn't account for his stupidity and he took the wrong bag, so they only had Minstrels to eat, but she didn't seem too bothered.

Despite his reason for being there, it was so good to be up on the hills. The welcoming wind and the vibrant shades of green were a heady cocktail that left him feeling energised and happy. All his worries and stresses were being held at the border between civilisation and this area of natural beauty.

When he picked up on something she said about needing to hide, and it didn't get him any closer, he thought that opening up to Billie about his own family might encourage her to do the same. Adam watched Billie intently as he told her how his mother had died when he was only seven, and about his father's subsequent journey into alcoholism. He also ended up telling her about his uncle, the one true shining light in his life. His uncle had recently moved to the area due to financial difficulties which had lost him his home, and whilst this was sad, it was great for Adam as he got to spend more time with him. Billie's face remained almost impassive through his entire story. But he could tell she was listening intently, truly interested, and wanted to know about him. When he stopped talking, she didn't offer anything about herself. It puzzled Adam. How on earth was he going to draw her out? He thought he was good at that, but she was proving otherwise.

He hated that he had been so frank with someone who, in the cold light of day, didn't deserve it. It was going against all his morals and principles spending time with her and being nice to her when he knew what she really deserved was to be humiliated and despised. But he would make sure that happened, he reminded himself. Focusing on the damning article he would write, he concentrated on his task. Surreptitiously turning his Dictaphone on, from inside his pocket, he tried different ways of bringing the conversation around to her past. He tried talking about her parents, but she shut him down. Admitting only that she was estranged from her entire family and had been for a while. He didn't bother asking why because he wagered she was ready for that question. Instead, he asked her where she had gone to school and where she grew up, but again she just brushed him off, saying, "Oh just a public school up north, you won't have heard of it." She wasn't giving anything away. He decided to leave it and try again via text message. She seemed to be more confident in virtual communication. He was going to have to be smarter. After all, he knew she was a master manipulator; she wasn't going to be fooled easily.

# Chapter Five

## Billie

Adam was becoming a problem. He was pulling her away from her solitary existence and forcing her to acknowledge and experience what she had been missing. Since their walk in Malvern they had spent so much time together. He never wanted to do anything normal and she found herself agreeing to do crazy things she'd never thought of doing. They had gone kayaking down the Severn which was a hilarious disaster as Adam had terrible balance and she was useless with her left and right, so they had capsized more than once. The following week Adam had said he needed her help with an article, and so she was dragged along to the Coffin Works museum. It advertised a journey into changing attitudes to death, but for her it was an insight into Adam's sense of humour. His dry observations and immature comments had her in stitches, much to the disapproval of the staff. Most of the things they did were for Adam to write about in his column, but it was obvious how much he thrived on doing things that were out of the ordinary.

When they'd gone for the picnic in Malvern, he had revealed what a miserable childhood he'd had because of his alcoholic father. He'd said he knew his mother would have wanted him to have a full and vibrant life, so he was doing his best to live up to that. His honesty and openness with his past and his feelings put Billie to shame. It was partly the reason that she was so amenable to his requests; she knew how much parents could shape your life, and she wanted to help. She also enjoyed herself not that she would admit it to herself. It was like Adam had replaced her common sense and fear with excitement and fun, and she couldn't help but let herself be pulled along for the ride.

Billie felt a connection with Adam, especially through their lack of decent parents. It was nice to hear that Adam had someone dependable in his uncle. Billie had no one. But she was in no way ready to share the tragic circumstances of her upbringing.

Adam's outlook on life was astonishing. He'd taken the difficulties in his childhood in his stride, chosen to focus on the positive things in life, and not let them define him. Whereas she had let her struggles defeat her. His zest for life and positivity was infectious. Even though each night she berated herself because she knew this could only end badly, she couldn't help it. By spending time with Adam she was being enticed to dip her toe in the waters of the world; to explore what life had to offer.

# Adam

Billie was really getting under Adam's skin. When he first met her it was easy to believe everything he knew. But it was the old cliché, the more he got to know her, the more he couldn't believe it. There were so many things she had said and done that just didn't add up. He had made it his business to be observant, and her micro expressions and instinctive reactions were strange. He had noticed these red flags before but didn't want to acknowledge them at first.

When she made the comment about people needing to hide, he'd caught a flicker of emotion. It wasn't shame or guilt, but pure unadulterated terror. She seemed to realise that she had spoken without her usual careful consideration because she quickly altered her face into a shy smile. He tried to prolong the moment, to get her to keep her guard down and confide in him, but it was too late. It stayed with him though, the way her whole body had appeared to shudder, and her vivid green eyes had widened in fear. He'd never seen anyone look so afraid. From then on, he vowed to watch her more carefully.

After all, she could be the world's best actress. He couldn't afford to fall for her lies if she were deceiving him. The whole point of this was to get justice, not become another victim. He was relentless in spending time with her from then on. It seemed to be working; after every date he felt like he was making progress. He was getting to know her, but wasn't finding the evidence he needed. In fact, he was enjoying himself. Her witty and warm personality fought off any negative thoughts he had about her when they were together. When she wasn't so guarded, she had a wicked sense of humour. It was getting easier to persuade her to lower her guard, but it was getting harder to keep up his own.

He tried to draw her out, to bring the conversation around to her past, but each time he did her body stiffened, and her eyes looked at everything but him. It was as if he'd jumped on a button that switched on her defences. She would not admit anything, and he couldn't insinuate anything, because then he would tip his hand and he'd never get to the bottom of what happened. He just needed to get closer. If he kept digging, he might be able to find the evidence he needed.

They were in the car coming back from a trip to the Cotswolds, they'd had lunch at a nice cafe in Bourton-on-the-Water. They had lapsed into companionable silence. They had so much in common and the conversation had flowed smoothly between them. She didn't judge him; she didn't expect anything from him. She just wanted to spend time with him. Adam had had a very lonely childhood. No one had wanted to go to Adam's house in case his alcoholic father landed back. He stopped trying to have friends because the relentless burden of his father burnt his bridges before proper bonds could be created. A year or so after his mother's death, he stopped getting pity invites to parties, and was never invited anywhere else as the other parents didn't enjoy listening to his father's drunken rants or his destructive behaviour. He'd had a few friends at university who he went to the pub with every now and then, but he had never let anyone get this close to him. He'd had a few flings but he was the classic late twenties commitment-phobe. He guessed he was just used to being independent and the thought of relying on someone, or someone relying on him, was terrifying.

Which was why it was surprising that spending time with Billie felt so natural. He'd even held her hand today for the first time. He didn't want to enjoy it but it felt so right. Walking through the 'Venice of the Cotswolds' with her, having silly banter about the sheer amount of elderly people around them. Until today, every time he had accidentally made physical contact with Billie it made him feel like a monster. Once he had brushed her back with his hand to lead her through a door of a museum they visited, and she had flinched and shrunk away from him. Within a split second she had recovered, and laughed it off saying she had thought it was a ghost they were in the Coffin Museum so he'd let it go. But he had tried again to touch her when they'd gone for lunch at the West Midlands Safari Park. They had sat down for doughnuts, which had smelled irresistible at the time but were regrettably sickly after just one, she'd had sugar on the corner of her mouth and he'd thought it was the perfect excuse to initiate some physical contact; create intimacy. As soon as his finger had touched her face she lurched back so far that she fell off the bench they were sitting on. Adam had laughed when he saw her legs sticking up while the rest of her lay on the floor. But inside he was concerned and confused that she was so uncomfortable with his touch. It didn't add up to what he knew about her. He realised later that he was hurt she had rejected him. Oh dear. That was not good. He had punished himself with one hour on his treadmill when he'd got back to his flat. But this time, this time she hadn't minded when he'd held her hand. He couldn't resist and had even prepared himself for rejection, but he was delighted when she didn't do anything but gently return his squeeze. As he looked over at her in the car, he was wondering, if it had taken him just over two months to hold her hand, how long exactly would it take to get her deepest secrets?

# Billie

Billie was attempting to clean the kitchen when there was a knock on her door. It was only an attempt to clean every time she moved on to clean something else, Bobby would jump up onto whichever surface she had wiped down, and roll around leaving wisps of fur everywhere. He looked so cute doing it she somehow ended up rewarding him with cuddles. Pleased to have a distraction she opened the door, smiling in anticipation of seeing Adam. Long gone were the days when she would have hidden under the bed at the sound of someone at her door. Adam looked just as handsome as ever.

"I've got something for you," he told her with a smug smile. God, she loved that smile. He crossed the threshold and sat himself down in her worn, black chair. "Come here then." She walked over to where he was sitting and perched on the edge. She was getting a lot more comfortable being physically close to Adam. The instinct to flinch and recoil had all but disappeared. She had never, ever thought she would be able to have anyone touch her again without it striking the fear of God into her, but here she was. She was staggered that she was now holding his hand and hugging him. Small actions, but they were momentous milestones for her. She blushed at the thought of Adam's arms surrounding her. She wasn't exactly a slip of a girl, but his arms held her tightly and she felt like she was invisible to the world. Adam made her feel like they fit together. His large frame wrapped around her almost protectively. Feelings of safety and happiness warmed her heart. Travelling through her nerve endings until every single part of her felt content and relaxed. She hadn't wanted to let go. It was the first time since she was eleven years old that she had felt safe. It was as overwhelming as it was amazing.

Adam pulled a box from the inside pocket of his jacket. At the sight of a jewellery box she felt sick. The memory of the last time she'd been given jewellery was beating at her brain, taking advantage of the situation and trying to be relived in her mind. She swallowed the memory and forced her mouth to smile. Everything was all right. Just breathe and smile. She took the box from him with shaking hands, it took a couple of attempts to open it. If Adam noticed, he didn't say anything. She was generating an appropriate response in her head when her eyes processed the style of bracelet she was looking at. This time, she was sick. The box fell to the floor as she ran to the bathroom, slamming the door behind her. She just managed to get her head to the toilet before the bile reached her mouth. Her mental defences collapsed and memories flooded her mind. Vivid images, horrific sounds and evil whispered words invaded her thoughts. Her body crumpled to the floor. She was utterly spent. She weakly grabbed at the flannel on the sink and tried with every fibre of her being to compose herself. The door creaked as it opened.

She didn't meet Adam's gaze as she spoke, "I'm not feeling well. You should probably leave."

"You were fine two minutes ago. What the hell? I give you a present. You look like you've seen a ghost and then this? I want an explanation."

Her body quaked in fear at his raised voice, unable to take any more stress after the onslaught of memories that lingered in the back of her mind.

"Please, Adam, just go."

"Well, at least put the bracelet on. I spent hours choosing it."

The strength of her voice surprised her as she yelled, "NO! I don't want it."

"What? Why?"

She wracked her brain for a way to explain without telling him the truth. The truth that had the power to reduce her to a cowering wreck on the floor of her bathroom. A small part of her wanted to tell him, but she couldn't. She wouldn't go there.

"Please, Adam, you shouldn't have got me anything. I'm not your girlfriend, we're just friends."

"Bollocks. I care about you and you care about me. I don't understand you. What's going on? Talk to me. Please?"

"I'd like you to leave." She inwardly cringed at the desperation in her voice. She could feel her mind shutting down, her body was so weak. The familiar numbness was overtaking her, trying to protect her from a full scale breakdown.

"Whatever, see you around," shouted Adam, the hurt in his eyes seared her heart. He must think she's a psychopath.

Oh Adam, she thought, I wish you knew.

The slamming of the door released the sobs she hadn't known she was holding back.

# Adam

Bloody hell. It was just a sodding bracelet. Adam punched the steering wheel. It did nothing to relieve his frustration. Well, she was making it easier to hate her now. Ungrateful cow. He wished he'd never bothered. You'd think he'd just offered her a bomb. All the way home he fumed, swerving in and out of lanes and speeding where he shouldn't. He told himself to get a grip. After all, it shouldn't bother him so much. It wasn't like this was a real relationship. Even she didn't consider it one. But his anger was relentless. He couldn't help it. It was like fire in his veins and he just wanted to lash out at someone or something. He was so sure that she'd love it. He'd spent all day yesterday in the Bull Ring shopping centre trying to find something perfect. Something to help him woo her. It was an unwritten rule of dating, you like the girl you buy her gifts. Well, that's what they did in the few films he'd watched by accident. He was more of a man's man when it came to films. He'd never bought a girl anything, so a few days ago he had persuaded his uncle to meet him in Birmingham so he could help him get it just right. He was so glad he had, because he knew just what to go for. After looking at everything on offer in his price range he was only a columnist he'd gone with his uncle's first suggestion. Pointedly ignoring the smug look he shot him when he handed over his card.

"Trust me, son, she'll love it. I know what works with women. Haven't I always steered you right?" he asked, as he ruffled Adam's hair like he was seven again.

"Yes, yes, you were right. Now get off," said Adam, playfully pushing him away.

"Besides, the way you've been going on about this girl I feel like I know her myself, so I think this would suit her down to the ground."

Adam had felt instantly defensive. It was bad enough that he was aware that Billie was getting under his skin, he couldn't stand to look a fool in his uncle's eyes. He didn't realise how important it was for Adam to get this story. He'd been vague with him about what he was doing with Billie. He'd even changed her name when he had asked about it. Adam couldn't take any risks. He needed to find out what had happened and that meant doing whatever it took to get Billie to trust him.

"I don't talk about her that much! I told you, I'm just doing it for a story. I don't really like her; this is just part of my plan." The lies tasted horrible on his tongue. But once he'd written his story, once he'd made Billie suffer the consequences of what she had done, then his uncle would understand his manipulation of the truth.

"All right, son, I was just teasing you. Can't a loving uncle tease his beloved nephew?" questioned Eric, while wrapping his arm around Adam's neck. "Come on, let's get dinner and we can talk tactics for wooing your fake girlfriend."

Adam pulled into his parking space and sat in the car, trying to slow his breathing and calm his thoughts. Why was he so wound up? Probably because he was fed up of not knowing the truth. No matter what he did, she just would not trust him. It was infuriating. He knew what the police reports had said. He knew what the press at the time had said. He knew what the people she hurt had said. But he didn't know what she knew, no one did. The way she had reacted when he gave her that bracelet. He replayed it in his head in slow motion. He remembered her nervous energy when he pulled out the box. Now he thought about it, he could see her wincing at the sight of it, like she didn't like jewellery. He'd never seen her wear any, but still, it didn't make any sense. Once she had opened it, her eyes widened and her face paled.

She had launched herself into the bathroom and slammed the door. He had just stared after her, baffled.

Why would she get so upset over a bracelet? The reports had described her as cold, calculating and manipulative. Was this part of her manipulation? But why would she fake being sick over a bracelet? Unless it brought back bad memories? Was she sick from the guilt? But what does a bracelet have to do with anything? Maybe he was missing something. No. No. He shut down that thought. He had heard the stories of those she'd hurt and there was no way they were lying. Adam's head pulsated with pain. He just needed to hear it from her. He knew there was more to the story. *He needed to hear it from her*. After all, there are two sides to every story. He had spent enough time with her to study her reactions and her body language. Once he had heard it from her, he would know the truth. He pulled out of his drive and set off back to Billie's house. He would make this right and continue with his quest to find out the truth. He had invested too much of himself to quit now.

# Chapter Six

## Billie

"I'm sorry." Adam stood at her door. The very picture of a dog who knows he's screwed up but hopes his cute face will get him out of trouble. It was like a punch to her gut, he hadn't done anything wrong. She should be down on bended knees, thanking him for coming back. She couldn't understand why, after a lifetime of bad luck, she was being blessed with a man like this. After everything she had done in her past she didn't deserve him.

"Please can we talk?" his earnest voice and sad eyes sparked her tears. She moved aside to let him in, but to her surprise he followed her, and his large hands took her face and held it gently. It was such a tender gesture she didn't even flinch. "I'm sorry I upset you so much. I was just trying to do something nice for you. I didn't mean to overwhelm you." Words failed her, he was so kind. She had barely any experience with relationships. Did she have to tell him the truth now? Or could she just apologise and they would move on? What was expected of her?

Like he could read her thoughts, he continued. "Look, why don't we put all of this to one side for the moment and spend a nice evening together. I really care about you and I don't want … whatever this is, to end." He pulled her close to him and held her tight, as if he was trying to quash any thoughts she might have of running away. She sagged into him, wishing that she'd had someone to hold her like this all the times she'd cried herself to sleep; this was the most soothing feeling she'd ever experienced. It felt like his strength and warmth was seeping into her and flooding her body. Adam pulled back and his hands returned to her face.

"Billie, would you mind ... I mean ... would it be okay ... could I please kiss you?" His gaze was soft and inviting. When she slightly inclined her head he moved slowly towards her, until his body was pressed up against hers. A finger tenderly traced the line of her cheekbone and jaw. His mouth moved towards hers and she felt his breath brush across her face before the warmth of his lips touched against hers. Her heart jolted and her pulse pounded. She had only been kissed by two other people in her life, but she knew she would never experience a kiss like this again. It was gentle, yet so intense. He raised his mouth from hers and gazed into her eyes. She was weak from the intensity of the emotions she'd just experienced. She finally understood the clichés that talked about being weak at the knees.

"Should we watch a film?"

Billie blushed as she almost said, *no let's do that all night.* Reading her mind Adam reclaimed her lips, more demanding this time. The kiss sent the pit of her stomach into a wild swirl. Everything else just melted away. All she knew was the feel of his lips against hers, his hands caressing her face and his powerful, warm body pressed up against her. With confidence she never knew she had, she wound her hands under his jacket, circling him. Under his shirt she could feel the strong muscles in his back.

After he had gone, Billie lay in her bed and made a decision. She was no longer going to worry about her relationship with Adam. If she kept forecasting its end she would never get to enjoy it. So much of her life had been ruined by fear she would not let it take this away from her. He made her realise that she could be happy. She wanted to trust him. So, she would.

# Adam

Adam ran from his car to his flat, trying to escape the stormy weather that was viciously attacking him. It only took a matter of seconds to get to the front door but he was thoroughly drenched. He shut the door on the brooding grey clouds that were gathering in the sky. It matched his anger. This time his anger was at himself. He should not have kissed her. *Why did he kiss her?* He knew that he was getting too close, and that kiss … it was unbelievable. He'd kissed plenty of women, but the connection between them when he'd kissed her had electrified him; pleasure had radiated through him. He couldn't stop. He should not have kissed her.

He poured himself a whisky hoping to drown out the feelings the kiss had awakened. When the whisky didn't work, he went over to his desk in the corner of his room and pulled out the file on Billie. He looked at the pictures, read the statements and the lies and about her deceit, until the words blurred on the page. That night for the first time since he was a child, he had nightmares. Images of Billie kissing him and then, as he turned to leave, stabbing him in the back with a steel kitchen knife, plagued his dreams. When he awoke, he knew he needed to get answers.

# Billie

Intimacy had not been something that Billie had missed. But since that first kiss, Billie found herself craving Adam's touch, his kiss, every time she wasn't around him. To the extent they spent most of their time together kissing and holding each other. She couldn't doubt his feelings now and she could feel herself trusting him in a way she never thought possible. She no longer panicked at his touch and she could feel her confidence growing when she was with him. He had even convinced her to go for a drink with his friends. They had been seeing each other for a while and he knew exactly how to get her to do things she didn't want to mostly by kissing her until she forgot the reasons she didn't want to. So, she walked behind him all the way to the pub, her stomach whirling in turmoil. It was one thing to be comfortable with Adam, but another to sit in a group of people. Her protests were met with sensible discussions about facing her fears. As she couldn't explain to him that her fear didn't come out of shyness, more self-preservation, she had no choice but to go with him.

They reached the pub and she was momentarily distracted from her fear by the beautiful wooden beams that lined the ceilings and walls, and the incredible uneven floors. It was so rustic and olde-worlde. They approached a group of people who were chatting amiably. She would have put her chair behind his chair to hide but, as if he had read her mind, he guided her to a chair next to his so they were all sat around a table where she couldn't possibly be missed.

She was terrified as soon as she looked around the table and saw four smiling faces looking at her. First, Adam introduced her to Tom. He was sat next to her and he smiled with kind eyes that were framed with stylish black glasses. He looked a bit like a computer nerd, with his scrawny body and his shirt with a jumper over it. He sat hunched over as if he didn't have any confidence. She liked him immediately. Sat next to Tom was Stacey. Billie noticed with relief that Stacey was a similar size to her. Skinny Barbie types gave her shuddering flashbacks to her secondary school years.

Her relief was dispelled when Stacey got up and wrapped her arms around Billie in greeting. "So happy to finally meet you, we've heard so much about you!" Billie was instantly on edge. She had only just got used to Adam, and this bear hug from Stacey was a shock to the system. Adam must have noticed her discomfort because he suddenly spoke up.

"Put her down, she's shy. Don't go scaring her off." She was released and she sank into her seat next to Adam. He immediately put his hand on her knee, but she didn't tense up. He was her only ally here so she was glad to feel connected to him. Protected even. Billie looked around the table apprehensively. It had been a very long time since she had sat in a pub with a group of people. She pushed down the memories that were bubbling to the surface and instead resolved that she would have a good time. Adam was there, he would not let anything happen to her. She tried to lower some of her barriers and attempted to join in their conversations.

She tried to think back to the last time she had voluntarily entered a conversation with someone. During her first year of university she'd managed to make a couple of friends in the flat she was in, but her past soon put paid to that. Her friends wanted to go out clubbing and have a good time. They were carefree and excitable whereas she saw danger everywhere she went. The man she picked up her mail from had a twinkle in his eyes that meant something bad was about to happen. The boy dancing next to her in the club was going to beat her if she didn't have sex with him. All these possible dangers pervaded her consciousness and she couldn't relax. More often than not she ended up hyperventilating in the corner or running all the way back home.

She was so damaged by her past that it was impossible for her to have a normal university experience. The girls in her flat slowly gave up trying to tease information out of her. Eventually, they got fed up of their invitations being rejected and they left her to it. Since then, she'd learnt it was easier to be invisible. Her time at university taught her how to move around without attracting attention. She knew how to blend into a crowd, and how essential it was to avoid eye contact. She managed to get an admin job in her second year of university so she could secure her own studio flat. John, a flatmate in her first year, had asked her where she was living the following year. He stood at the fridge, leaning on it whilst drinking a beer. She knew he was only making conversation but she felt uncomfortable being alone with him. He had piercing eyes that stared too intently at her. He nodded enthusiastically when she admitted she'd be getting her own place, telling her that she was doing the right thing as the screaming in the middle of the night had kept him up for nearly a month before he'd got used to it.

The sheltered cocoon she'd been living in meant she understood little of the banter between Adam's friends. It wasn't until Stacey mentioned a book that she had just finished that Billie felt able to contribute something interesting to the conversation. To Billie's delight, this led to an animated debate between herself (who hated the book) and Stacey (who loved it). Her passion for reading, and the stories she had absorbed like oxygen, overshadowed any fear or shyness she might have felt. Making this connection with Stacey seemed to unlock her old interactive skills and as the evening progressed she felt like she was fitting in. She spoke up, and even joked around with Tom about his love of *The Big Bang Theory* and how he could be a Sheldon Cooper lookalike.

As the night drew to a close, Billie and Adam left the pub hand in hand. The wind was blowing the autumn leaves across the pavement as they walked to his car. But Billie didn't notice the wind; she didn't notice anything. Tonight, there were no shadows across her heart. It felt like her insides were glowing, happiness bubbling in her veins.

Billie kept glancing at Adam during the drive back home and a rush of heat filled her chest. She couldn't put her finger on how she was feeling. Before she had met him she was convinced that no one could be trusted, but Adam was showing her how naïve she had been to tar everyone with the same brush; that she was keeping herself safe at the expense of happiness, denying herself all that life had to offer. All those times she'd watched conversations in the cafe from her place in the shadows, she recognised now that she wasn't eavesdropping for entertainment, but because deep down a part of her wanted to overcome her past and re-join society make connections, relationships and have friends. She had lectured herself time and time again, trying to convince herself that she didn't need anything or anyone. But tonight had exposed the falsity of her beliefs.

Adam had done that for her. Her gratitude was trying to burst from her and she wanted to find a way to show him what he had done for her. She contemplated sitting him down and telling him everything. After all he had done for her, whether he appreciated it or not, it was the least he deserved. That thought was like a bucket of cold water to her face. No, she wasn't ready yet. But she couldn't help acknowledging the progress she was making by even contemplating doing so. She felt wrapped in a silken cocoon of euphoria, and was beginning to think that she might get the happy ever after she had thought impossible for her.

# Chapter Seven

## Adam

Life was becoming confusing for Adam. His world had been turned upside down and everything he thought he knew felt unstable. The foundations of his beliefs and ideals were being shaken to the core. He felt like he was living on a see-saw. One minute he was thinking about all the bad things that Billie had done, and hating her for drawing him in. Then he was kissing her with a passion he didn't even know he was capable of all thoughts of what she'd done vanishing into the aether. No matter how much he wanted to deny it, there was no doubt that their relationship was deepening. He was losing sight of his end goal. The whole situation was crazy because he knew what she was capable of. Or did he? He wanted to test her. He had been investigating the exact details of what Billie had done. Yesterday his source in the police had come through with some more information, giving him what he needed. It didn't make for pleasant reading and he felt sick and drained as he digested it. He almost wished he hadn't read it. But he needed to concentrate on getting to the truth. In the back of his mind he was beginning to question exactly what that was.

Billie was lying with him on his sofa. Man, he was so turned on. It would only take one simple manoeuvre and he would be on top of her, where he really wanted to be. He was a man after all. Emotions didn't come into it when an attractive girl was lying right next to him. Fiery red hair splayed across his chest. Her ample breasts pressed up against his side. He needed a distraction. He scrolled through the channels on Sky. The whispers of a plan came to him as he saw the programme *Rome*, one of his favourite series. He knew this episode. Hmm … given what he'd learnt from the police file, this might be a way to provoke a reaction from her; a trigger for a conversation about her past. He let the episode play on, hoping that he might be closer to finding out who the hell this girl really was so his brain could stop hurting.

It was towards the end of the episode that the violence really started. He had begun to drift off he had forgotten how long these episodes were when Billie tensed up next to him which jolted him from his doze. He watched her out of the corner of his eye. From his elevated position he could see her, but he didn't think she could tell he was watching her. Her hand had moved from his chest and she was clenching it to her side. He was shocked when he felt her body shaking next to his. He was about to start the conversation he had been longing to have, when she stood up and ran towards the door. She yelled that she was feeling ill before running out of the room but not before he saw the tears streaming down her face. Oh, man. She really had done it. Disbelief and anger burned in his stomach. Damn. He'd fallen for her act, exactly like her previous victims.

# Billie

Adam, Adam, Adam; her heart sang his name, his face was the screensaver in her mind. She was becoming a different person. She seemed to be herself first and remember to be scared second. She was at his apartment, and had managed to wriggle herself into a position so that every part of her was touching a part of him as they lay on the sofa watching the television. She loved the feel of him. It caused emotions to whirlpool in her stomach. She had let him choose the programme, she was content just to feel normal.

Her focus on the show was zoning in and out, she found watching Adam a much more attractive alternative. Screams from the TV drew her eyes away from Adam, and she was greeted by scenes of a woman being sexually attacked. The image burned into her retinas. Her breath shortened and her muscles clenched as if in preparation for an attack. She tried to calm her breathing but the sound of her heart pounding in her ears, and her tingling lips, signalled that she was no longer in control. She glanced at Adam but he was glued to the television. She didn't know if she was relieved or disgusted. He was watching the most atrocious act like it was nothing. Like it happened every day. She knew she was being irrational. It was the television's superpower normalising the violence. Capitalising on the darker base instincts of man. No one thought about the families of the people being killed as easily as stamping on an ant. Her experiences had altered her entire life and would control her, and influence her, until her last breath. The people who watched scenes like that would probably forget about it by the time they went to bed. If only she could.

How could Adam, her perfect Adam, watch this? Why wasn't he switching it off? Why wasn't he angered or repulsed? His face was impassive. But then he didn't know what had happened to her. She realised that she was being unduly harsh. She was sure if he had known, he would never have put her through this. Panic was taking control and she wasn't ready to show Adam how damaged she was. She got up abruptly and, as she grabbed her stuff and walked out of the door, she told him, "I'm sorry, I have to go, I'm not feeling well." She shut the door firmly behind her before he could say anything.

She walked to a sheltered alleyway and cried silently; waited for her memories to fade and her strength to return. Once home, she was convinced that their relationship was over. She couldn't be with someone who could watch something like that, and he probably thought she was crazy because of her disappearing act. She felt awful. He was probably sat at home wondering what it was he'd done to make her leave. After all, it was very rare for an illness to come on that quickly. *Oh, Adam.* She wished she could find the strength to tell him what had happened to her. But she knew if she did it would bring it all back and she couldn't deal with it.

After her disastrous first year of trying to fit in with her fellow university students, she realised that she needed to do two things. Firstly, stay away from people it was the only way to stay safe. Secondly, she needed to compartmentalise concentrate on burying emotions and memories she just couldn't handle.

Being with Adam was distracting her from keeping those past experiences at bay. He was edging her out into the world and she was starting to look up and take it in. Opening herself up to triggers which brought images that sent her reeling. But being with him was more seductive than the prospect of hiding from the flashbacks. His positive energy and his gentle, loving nature were addictive. Unlike anyone she had ever met, his unpredictability was the perfect antidote to her instinct to hide away. He was a lovely man and she couldn't help but trust him. Even after a couple of blips, he hadn't given up on her. On their first date he had hinted that he knew something had happened to her, and she had reasoned that was why he hadn't thought she was a crazy weirdo he needed to stay away from. If anything, each time something happened it seemed to bring them closer. If she needed proof that they were right for each other she only had to think back to his sensitivity around her. Before he took her hand, or kissed her, he always hesitated; giving her the chance to refuse him. It was like he instinctively knew how to make her feel safe around him.

She could admit it to herself now, she didn't want things to end with Adam. She was the one with the problem, but she needed to make the decision to overcome it and stop relying on Adam. For the first time in their relationship, she would go to him and make the first move. She jumped up from her bed and, before she changed her mind, she put on her nicest dress and matching cardigan, and put a touch of makeup on. She was ready to take control of her life for a change.

Billie had wanted to get a car for a long time, but she couldn't afford it. She lived on the outskirts of Worcester, whereas Adam lived over by the river in St John's. She was used to walking everywhere, but a glimpse at the relentless rain battering her window had her dialling a female-only taxi driver service her go-to solution when she couldn't face the weather. At the beep of the horn she rushed out. She spent the whole journey shaking, her courage seemed to have stayed at home. But she reminded herself that she had absolutely no reason to doubt Adam; he'd done nothing but show her patience and kindness. She had to take a leap of faith.

# Adam

Adam had to clamp down his smile. He had done it. Much to his surprise he hadn't pushed her too far. Her rapid departure had convinced him that his chance of getting her story had also fled. But no, this was it. Part of him was relieved it was nearly over. He would no longer have to deal with his growing feelings for her. He'd just settled down for the night, sprawled across the sofa, ready to binge-watch *Game of Thrones* on his almost wall-size television, when the door went. He'd hoped it was his uncle. He hadn't spoken to him for a while and he regularly turned up unannounced now that he lived close by. He couldn't believe it when he saw Billie; her hair plastered to her face, rain running in rivulets down her, soaking her clothes. This was unexpected. Since they met, Adam had done all the running. It was up to him to steer the course of their relationship, navigating round the bumps along the way. It must have taken her a lot of courage to take this step. As he let her into his flat, a broad smile broke out across his face as he realised the significance of the gesture. She wanted him. But it was easy to dampen his smile when a rush of guilt flooded in, leaving him feeling queasy and unsettled.

Her flight reflex was evident from their very first meeting, but now she had come back to him on her own. He'd broken through her barriers and she was now ready to admit her feelings. He reminded himself of the emotions that he had rippled across her face when she left his flat. It was the first break in her composure that shed some light on what had happened. She couldn't stand to watch a woman being attacked because of what had happened in her past. When he first heard about Billie, before he had met her, he was expecting a shrewd, scheming, emotionless woman. Not a terrified, flighty girl with a deeply buried inner strength who had created protective barriers around herself. He tried so hard to break those defences so he could understand how she could have done what she did. He had originally believed that the meek and mild persona was an act. But he knew now there was a lot more to the story. She had undoubtedly ruined lives, but he felt sure there were circumstances that he wasn't aware of. He hoped to God that he was about to find out. If only he had known the Achilles heel to her defences before he'd become so emotionally involved. He wasn't sure he was going to come out of this unscathed.

He had been questioning whether everything he knew about Billie was right, but now he knew he was close to the truth. His feelings would take a back seat now; it was time. Here she was, at his door, taking the first steps to fully trusting him. It would not be long until she told him everything, and he would have the story he needed to get justice for the people she'd hurt, and further his career. He just had to make sure his emotions didn't get in the way.

# Chapter Eight

## Adam

Adam had always been a light sleeper. It became a habit after his mother died. His father would come home perspiring alcohol, and Adam had to make sure that he didn't choke on his own vomit. Tonight though, tonight he couldn't sleep because, for the first time in a long time, there was a woman in his bed. He hadn't got the story he was hoping for, but it was a giant leap towards getting it. Since she had come to make peace, their relationship had solidified. Well, for Billie anyway. Adam was still trying to keep an emotional distance. He couldn't forget what she had done; whatever the mitigating circumstances were that he was secretly hoping to hear. But he was failing. He put it down to being too close to her, and he was sure that, once his purpose was realised, he would regain his senses. He had to put all his focus into Billie and developing her trust and feelings for him. That night, Adam had taken Billie disco rollerblading. She loved the eighties and nineties dance music, and he was elated when she let her guard down and moved to the music and showed a natural talent on skates. It was exhausting, but fun, and Billie had fallen asleep on the journey back. She had looked so peaceful, and his flat was nearer, so he took her there instead of to hers which was the original plan. It was a big step. They'd only ever spent days or evenings together, never the whole night. Adam told himself that it was all part of the plan to get her to open up to him. She needed nudges to move their relationship to the next level, and it needed to to for her to admit what she had done. There was no doubt she was getting closer to trusting him completely, but he was impatient. A night staying at his apartment without anything bad happening would surely gain him some trust points. He was so close to getting her story he knew it. She must have been deeply asleep, as he managed to get her out of the car and up the stairs to his flat without her stirring.

Adam was proud of his flat, it felt like the only good thing he had accomplished in life. Everything was state of the art. He was proud to say it was one hundred per cent a 'man cave'. The massive flat screen television took centre stage in the living room. Directly opposite, was a black leather L-shaped sofa that had taken four grown men to get up the stairs and in the flat. From the sofa he could see the television, but he also had a stunning view of the River Severn. On the right-hand side of the sofa was the balcony. He spent a lot of time on the balcony, watching the powerful current driving the water down to the city. It calmed him and made him feel less alone. He was on the balcony now. It was helping to quiet the discomfort he was feeling at his growing affection for Billie. He was frustrated with himself: how clichéd was he, falling for a girl he was supposed to hate? The sounds of the cascading river were easing his conscience and he felt his muscles relaxing.

A scream pierced the night. It came from inside his flat. It reverberated through his chest as he flung open the balcony door and ran into the bedroom where he'd left Billie. His heart was pounding with fear; the scream was haunted, filled with terror. Relief calmed his racing heart when he saw that there was no one in the room but her. Approaching the bed, he tried to untangle her from the sheets that bound her. She had her arms around her head as if warding off an attacker. Her breathing was erratic. She was pleading, "Please, don't hurt me." Adam was scared by her words. They were desperate and laced with pain and fear like nothing he'd heard before.

He called her name, trying to wake her up, but to no avail. She was hyperventilating but her gulping breaths were lessening. Each breath was taking longer, like her lungs were giving up. He tried to grab her arms to uncurl her but she shied away from him, eyes still tightly shut. He gripped her ashen face in his hands.

He tried to force open her eyes but they were rolled back in her head. He tried shaking her awake but she was screaming and writhing in his trembling hands. He didn't know what to do, he'd never seen anything like it. What was wrong with her? He was about to let go and call an ambulance when he felt her eyes focus on him. Fear, stark and vivid, glittered in her eyes. Her clammy hands dug into his arms.

"Help me," she said weakly.

"Billie, you need to breathe."

"Please don't hurt me!"

"I won't hurt you, I just need you to breathe slowly."

He could see that she was beginning to calm down, he could barely see her chest moving as she inhaled. Anything was better than the gasping sounds he'd walked in on. Suddenly, her arms dropped to the bed, her eyes closed. The room was deathly silent. Billie's chest had stopped moving. The moonlight cast its glow over her face, making her skin look deathly white. *She's dead.* With shaking hands he pressed her neck, trying to find a pulse, but he couldn't feel anything. He staggered away from the bed. His whole body shaking. His back hit the wall and he used its stability to reach the phone in the living room.

He asked for an ambulance, or the police, or anyone, and gave his address. The phone dropped from his hand as a violent tremor wracked his body when he caught sight of Billie, prone on the bed. He slid down the wall and cradled his head in his hands. She was dead. It was all his fault. Why didn't he call for an ambulance straight away? What the fuck was he doing? What was he going to tell the police? They would find out what he was doing. They would blame him. He had tricked her into coming, he didn't get her permission. She had woken up terrified and now she's dead. How was that possible? Did she have a heart attack? Getting justice was so important to him, he'd lost sight of the fact she was an actual person. With real feelings. He was just messing about with her to get what he wanted. Tears poured down his face. His body betraying the feelings that his mind would not admit.

He vaulted up as soon as he heard the bell. Unable to speak, he felt dizzy, he directed them to the bedroom and sank back to his position on the floor; unwilling to hear or see the inevitable. A paramedic knelt in front of him. "Are you hurt?" Adam shook his head. He didn't trust his voice. The other paramedic called to her colleague and Adam was left alone. Time stood still but then suddenly the paramedic was back, kneeling in front of him with a kind smile on his face. "She's okay, son." Adam looked up at the familial term, thinking for a minute that it was his Uncle Eric. "Did you hear me, son? I said she is all right. It was a panic attack." The words reverberated around his head but he couldn't understand them. They refused to make sense. His chest tightened, his head throbbed. The paramedic pulled Adam to his feet; supporting his weight as he half dragged him through to the bedroom. Adam saw an oxygen mask on Billie's face. Colour was slowly returning to her cheeks. He saw her eyes flickering as she grasped at consciousness. His relief left him weak-kneed. If he were not being held up by the paramedic, he would have collapsed.

An hour after the paramedics left, Adam was in the kitchen drinking a glass of vodka. The whisky hadn't worked it did nothing to calm him. Billie was asleep in his bed. She had gone into a deep sleep a few minutes after regaining consciousness. The paramedic had assured him that this was normal. Her body was exhausted from the episode and, after some rest, she would make a full recovery. Adam couldn't even go in and look at her. His thoughts were troubled. He was overwhelmed by his guilt. It hurt him to have caused her so much fear and pain. He needed time to process his thoughts because her panic attack had prompted his brain to make connections that he'd not considered until now. Adam fixed himself another stiff drink and tried to sort through the emotions and thoughts burning in his head.

What happened tonight made him look at his time with Billie in a different way. Memories of her that he hadn't given enough attention swam around his head. The way she would shake uncontrollably whenever she was near people she didn't know. The way her eyes would dart around rapidly as if looking for something. Was she expecting danger? The pain in her eyes when he brought up her parents. The sadness within her the first time he met her. When she'd run out of his flat, crying, after watching the violent attack on the television, he'd put that down to guilt. If he was beginning to doubt her evil character, that meant it was genuine fear and disgust that she had shown. And the bracelet. Oh God. How did he not make that connection? And then there was tonight. The unadulterated terror and pain in her eyes; you couldn't fake that. Guilt couldn't cause that sort of reaction. Why would she be so scared if she was the villain? It didn't add up. No matter how much he wanted to, he couldn't believe that she was this good an actor. His instinct wanted to believe she was telling the truth. Although the repercussions of that were too horrible to consider, there was no doubt that she wasn't the person he had been led to believe she was. He needed answers, and there was only one place he was going to get them.

# Billie

Billie sank into her bed, feeling the soft fabric comforting her skin. Her body was exhausted but her mind was racing. Shame hung over her like a bad smell. She couldn't believe she'd had a panic attack in front of Adam. They were a nightly occurrence for her, a result of the awful nightmares she experienced. She always knew when she'd had one because of the full-bodied exhaustion and tightness in her chest the next morning.

She didn't really remember very much about last night. Flashes of a figure hanging over her, trying to pry her arms away from her head were all the memories she had. The first thing she was aware of was a paramedic shaking her into consciousness, explaining that her boyfriend had called them when she passed out. She responded to their questions with the answers they needed to hear in order for them to leave her alone. As soon as they had gone, she had given in to the exhaustion that had been clawing at her, trying to drag her under. She had sunk gratefully into the sweet oblivion of sleep.

When she awoke, Adam was perfect. He didn't ask any questions. He had always shown her kindness and attentiveness, but this time she sensed something different in the way he was treating her. More than once she caught him looking at her with a complicated array of emotions flickering across his face. His touches lingered and his kisses were intense. When she had opened her eyes she had felt humiliated, but that soon disappeared when Adam, realising she was awake, lay on the bed next to her and wrapped his arms around her. His muscular arms were holding her so tightly they should have been suffocating but they weren't. He didn't question her, he didn't even mention it, he just made sure she was okay and nuzzled into her. Holding her to him like she was his oxygen. It was just what she needed. Warmth and affection were the medicine she didn't know she had been missing.

After some breakfast, dutifully cooked by a quiet but attentive Adam, she insisted she wanted to go home. She'd put him out enough and she needed some time to be alone to absorb and contemplate everything that had happened. He'd texted her every hour since, to check in and see if she needed anything. It was so endearing. She sensed that seeing her in such a state had intensified his feelings for her. Deep down she revelled in the knowledge that someone cared about her and was worrying about her.

So now she was lying in her own bed, petrified at the decision she had made. She was going to tell Adam everything. He had shown her that he was trustworthy, honest and compassionate, and she knew that he cared deeply for her. He wasn't going to shy away from her past. If he could see her having a panic attack and not run for the hills, then she could have faith that he would be able to handle her troubled background. She had never told anyone what had happened to her, and she had never wanted to. But Adam had always been honest with her, it was only fair she gave him the same respect.

She had realised around a week ago that she was falling in love with Adam. It was after one of his mad ideas, flying a large kite that needed two handles to control it, at the top of a place called Lickey Hills. It was for his column, but Billie wasn't so sure. Adam was like a big kid, whooping with childish abandon. It was nice for her though, as it kept him entertained and she could sit back and read a book. The sun gently warming her, soaking into her skin, until she was cajoled into having a go. By that time, it was so windy she was swept off her feet by the force of the kite. She only avoided being injured because Adam had managed to grab her at the last minute before she plunged down the hill to the promise of death, or a few broken bones at least. He wanted to live life to its fullest and it was infectious. After hibernating for so long, she had to admit she was loving every minute of their crazy cycle rides that had no destination, walks to everywhere and anywhere, and kissing in the maize maze. Adam shared her adoration of nature, and it made it even more special to visit sites of natural beauty and have someone who also appreciated the sight of a rabbit darting across a field of luscious green.

As Adam drove them home, Billie had taken the cover of darkness and his preoccupation to look at him. She stared at him, his angular face; she knew every expression that face could make. She felt like she knew everything about him. Her heart grew in her chest as she took in the hint of stubble on his chin and down his throat. When she first met him, she had thought he was handsome. But now she had got to know him it was as if his appearance had changed. She no longer saw just a handsome face; she saw the creases at his eyes when he laughed, she saw the spark in his eyes when he was about to kiss her. She saw the way his lips would slightly pout when he was deep in thought. When she looked in his eyes she didn't just see the pale-green colour, now she saw his feelings, the happy gleam, the darkening of anger, or, her personal favourite, his wicked gaze that made her want to find the nearest bed straight away. Wait, did she just think that? What happened to the fearful, timid girl she was only months ago? When she looked at his body, she didn't just notice the clothes that fit tightly to a well-toned figure. She saw the safety and strength it could provide. As she considered all this, Adam absently took her hand like it was the most normal thing in the world. She closed her eyes and focused on the feel of his hand around hers. It felt like her chest was constricting with all the emotion she felt, and that is when she realised she was most likely in love with him. She couldn't tell him though, she wasn't ready for that.

But she wanted more than anything to tell him everything else how she felt, who she was, who she had been and who she wanted to be. He had made her a better person. He'd taken away her fear of life. Okay, she was still scared of strangers, and when she wasn't with him she would shrink back into herself. But when she was with him she felt invincible. With his strength and security wrapped around her she could walk with her head held high; she could look at other people and not be filled with ice-cold fear. He had shown her all the things she had been missing when she had sequestered herself away, and she loved him for that. He made her feel good about herself and not just like a piece of meat. In fact, he hadn't even mentioned or tried anything sexual. She had been holding her breath after each kiss, waiting for him to try it on. But he hadn't. It was like he knew what she needed, sometimes even before she knew. She'd never been in love before but she knew what she felt for Adam was beyond friendship. Her favourite book was *Jane Eyre*. Until recently, Billie had never been able to understand the intense love that Jane had for Mr Rochester. She knew if she read it again she'd appreciate the love described, and how it can change you, instead of just skimming those pages. She hoped that they got their 'happy ever after' as well. The epic romances she had read swirled around her mind in a new light. She wanted to talk to the characters and say, "I get it now, isn't it wonderful? How do you cope with your heart expanding with love like it wants to escape and go to him?"

Reliving this revelation of how she felt about Adam settled her doubts and made up her mind. She was going to tell him everything. She called him, leaving a message when he didn't answer. She invited him to come over that night for dinner. She was going to pop to the shop to get the ingredients for his favourite meal: spaghetti bolognaise. She got out of bed, ignoring the protests of her tired body. It was four in the afternoon, she didn't have much time to get the flat spruced up and the dinner cooked. Even though the thought of reliving her carefully repressed memories was distressing, the feeling that this sacrifice was the first step to the rest of her life overrode her fear. She focused on all the opportunities her life now held with Adam at her side.

# Adam

Adam got out of the car and shuddered at the sight of the miserable grey building. He couldn't believe his exuberant kindly uncle lived in a bedsit here. The graffiti voiced the disreputable status of the area. It was worse than his uncle had said. The poor man. He never let Adam visit; it was always the other way around. He now understood why. Adam felt a twinge of embarrassment about the blatant showing off he had done when his uncle had visited his newly built studio flat. He hoped his uncle was home. He hadn't been able to reach him and he really needed to talk to him. He was the only one with the answers. He had barely slept and he couldn't function until he knew the truth.

He walked up to the block of flats, his stomach doing backflips. He wasn't looking forward to seeing the inside of the building when the outside looked so dismal. He checked the address his uncle had reluctantly given him a while ago. He'd had to pester him for it in case of emergencies. He checked the flat number and went up the grimy, concrete stairs, trying his best not to breathe in the nauseous aroma of urine and drugs. It wasn't right that his uncle should have to live here. Adam had tried so many times to get him to come and stay at his flat but his uncle was a proud man. He was quite happy helping other people but he would not take help for himself. He was so selfless which was why Adam was here. Uncle Eric always made him feel better, he would sit patiently and listen to anything Adam wanted to get off his chest and then he would tell him what to do. His support was always available and there was nothing he wouldn't do for Adam. He knocked at the door of number sixty-six, immediately wishing that he had used his foot, or something else he would not mind getting dirty. There was a shuffling noise from behind the door and it opened to reveal a dirty, wrinkled old man. He gave Adam the once over and scowled. Adam was taken aback by the unexpectedly dishevelled man, and struggled to remember what he was doing there. The man was ghastly: his grey hair was matted with what looked like bits of food stuck in it; his clothes had holes in them and looked like they'd never been taken off. Could this man be a friend of Uncle Eric's?

"Excuse me, I'm looking for my Uncle Eric?"

"Who wants to know?"

"I'm his nephew. Adam."

"Wait a minute." He walked off into the room and searched amongst a pile of takeaway wrappers. He came back with a stained piece of paper that presumably used to be white. "Let me see … aha!" He looked up at Adam and said, "He's out visiting a friend."

Adam's brow creased. "Why is my name on that piece of paper?"

"Why should I tell you?" He grinned at Adam, obviously enjoying whatever game he was playing. "How much is it worth?"

"Excuse me? I don't understand."

"Look, son, in case you haven't realised by now, I don't do nothin' for free. If you want to know the truth you need to pay me more than your uncle does. Oops … I wasn't supposed to tell you that." He looked anything but guilty, he looked like his lottery numbers had come up. Adam wanted to walk away. He didn't want to give this vile man what he wanted, but they both knew he would. He had to know what the hell was going on.

Pulling out his wallet he said, "I've only got twenty on me."

"That'll do," the man said, snatching the money out of Adam's hand. "Your uncle doesn't live here, he paid me to tell anyone who asked that he did, and gave me a list of things to say depending on who called here. Little did I know it would be such a money making scheme." He rubbed his hands together, the picture of greed.

"I don't suppose you know where I can find him?"

"You've run out of money and I've run out interest." With that, he slammed the door.

Adam walked back to his car in a daze. Why on earth would his uncle say he lived in a place like that if he didn't? More importantly, why would he pay someone to say he lived there? Once again, his journalist senses were screaming at him. He needed to do some digging. If he didn't find his uncle, he would not get his answers.

One of the things that Adam loved about being a journalist was that you could find out pretty much anything you wanted to if you were smart. He'd been doing his column and other freelance work for over five years, since he finished university, and he'd built up a lot of contacts. Journalism wasn't for you if you couldn't, as it was the contacts that would help you advance further. The industry is one hundred per cent 'who you know'. So, unsurprisingly, after a few phone calls he was able to track down an official address for his uncle. To Adam's surprise, it was in one of the most affluent areas of Worcester. He didn't want to believe that his uncle was lying, but his source had been certain. He was also offered a file on his uncle, but Adam couldn't bear to intrude any more than he had.

Arriving at the address, Adam parked surreptitiously down the street. A drive-by had confirmed that his uncle's car wasn't outside. Despite the sick feeling it gave him, Adam decided to have a look around. He didn't know when his uncle would be back and he needed answers. He walked up the driveway that led to his uncle's house. It screamed wealth. Not the abode of the broke, ruined man his uncle portrayed.

The driveway was surrounded by trees, the kind of privacy only the wealthy can afford. He took in the large white painted house. Windows of various sizes stared down at him. He passed manicured lawns as he headed towards the path between the garage and the house. Along the walkway was an archway of artful greenery and flowers. The house was beautiful but he couldn't truly appreciate it. He was too busy trying to understand why his uncle always looked dishevelled, and why he was always hinting how awful his bedsit was and much how he hated living there.

When Adam reached the back of the house, he stopped abruptly. What he saw was like paradise incarnate. A glowing green lawn was surrounded by carefully coordinated bursts of colour. Two majestic white lions posed in the elegant water fountain and competed in shooting water high into the sky. The decked area had its ceiling and walls made of climbing flowers and green leaves, like nature was claiming it back. The swing chair swayed gently in the breeze, perfectly positioned to take in the soothing sounds of birds and bees. It was like someone had taken the garden of a stately home and transplanted it there.

The vast conservatory, complete with Roman-style columns, was his first port of call. He had spotted the CCTV on top of it and his hopes of getting in were doubtful. When he got to the conservatory doors there were two large plant pots, so huge it was as if they'd been chosen as guards for the door. He checked behind and underneath each one, and was relieved when he found a key. At least something about his uncle remained predictable. He entered the house and found the interior as awe-inspiring as the exterior. His uncle had always been cool. He was not one for dressing his age so it wasn't too surprising that he had modern tastes. The scale of his home and the magnitude of his wealth was what Adam couldn't understand. His thoughts were interrupted by the piercing sound of an alarm. How could he have missed the keypad right next to him? He tried a few numbers. Surprisingly it was Adam's date of birth that stopped the sound. The silence was magnified in the wake of the screaming alarm.

Adam did a quick tour of the house, getting his bearings. Three bedrooms overlooked the front of the house, but only the fourth room at the back looked used. The one that overlooked the garden. He realised it was his uncle's room when he recognised his clothes neatly folded on a dresser. He walked over to the built-in wardrobe. His head pulsed in pain as he took in the designer labels on most of the clothes in the wardrobe. Adam would have chosen to wear some of the stuff. But on the other side of the rack were the clothes that Adam had seen him wearing worn corduroy trousers, and jeans with holes in them. Adam knew his uncle used to be a very wealthy man; a tragedy had lost him his fortune and now he was living on his pension. Or at least that was what he had led Adam to believe. Things started slotting into place leaving Adam with a nauseating feeling. The rose-tinted glasses came off and Adam had to accept that his uncle was not who he thought he was.

Adam slumped on his uncle's bed, trying to grasp the magnitude of what he had discovered. His uncle, his own flesh and blood, was possibly the best manipulator he had ever known. He had lied, deceived and controlled Adam his entire life. He had taken advantage of the fact that, as a young boy, Adam had been crying out for a father-figure, a role model, and had used it for his own gains. Adam had done anything and everything that his uncle had wanted. His entire life had been shaped by their conversations and his uncle's direction.

He tried to keep back the nausea, and was about to stand up when he noticed a crack running down the middle of the right-hand side wall that shouldn't be there. It looked as though this wall was only there for decoration as there was a large free-standing lamp right next to the crack. Perhaps it had been put there to hide it until it could be fixed? As Adam got up and walked closer, he saw the crack ran in a rigid straight line and went all the way to the floor. It wasn't a crack at all. There was a gap between the wall and the floor. He pushed at the wall, trying in different places, until it began to give. His suspicions were confirmed. It was a door.

Adam pushed the door and it gave way easily. He found himself in a small, narrow room. The light from the bedroom behind him lit it up a sliver, casting ominous shadows into the darkness. A cold draft tickled his neck causing his hair to stand on end. Adam felt along the wall blindly until something hit his head; groping in the air he clasped a handle and pulled. There was the tinkling sound of a light bulb waking and the room flooded with light. He was in an extremely narrow hallway the grey concrete walls made him feel claustrophobic that looked like an artificial passageway between two rooms. It was empty apart from an old brown wooden desk at the end with an executive chair. As he moved towards it he could see the leather was faded with wear. When he stood in front of the desk, he saw photos covering the walls; some Polaroids, some standard prints, but they all had the same person in them. Sometimes his uncle was in the picture, but most of the time it was just one little girl, growing older in each image.

The desk was full of leather-bound books, some had more photos in, some had been written in like a diary. His head was thumping in horror as he began to understand what he was seeing. Words jumped out at him from the pages: 'my favourite'; 'so easy to control'; 'my precious'. A miniature television was on the other side of the desk. When he switched it on he saw a grainy image of a man. He moved closer, his face was right up to the screen, and he swore when his uncle's face came into focus. He gasped in horror as he recognised Billie's flat. Without thinking, he burst from the hidden room and ran to his car, his fear spurring him on. He dialled Billie's phone on the way but it just rang out. He saw that she had left him a voicemail and he felt a stab of pain when her happy voice told him to come over this evening as she was going to buy ingredients especially to cook his favourite food. His uncle was obviously looking for Billie; he didn't know why or how, but he knew he needed to get to her. He thanked God, as he drove, oblivious to the orchestra of beeping horns when he swerved in and out of lanes, that Billie was a creature of habit and he knew exactly where she would be.

# Part Two
# The Past

*"Beware of the heartless who make your heart beat quickly. They're just using your heart because theirs won't start."*
Unknown

*"Some people would push you off a ledge, just to catch you and say they saved your life."*
Unknown

# Chapter Nine
## 1998

### Adam

Adam gripped his mum's hand, hoping that, if he squeezed hard enough, she'd wake up and tell him off. When it didn't work, he loosened his grip and went back to staring at her, trying to make sure he would remember exactly what she looked like. The doctors said it would not be long now till she went to heaven, so he didn't want to forget anything about her. His dad sat in the seat on the other side of the bed on a matching grubby hospital chair. He would not even look at her. It made Adam angry. It made him want to smack his dad like his mum smacked him when he was naughty. It wasn't fair. His dad had so many more 'remember when' moments than Adam had. He should be using them to stay brave for his wife as Adam kept being told. He'd been sent to a school counsellor when his mum's illness had started to worsen. His counsellor, Emma, would play games with him, like 'remember when'. Emma said that whenever Adam got upset about his mum leaving, he was to play this in his head, and think of all the funny or happy times that he had had with her. When he thought of the happy times it made it easier to sit next to her and talk to her. It kept the crying at bay.

His dad had sneered at Adam the first time they saw Mum. He'd cried at the sight of her pale cheeks, and the way her body had shrunk like his T-shirt had when she'd washed it on the wrong setting. "Only girls cry. Cut it out," said his dad, clipping him around the back of the head. So, before every visit, Adam focused on which stories he would tell his mum this time. If he concentrated on that, it would stop his tears. He could pretend that his mum was just sleeping.

Adam hated the hospital; the beeping sounds of the machines gave him a headache. The tubes and wires that were stuck in his mum made him feel sick every time he looked at them. He blamed the hospital for making her sick. Each time he came she looked worse; she was supposed to get better in here. The doctor had told his dad when they thought Adam wasn't listening that they had operated on her but they couldn't remove all the tumours. Adam didn't know what a tumour was. He had asked Emma and she said it was a bad thing that was making his mum poorly. This made Adam think there was an alien inside his mum. As much as he hated the hospital, he hated going home more.

When his mum was there Adam loved going home. The bell would ring at school and he would race to the gates, anxiously seeking her out. She would always be waiting there in the same blue raincoat, even when it wasn't raining, with a broad smile. She would always give him a hug, which he would pretend not to want, but secretly he loved his mum's hugs. It was like being wrapped in a cloud.

Adam was very proud of his mum. She was very pretty with long brown hair and she was always clean and slim. Some of the other kids' parents, especially Jamie's mum, came to school in their pyjamas, and never washed their hair. When he asked his mum why, she told him that she 'always wanted to look good for her favourite little man', then she would ruffle his hair until he managed to escape her clutches.

They would walk home together, telling each other stories about their day. Mum's stories were always funny and not always true. His favourite was about the elephant that liked to sleep underneath Adam's bed. Apparently, she'd had to coax it out with peanuts so she could hoover under there. Adam used to protest he wasn't young enough to believe in Colin the elephant anymore, but she wouldn't listen and he still laughed despite trying to remain serious. Once home, she would sit and help him with his homework then feed him his tea. After a quick bath, which he could do alone now 'get out, Mum' she would put him to bed and regale him with the most imaginative and crazy stories. They made him have weird dreams about cowboys who hated tomatoes but he loved that special time with her. Not that he would admit it.

He wished he had now.

He'd give anything to tell her how she was his world. He didn't know how to live without her; his world had darkened now she wasn't there. Walking home from school was a long, unnerving and lonely task. He never knew what he would find at home. Adam was so scared of his dad. Before Mum went to hospital, Adam only saw his dad at the weekend. A high-powered businessman, he would commute to London every weekday and Adam didn't see him until the mandatory family time at the weekend. It was his mum's rule: even if one of them was ill they had to do something. It could be just watching a film. His dad could be quite grumpy on those days, tired from all his long train journeys, and he didn't have much patience with Adam. But Mum brought out his good side. Each time his dad began to raise his voice and lose his temper, her reassuring hand on his arm calmed him right down.

They both adored her. It sometimes made Adam jealous when he saw his dad holding his mum's hand and making her laugh and smile. Adam wanted to be the only one who could do that. His dad was a big man, taller than all his friends' dads, and his height hid his weight. Adam's friends didn't like his dad very much because his loud voice and towering body scared them, but they all loved his mum. She was an excellent cook and she didn't mind Adam and his friends eating junk food. Whilst serving chocolate rice crispy cakes to them she would always say that kids should be kids and worries about chocolate could come later in life.

Without his mum in the house there was no one to protect Adam from his dad's nasty temper. It hadn't been too bad at first, but when they found out she would not be coming home he changed.

Adam's dad became a different person. He lost his job and lay around the house drinking and yelling at the TV. The house was a mess and it was obvious that his dad had never cooked or cleaned before. Adam had to clear away boxes and wrappers from various takeaways to do his homework at the table. The clothes that hadn't been washed were piling up in front of the washing machine.

Adam was always sent to his room as soon as he got back from school. He was only allowed back downstairs when his dad needed something. Simple tasks his mum had done, that he'd taken for granted, became harder. Adam's mum had made him promise never to use the bath if he was on his own. He'd had to try but the water wouldn't heat up, so he had to wash in the sink with a flannel, he couldn't face an ice-cold bath. He tried to wash his hair but he banged his head on the tap and didn't want to try any more. Life without his mum was horrible. He had no routine no one to rely on to help him with his homework or tell him what time to go to bed.

He often heard his dad crying in the kitchen that was where he slept now. Adam wanted to go downstairs and cry with him. He missed his mum too. They could be sad together. But the last couple of days had taught Adam to stay out of sight.

At school, the third week after his mum went into hospital, Adam was called to see Emma. He was scared. They weren't supposed to meet again until Thursday. Emma gave him a smile and a hug as normal, but her smile didn't reach her eyes. His mum had told him that was how you knew someone was pretending if you couldn't see their smile in their eyes. *Happiness comes from within, my dear Adam. How a person really feels can be found in their eyes.*

"Hi, Adam." Adam didn't answer, he was worried. Emma seemed to realise as she quickly reassured him that his mum was still alive, and she just needed to ask him some questions. "Adam, love, why did you ask Jamie if he knew how to work a washing machine?" She used the tone that his mum used when she already knew the answer but she just wanted to hear him say it. He didn't want to get his dad into trouble, but his mum had always told Adam that he had to be honest. Even if it was hard. 'Honesty is the best policy' was what she would always say.

Looking at his knees, he answered reluctantly. "I don't have any underpants left. It isn't dad's fault, he don't know how to use it either. It's a big machine, with lots of buttons."

"Okay, sweetie. Thank you for telling me. And when was the last time you had a bath or a shower?" Adam's cheeks flamed red. The boys in his class had been picking on him, saying he was 'grease man' with sticky hair. They said he had the lurgy. He had washed it with soap in the sink, but it still didn't go as shiny and soft as when his mum did it. Adam was worried that his dad would get into trouble and it was his fault. If he weren't so useless he would know all these things. I bet the other boys did.

"It's not Dad's fault. Please don't be mad at him. It's just with Mum ..." he trailed off. He couldn't say the word 'hospital'. It made him cry, and only girls cry, his dad always said.

"Don't worry, Adam. No one is in trouble. Do you have any other family?"

Adam thought about this. "Not really, Mum's an only child and all my grans and grandads are dead. There's Uncle Eric. He's Dad's brother. But he lives up north. Mum doesn't like him because he rides a motorbike. She said it's a midlife crisis."

"Alright, thanks, love. I think we should get in touch with Uncle Eric. Dad is very sad, isn't he? It might cheer him up to have his brother there, don't you think?"

Adam had once heard his parents discussing Uncle Eric on their way back from Wales. His dad had said that they were never close because when they were younger, Eric was always getting him into trouble. He said he could wrap everyone around his finger and it got on his nerves. Well, he actually said a rude word but his mum said he would get his mouth washed out with soap if he ever said naughty words. That made Adam laugh for ages as he pictured his dad's mouth full of soap. Adam didn't tell Emma this because he liked his Uncle Eric. He was fun. He always brought Adam a cool present that he could take into school and show off. His favourite so far was the two metre-long Scalextric.

The next week, Adam had answered the door after unsuccessfully trying to wake his dad. He was shocked to see his Uncle Eric. Adam was ashamed to let him in the messy house with rubbish decaying everywhere, and unwashed clothing and sheets lining the floors. Uncle Eric had stood stock still; the open-plan design meant he was able to see all the mess in the kitchen and living room in one go.

He walked over to his brother's snoring figure, sprawled across the sofa, and smacked him hard across the back of the head. "What the hell do you think you're doing, sleeping in the day when your house looks like a shit tip?" Ignoring the cursing coming from the sofa, he thrust open the living room curtains and yelled: "Rise and shine, you lazy git." Adam giggled in the corner with nervous relief. Hearing the sound, Uncle Eric walked over to him and bent down to his level. "Now, how would you like to take part in a very special mission? It is called 'Operation Cobra Clean'." Adam readily agreed, happy that there was someone taking control of his life.

Over the next few hours Uncle Eric showed Adam everything; patiently talking him through each chore, bestowing smile after smile when Adam had mastered something new. "You're a growing lad now, son, no reason you can't do chores like a real man." They got the house almost back to how it was before his mum had left. Although without her, it felt like an empty shell. Uncle Eric promised he would stay for as long as he was needed and Adam settled in a happy routine; no longer having to walk home alone or struggle with his sums. Uncle Eric was right there. He didn't treat Adam like a child, he didn't try and replace his mum. He was just whatever Adam needed him to be. He would show him things, teach him to be a grown-up, but he made everything so much fun it didn't feel like a lesson. Adam was so happy, he wished that Uncle Eric was his dad.

# Chapter Ten

## 2004

### Billie

When Billie first met Eric she was eleven years old and her gran had already moved in with him. Her gran, Sylvia, was one of the cool ones. You would not have thought she was fifty-nine her curly auburn hair and her stylish clothing had everyone deceived. Her gran's youthful looks reflected her lifestyle. She had bounced around from one relationship to the next for as long as Billie could remember and she was always moving around the country. So, it wasn't really a shock to find she had a new man and, within a matter of weeks, had ingratiated herself into his life and his home. However, it was a surprise that his house happened to be only a couple of streets away from Sylvia's daughter, Megan, and her two granddaughters, Billie and Holly. She desperately hoped that Eric was here to stay and Sylvia would begin to settle down like ordinary grans.

Eric was amazing. Billie and Holly met him when their gran had insisted that they come and meet 'Grandad Eric'. Billie's mum had refused the invitation, unsuccessfully whispering under her breath that she'd met enough new dads to last a lifetime. They had walked into his house, the only detached in the village, and they were awed by its size and the luxury he lived in. Eric was standing in his massive oak kitchen that had beams running the length of it. It looked so homely and welcoming, matching the smile on Eric's face. He walked over and hugged both Billie and Holly tight, insisting that they were going to be the best of friends. He then pulled out two state-of-the-art Walkmans as presents and said, "Call me Uncle Eric." From that day on, he spoilt them rotten. Billie could tell that Holly wasn't as enamoured by

Eric and she couldn't understand why. Like her gran, he didn't look anywhere near the age he said he was. He had a full head of dark-brown hair, sparkling brown eyes, and a slim frame that showed no signs of frailty. He always had a ready smile and was full of energy. Better still, he wanted to spend time with them. He would pop over to their house on his walks and, without fail, he would invite them to go along with him around the countryside, or bring them a gift. He was always thinking of fun things they could do and Billie always accepted his invitations as she really enjoyed spending time with him. He listened to her, and he had a wicked sense of humour.

Billie's mum, Megan, was a solicitor and she was always working. As soon as she realised that Eric was retired from his job as a postman, and he actually wanted to spend time with her children, she scrapped the expensive childcare and handed them over to Eric whenever she needed to much to Billie's delight. She had never had so much attention. Holly was only nine years old so she was still cute and babyish and, more importantly, the apple of their mother's eye. Holly didn't need Eric's attention because she got more than enough at home. At Eric's house, Billie ruled the roost and she could convince him to do anything she wanted. She remembered when he let her wrap him up like a mummy in bandages, to the point where only his eyes and mouth were visible. Then there was the makeover and painted nails. She had never had so much fun.

Billie was a loner, and instead of following her mother around the house, chattering away like Holly, she was in her room. As a result, her social skills were not very good. At school her bright-red hair was a beacon to the bullies, and she never knew how to stand up for herself. But since Eric had joined their family she had started to not care what other people said. She remembered the first time he had heard her singing to the radio; on the way back from a school trip to the Sellafield power plant that he had picked her up from. She had become so relaxed in his company that she had forgotten he was there.

"You have a beautiful voice," he said. She blushed furiously. There wasn't very much that Billie felt she was good at, but she did love to sing that was when her stepdad, Matthew, wasn't yelling at her to shut up and keep the noise down. She wanted to join the choir at school but she just couldn't do it. There was a group of boys and girls at school who made her life hell, and some of them were in the choir. If they weren't laughing at her bright-ginger hair, it was the weight she had gained over the summer. It was also because she knew that some of those girls were really good singers. There was always someone better than her at everything she tried, and she longed to find something that she could be good at. Day after day she sat in the school canteen where she was purposely avoided and isolated. She tried desperately to act like she didn't care that she was alone when she was gripped with embarrassment and terrible sadness. Then she would go home and her mother would be at work; her stepdad was so strict it was better to avoid him and her sister. She did enjoy her own company so she went to her room and read. Each day she felt the pointlessness of her existence grow. So, to have a compliment like that lit her up inside and made her euphoric.

"Don't be silly," she scoffed. "There are so many people that are better at singing than me." He looked at her for a moment, with what seemed like sadness in his eyes. "Billie, there is always going to be someone you think is better than you at everything, but none of those people are you and they can't sing like you." He kept switching between looking at the road and back at her.

"They can't do anything like you because you are unique. So you are the best at being something, you are the best at being you. It is your responsibility to be the person that you want to be, and not think about anyone else or let them influence or change you, because you have to live with yourself. You just need to keep being your amazing self, no one can ever take that away from you. Anyone that tries to is just jealous and not worth your time. Have something confidence in yourself, you are an incredible young lady." She wasn't sure how to respond to that. It was like he knew everything that was inside her; all her worries and fears and he knew how to soothe them. She didn't need to respond as he changed the subject, his tone lighter. "I want you to sing for me and your gran when we get home. I've got an old karaoke machine in the spare room. I'm going to dig it out."

They got home and, sure enough, he found the machine and plugged it in. He even sang the first couple of songs with her, much to her gran's amusement. Her gran's wild days seemed to be over, as she had come into the room and sat down to work on her latest hobby, tapestry. Eventually, Billie found the confidence to sing alone and she loved it. She could see the love in their eyes and feel their silent encouragement. She felt like she was glowing inside. She tried to imagine her parents ever giving her this level of support, or taking the time to do something like this with her, but she couldn't picture it. She wished she could live there with her gran.

After a couple of hours it was time for Billie to walk home for her tea. Eric put on his stylish black raincoat that was a little too big for his wiry frame. He didn't look or act like an old man. He hadn't worked as a postman for a long time since a dog took a nasty bite out of his leg on one of his deliveries. He had cleverly invested his compensation money and he was set for life.

They walked towards her home in companionable silence, until just before the turning for the alley that would lead to her house. He turned to her and lifted his hand to stroke a finger down her face. "I really enjoyed hearing you sing today, you look so beautiful when you let go and do something that you love." With that, he walked towards his house, leaving her to travel the short distance to her own. She practically floated home. No one had ever been so nice to her.

She loved Eric; she was so happy that her gran had chosen to be with him. She liked to pretend that he was her dad. Billie's dad had left when she was a baby and she'd grown up with no one to celebrate Father's Day with, and no one to take to father-daughter events. On the rare occasions she went to a friend's house, she would see their fathers and would watch them interact with such a jealous envy, that she struggled to stop herself from saying something. She would have been such a great daddy's girl. Billie's sister, Holly, had a different dad to her Alistair. Unlike Billie's dad, Alistair still wanted contact with Holly, so every weekend Holly would leave Billie at home alone; only interacting with her parents when one of them wanted a cup of tea or help on the computer.

Her mum did her best. She didn't do anything horrible to Billie, she just didn't see that Billie needed to be supported, especially when school was so bad. Billie walked through the back door of their home; it was an end of terrace house. As she entered, her mother came down the hallway with a basket of laundry, heading towards the utility room. She had her head turned and she was in deep conversation with Holly, who was always one step behind her. They were so busy bitching about whoever had irritated her mother that day, they didn't even notice Billie come in. After such a great afternoon, brimming with confidence and happiness, she felt deflated. Once again, she wished she could live with her gran and Eric.

Billie's mother wasn't a bad mother, she was one of the good ones really, but she wasn't good at showing her affection. She was so caught up in her own life it was difficult to start a conversation with her that would stay about Billie, and not diverge into something about her own life. Billie tried everything she could to make her mother proud, but it was only when she asked her that she would say it; it's not the same when you have to ask. Her mum didn't do compliments or sympathy; she loved drama and gossip. Unless Billie wanted to gossip, and listen to the same story over and over again, these were the only conversations her mum liked to have. She didn't really take the time to talk about things Billie wanted to talk about, but when Billie thought like this she became wracked with guilt because she knew she was lucky to have her mother at all. Her mum was all she had and, although she might not give her attention and understanding, at least she hadn't abandoned her.

It didn't help that Holly was, unequivocally, her mother's favourite. They were always together, Matthew joked that Holly was her mother's shadow. Every time Billie came to say goodnight to her mum, Holly would already be there and whatever intense conversation they were having, cuddled up in bed together, would stop. They would look up at her waiting to see what she wanted. All she wanted was to be invited into bed to cuddle. Instead, she would wish her mother goodnight and pick up her battered copy of *Harry Potter*, who had no parents, to try and remind herself she was lucky.

A couple of years ago, Billie's mum married Matthew. Billie loved Matthew and he was a great stepdad, albeit very strict, but he had two children from his previous marriage. She knew that he would never be her dad, he would always have someone else more important to him than her. She was under the impression that being a dad meant your child came before everything and everyone. When she spent time with Eric, he made her feel like that. Everything he said, every look, the way he bought her presents for no reason.

The only thing that upset her about Eric was every month he would go away for a weekend. The weekends were when she got to spend the most time with him and she hated that he just disappeared. He said he had to go to a hospital in Newcastle to get treatment for his back. He said that all those years walking miles and miles delivering mail had ruined it, and so each month he had treatment for it. It reminded Billie that Eric was getting older and soon he would not want to play with her, or do all the exciting things they did together because he would be too old. It terrified her because she didn't want to go back to a life where she was ignored and had no one to make her feel as special as Eric did.

# Chapter Eleven
## 1998
### Adam

Adam sat with his eyes closed tight, praying that he would hear another beep from the monitor. The doctors had just turned off his mum's life support machine and, even though they had gently explained this meant she would go up to heaven, he was begging with every fibre of his being that she would prove them wrong and wake up. He knew the one long beep meant his mum's heart was no longer beating, but he thought if he listened hard enough he'd hear something else. Perhaps her heart was beating so quietly that no one could hear it. A hand on his shoulder made him open his eyes. His Uncle Eric was looking down at him, glistening tracks of water running down his face. "I'm so sorry, son; she's gone." Adam wanted to jump on the bed and tell everyone that it was impossible, her body was still there, her eyes were still open, she couldn't be gone. He wanted to shake his mum back to living; to beg her not to leave him.

But he was a grown-up now. Uncle Eric had said so. An eight-year-old adult. So, he listened to the other grown-ups around him. The doctors giving their condolences to his dad. His father was holding his mum's hand, he kept kissing her hand, sobbing uncontrollably. Adam didn't like it. Dad was a grown-up, and he always said that only girls cried. And Adam loved his mum more than he did. He was always working, it was Adam who had spent the most time with her. It was Adam she would sing to sleep. It was Adam who she said was her 'favourite man'.

They went home and it felt different. There would be no more trips to the hospital. There would be no more hope. This was his life from now on. He didn't even think that he liked his dad, how was he going to live with just him? Uncle Eric had come up to Adam's room and sat on the end of his bed. "How are you doing, son?"

"Can you come and live with us?"

"I can't, son; I would if I could but I can't."

"Why not?"

"I've got a family back up north, you know that."

"Your sons?"

"Yeah."

"They could come and stay here, too."

"They can't, son; they've got their sons and daughters in school up there and jobs."

"Can I come and stay with you then?"

"I'm sorry but there's no room. How about this? I promise I'll come and see you one weekend a month. More if I can." Adam knew he should be grateful he was getting that at least, but he was too wary of what his life was going to be like.

Uncle Eric stayed until the week after the funeral. Before the funeral he pestered and raged at his brother, trying to get him to snap out of being a 'pathetic, selfish, lazy zombie'. Nothing worked. He still refused to sleep in his bedroom, he stayed on the sofa and didn't move unless he needed a drink or the toilet. He ate only when forced and never spoke to anyone. The funeral seemed to wake him up a bit. Out of respect for his wife he got showered and dressed and went to the funeral. He even held Adam's hand as the coffin was lowered into the ground. The wake took place at the house, which Uncle Eric had cleaned. When Adam's dad had a whisky he seemed to become his old self. He talked with people and laughed at their jokes. Adam wanted some of the whisky too, he wanted to be able to smile and laugh with people. Instead, he was struggling to hold back his tears. Only girls cry, he repeated in his head. He wanted to scream at the people who were telling him how brave he was, and that they were going to miss his mum. They didn't know anything about her. No one could miss her more than he would. He wanted to get a tumour so he could go up to heaven and join her.

Whatever heaven was, it was better than being without her. But when he told his uncle this, he said his mum would be really mad if he went and joined her too soon, and he shouldn't worry. "Your old Uncle Eric will take care of you."

# Chapter Twelve
## 2006
### Billie

It was a balmy Saturday afternoon. Billie had tried playing outside with the kids from the village, but it had not ended well. She'd managed to convince two boys to let her play football with them. They had shoved her in goal and obviously enjoyed belting the ball as hard as they could at a girl. However, she hadn't minded, it was nice to feel included. She jumped and dived for the ball each time with childish abandon. She was beginning to get tired when her pink, woolly poncho tightened around her neck. She grabbed at it, trying to pull it away from her throat. Behind her, she heard the cackling laughter of Caroline. Dread twisted her stomach. What was she thinking? She'd been playing outside like a brazen rabbit, hopping around in the open, forgetting about the sly fox that hunted it.

"What are you doing out here? Are you trying to work off some of that fat? Because you've got no chance." Billie struggled to get free.

"Let go!"

"Why should I? I should put you out of your misery, fat girl." She tugged at Billie hard enough that she fell to the floor.

One of the boys she had been playing with shouted out, "What are you doing to her?" Caroline swivelled her head and stalked over to him, no doubt to put him back in his place. Everyone knew not to cross her. Billie felt a twinge of guilt as she rolled to her feet and ran to Eric's house which was closer than her own.

He answered the door with a knowing smile and took her in his arms until she had stopped shaking and crying. When she was calmer, but exhausted, he led her through to the living room and she fell asleep on the new black leather sofa that had arrived the previous week. As sleep took her, she absently wondered about Eric's money, if it would ever run out. When she woke up, she looked over at Eric to see him bent over a dusty red book that had spidery gold writing creeping up the spine. He looked completely entranced, as if he wasn't aware of his surroundings. She envied him for that.

"What are you reading?" Realising she was awake, he carefully sandwiched his bookmark between the pages of the book and gently placed it on the coffee table, like he was handling a jewel.

"I'm reading Shakespeare. I've had this collection since I was a boy."

"I can tell," she smirked. "I hate Shakespeare. I don't understand any of the words and I don't understand why my teacher thinks it is still relevant."

"Of course it's relevant. Shakespeare's influence has transcended through the ages. It has shaped our language irrevocably." He laughed at the bored expression she made at him.

"I heard you quoting Shakespeare last week."

"No, you didn't."

"Yes, I did. You said your mum had dragged you on a 'wild goose chase'. That is from *Romeo and Juliet*."

"So what? If we already use the words, why do you still read it?"

"You don't understand. I read particular plays in Shakespeare because they have themes and ideas that I can relate to. That is what makes reading such a fantastic way to spend your time. It helps you understand things going on in your life, or take you away from them. Look, come with me." Billie walked over to the wall of books that she'd never really paid attention to. Eric deliberated and then pulled a faded green book from the shelf and gave it to her. In silver script, she read, *Jane Eyre*.

"Promise me that you will read this," Eric said.

When she got home she proudly showed her Mum and Matthew the book she was going to read. To her dismay they laughed at her. "You'll give up after ten minutes," said her mum, before she turned back to plaiting Holly's hair. Determined to prove them wrong and keep her promise to Eric, she began to read. After one chapter, she got it. Eric's words clicked. Jane's struggles became her struggles, and she couldn't put it down. When she next saw Eric, they had a fascinating discussion about the book and it made her feel so connected to him. In a way, she wished that she could do that with her mother. He gave her another book to read, and she couldn't thank him enough for giving her this gift of other worlds to escape to.

# Chapter Thirteen
## 2003
### Adam

Adam's life was dull and miserable. Uncle Eric kept his promise and came to see him for one weekend every month. Adam lived for those weekends, they were the only shining light in his dark and sad world. The love and happiness he experienced with his uncle got him through the lonely existence he now had. His dad had become an alcoholic. That is what the paramedic had said, when they came and removed his tongue from the back of his throat when he'd swallowed it. They told him he was a brave boy for calling the ambulance so quickly. They asked him lots of questions. Was his dad an alcoholic? Was it just the two of them? At thirteen, Adam knew he was likely to get taken away if anyone found out how useless his dad was, so he told them that his Uncle Eric lived with them as well but he had gone away to visit someone. Uncle Eric knew the drill and would confirm his story if anyone asked. It had been his idea. He'd told Adam that he knew it was hard for him, living with his dad's drinking all the time, but he also said that going into care would be even worse. At least this way, Uncle Eric could keep an eye on him and help out, he could be sent anywhere if he went into care. Adam knew his uncle only wanted the best for him so he trusted that this was the best option. Anyway, he saw his uncle whenever he was free so it wasn't too bad. He couldn't risk never seeing him again.

It upset Adam that he never let him go up north to visit him. He was about to move in with his new girlfriend, Sylvia, but Adam hadn't met her. According to his uncle, she was jealous of Adam and the time they spent together, so it was best to keep them apart. It didn't bother Adam that much, because it meant when he did see his uncle it was uninterrupted quality time with him. Adam had found it very hard at school in the last five years since his mum's death. People stopped coming over to his house and spending time with him. It was all because his ex-best friend, Jamie, had come over, and Adam's dad had come in from the pub, stinking of beer, and was sick all over Jamie's shoes. They were his brand-new shoes which had flashing lights that flashed anytime he jumped. He was so angry he had told everyone at school about it, and no one wanted to come over in case his dad was sick in their shoes. It was awful.

Adam had called his uncle and confided in him. His uncle had told him to invite all his class on a trip to the nearby zoo; he would organise transport and pay for everyone. Adam was ecstatic. Everyone in his class was fighting to sit next to him in lessons and he was spoilt for choice in the playground. They all wanted to play with him and let him know how excited they were 'it's not even your birthday, your uncle is so cool'.

The zoo was awesome. His uncle was the life and soul of the party; he even took some of the shyer girls to look at the different animals so everyone else could run around and look at what they wanted. It kept them out of the way so it didn't slow Adam and his friends down as they raced around the zoo. The other parents were impressed by this charming relative, who was so unlike his inebriated brother, especially as he was paying for everything. That day his uncle was solidified as Adam's hero. He never let Adam down and he could always rely on him. Adam wanted to be exactly like him when he grew up. He was so kind and loving. Adam knew he was lucky to have someone like him in his life.

But after a couple of months he was a pariah once more, when his dad turned up in his classroom and demanded that Adam gave him back the money he'd stolen. He was almost taken into care that time, but his uncle had managed to calm the waters and had taken the car keys off his dad so he wouldn't be able to do anything like that again. But the damage to his reputation at school was not so easily fixed. It was fuel for all the bullies to use on Adam and no one wanted to be friends with someone whose dad was a drunk. So, the only person in the world who wanted to be Adam's friend, was his uncle.

# Chapter Fourteen
## 2006
### Billie

The Grimshaws were screaming at the top of their voices and Billie was sitting on the kerb trying to shrink as much as possible until she no longer existed. Their daughter, Caroline, had just slapped her across the face, in front of her sister this time, and Holly had gone straight home and told their mum. Billie had told her mum about Caroline before, but her mum had just told her to avoid her and began to talk about a client who had left the country without paying his legal bills. But now Billie's mum had stalked up to Caroline's house, which was only a few houses up from theirs on the same street, to talk to them and try to sort it out. When Caroline's mother had answered the door and stepped outside, she had begun to yell, and then Caroline's dad had come out and started shouting. Caroline's father was proclaiming her innocence, while her mother was exclaiming that she'd had a reason to do it. Billie's mother called Gran, and sure enough, Eric and Sylvia appeared.

Eric took one look at Billie. She could see the sparks of anger flaring in his eyes, his body went rigid and he walked straight over to Caroline's father. He began to roar at him, almost spitting. "How dare you call my granddaughter a liar, look at her, you can see the handprint across her face from here!" He grabbed the man by his shirt collar and continued to shout at him. "You should be ashamed of your daughter; she has been torturing my granddaughter for weeks now, grinding her down until she feels like nothing but a gutter rat. Your daughter is the lowest kind of human, scratch that, she's a monster, and I wonder who she learnt that from. Now I suggest you advise your daughter to stay away from my granddaughter, or you, my friend, will be very, very, sorry."

With each 'very' he shook Mr Grimshaw so hard his head rocked back and forth. His tone had gone from angry to menacing. Billie stared open-mouthed. He was the only one who had ever spoken up for her like that. Her mother had merely said, "Look what your daughter has done to mine, what are you going to do?"

Considering she was a solicitor, you would have thought she'd have had more fight in her. It felt like her mother was going through the motions, but the way Eric had reacted was so touching. How could she ever repay him? She had craved for someone to protect her like this, and he was doing it.

The bond between Eric and Billie grew to the extent that Billie felt like asking him to adopt her. He was the father she never had and she wanted to spend every day with him. He had not only defended her with the Grimshaws, but he was now standing up to her mother.

Eric had become her world and she told him everything her deepest fears about herself and the worst things that she thought. She had told him how she was fed up with Holly being the favourite child, and that she wished there was something she could do to become her mother's favourite instead. Eric had shaken his head kindly at her. "You shouldn't worry about that, you've got me. You'll never have to worry about being second best with me. I think you are amazing, and I always will."

# Chapter Fifteen
## 2006
### Billie

The first time Billie began to doubt that spending time with Eric was a good idea was on the eve of her thirteenth birthday, almost a year since she first met him. She was at his house, sitting on his knee on the recliner armchair, as she had done for the past year. She had the Sky remote in her hand and was tormenting Eric by choosing the channel where a dog and a duck speak to each other about pressing the red button to learn more about Sky it repeated every two minutes. Billie laughed hysterically at Eric covering his ears with his hands and moaning at the advert.

"What's wrong, Eric, don't you like this channel? You said this was your favourite," she chuckled mischievously.

He lurched towards her hand, which was holding the remote, trying to wrestle it off her. She half screamed in shock and half giggled. "Gran! Help me!" Billie pleaded, trying to keep the laughter out of her voice. Her gran just shook her head.

"I honestly don't know who is the bigger child." She too was trying to hide her grin behind a stern look. She then turned back to her tapestry and continued to sew.

"If you don't stop I won't give you your birthday present early like we had planned to." The remote clattered to the floor.

"Really?" squealed Billie. "Where is it? Where is it? Where is it? Please, please, please!" She bounced up and down on his knees in front of him. "Tell him, Gran."

"It's not up to me; Eric bought it," she replied, shrugging her shoulders.

"Okay, you can have it, but no more dog and duck adverts!" said Eric, laughing as he stood up.

He led the way up the hand carved wooden staircase, and on to one of the three spare rooms. She followed eagerly, poking him in the back to make him go faster. He opened the door and gestured for her to go inside first. On the bed, on top of the 'old lady style' duvet she always moaned about, was a large keyboard with a pink bow tied around it. She fell to her knees in front of it. Speechless. She knew her mother tried her best to get her everything she wanted, but she had never had anything that was as expensive as this. She knew the price as she had been begging for one for the past year and a half.

"Do you not like it? Is it the wrong one?" Eric questioned when she didn't say anything, concern etched on his face. She turned at his voice, stepped towards him and put her arms around him.

"Thank you so much, it's perfect," she whispered. She wasn't sure what else she could say. She couldn't believe it.

"There's more," he grinned. He walked over to the wardrobe in the corner of the room and, from inside it, behind a pile of clothes, he withdrew a long black box. He passed it to her, it too had a ribbon around it. She gingerly opened it, and inside lay a glistening silver tennis bracelet with diamonds set in it. He showed her that on the other side it was engraved 'to my special girl'.

"Now, this present has to stay between you and me. I know you get picked on by that awful girl, sweetie, so next time she is mean to you, you can think about me and this bracelet, and know that whatever she says doesn't matter because we know that you are special and she is wrong." He caught her chin with his finger and forced her to look in his eyes. "But it has to stay between me and you, you can't show anyone." His blue eyes drilled into her. "Otherwise, I won't be able to give it to you. What do you say, can I trust you?"

She tried to nod, but when his finger would not let her, she realised he wanted to hear her say she understood. "Okay."

She was elated. The bracelet was beautiful. It was just like him: he'd do anything to make her happy. He was always saying so. He knew how hard she had it. The other boys and girls at school had gradually stopped being so obvious and picking on her, but the girl that lived on their street, Caroline, had taken a particular dislike to Billie. It was most likely because Billie had stopped her from taking dinner money from a girl who had just started at the school. She wished she could go back in time and not throw her shoe at Caroline. Since then, Caroline had sought her out, insulting and slapping her. It was awful because she was so clever about it, she did everything where no one could see. Billie could now look at this bracelet and know that someone loved her.

But she didn't understand why she couldn't show anyone. She very rarely got anything nice, let alone a diamond bracelet. She wanted to go to school and finally have something that would make her fit in; she could show it off and then maybe they would leave her alone. She supposed it was a long shot. Oh well, she trusted Eric, he was nicer to her than anyone she had ever met. He was the only one she had confided in about how bad school really was for her.

Billie put the bracelet away in her bag and decided that she would only wear it when she knew she would not get caught. She began to get ready for bed, she was staying at her gran's house that night, because her parents were going to her sister's parents evening and then taking her out for a meal. They said they would see her the following day after school to celebrate her birthday.

She opened her bag and pulled out her black spaghetti strap vest that she always wore for bed with matching black shorts. Black was the only colour that covered up her roll of fat (her mother called it puppy fat, the kids at school called her ten bellies). She went downstairs and she jumped into her usual space on the arm of Eric's chair which was starting to look worn now two people were using it. She swung her legs across his and he put his arm around her and they watched television. He let her pick a programme to watch, tickling her in the side when she suggested the dog and the duck as she hadn't watched that for ages. Her gran brought her some milk then went back to studiously working on her tapestry. Billie thought that one day her gran would end up sewn to the tapestry stand, she spent so much time on it. Eventually, unable to keep her eyes open, she was forcibly sent to bed by Eric. She zombie-walked upstairs and she was asleep before her head hit the pillow; it was exhausting work turning thirteen.

During the night, she wasn't sure what time, she woke to the feel of lips on hers. Groggy from sleep, she thought she was still dreaming. But as her consciousness slowly took hold, she saw Eric retreating and walking out of her bedroom. Had Eric kissed her on the lips? The thought jolted her awake and she wasn't sure what to think. No one had ever kissed her on the lips. She used to joke with her mum and try to kiss her on the lips. But she pushed her off exclaiming, "Oh no, don't do that, only your husband should kiss you on the mouth!" Maybe her mum was wrong. Her thoughts were conflicted, what she thought she knew and what she felt were completely different. Maybe she was asleep and dreaming and it coincided with Eric coming to check on her? Yes, that seemed much more likely. She smiled at the keyboard that was next to her bed and turned over to go back to sleep, willing it to be tomorrow so she could play with it.

# Chapter Sixteen

## Adam

Adam was sitting in the common room on one of the armchairs. He was surrounded by his year group but he'd never felt more alone. He just didn't fit in. He had no money to buy the latest craze or newest brand of clothing. He had just enough to pay the bills, the mortgage and feed himself. His uncle had given him hope when he'd offered to take him clothes shopping, but it was short lived when he came out with pretty much all the clothes his uncle would wear. So, he was sat there, being ignored, a mini-me of his uncle. It was as if he'd blended into the orange of the armchair, the amount of attention he was given by his classmates. He had brought this up with his uncle one time, when he was full to the brim with self-pity and loneliness.

"Adam, my dear boy," he'd said, without looking over from where he lay on the sofa, "having friends is overrated. You are your own man. When you do have friends, half the time they aren't even your friends. Just people trying to use you for their own gain, or drag you down to make them feel better about themselves." Adam must have looked unconvinced as his uncle shuffled up so he was sat facing Adam and sighed. "Look, if you really need friends, look to the girls in your year. Easily pliable, great fun to be around, sexy and cute, and if you push the right buttons they will adore you." Adam just nodded, he didn't have the words to explain to his uncle that he didn't want a superficial relationship like that. He wanted a connection. He wanted the 'inside jokes' he saw the lads in his year having. He wanted to play sports and be invited places.

The next day he signed up to join the school football team. He'd been asked before as he was an alright player, but he hadn't had the guts to do it. Now his need overcame his nerves. After the first practice he knew he'd made the right decision. He couldn't believe how easy it was. The guys had been happy to include him. Jamie who had either forgiven or forgotten the shoe incident had even invited Adam to his house party. He'd run all the way home and dug out his best shirt. It was a bit worn, but it would do.

He made his way to Jamie's house, his heart pounding; mirroring the eagerness he felt. As soon as he walked in, Jamie grabbed him, slapped him on the back and said, "Alright, mate." That acceptance filled a hole in his life that Adam hadn't realised could be filled. He sat with Jamie; the guys around him, having greeted him, went back to their discussion about which of the girls in their year they would 'do'. Someone mentioned Elle and in his desperation to contribute, he told them that he'd gone out with her. He winced inwardly, it wasn't really the guy he wanted to be a liar. He was immediately pounded with questions about how far they'd gone. He brushed them off.

"I don't kiss and tell, guys," he said, sounding so much more confident than he was. They laughed and the conversation moved on. Adam could see, though, that when some of them looked at him throughout the night, it was with a sort of respect and curiosity. Even Anthony the team captain told him that he thought Adam had potential. It was the best night of his life. He wished his uncle were there so he could show him how wrong he was, that friends aren't fickle and that there are good people out there.

A couple of weeks later they were playing a home game against another of the local schools. Adam felt so proud to be playing; the reputation of his team was legendary and they were known as being the best. Each member of the team was given automatic respect just for being part of it. They had trained every minute of the day and Adam was beginning to feel part of something like he belonged. He'd told his uncle all about it and had brushed off his reluctance to share his enthusiasm. He'd thought of nothing but this game. He tackled the ball from the opposing team and was dribbling it up the pitch when the players in front of him turned to watch something. Adam heard raised voices behind him and spun around. He fell to his knees, and dread coiled around his stomach. No. Please no. His father was stumbling and lurching around the pitch; yelling Adam's name and grabbing each person he encountered like a man possessed.

"Stop hiding, boy!" His dad roared. Adam thought about running away. The coach approached his dad and tried to usher him off the field. To Adam's horror, his dad swung and punched the coach in the face, the force of his swing sending him tumbling to the floor as well. Adam couldn't move. Couldn't breathe. If he didn't acknowledge it, it wasn't happening.

The guy he'd just tackled spoke to Adam. "I wonder whose dad that is? How humiliating. What a dick, eh?" Adam ignored the him and continued to stare as his dad shouted his name pitifully from the floor. More teachers and adults crawled around the two men. The coach was helped up, blood pouring down his face. Anthony walked over to Adam's father, then he looked over to Adam and motioned for him to come over. With the heaviest feet, Adam dragged himself across. He could feel everyone's stares like pinpricks. Whispered voices spread the word that it was Adam's dad. He looked down at his father and never in his life had he ever wished him dead as much as he did then.

Anthony and Adam managed to get his dad into the school. He was probably going to be arrested, so they weren't sure what to do with him. They sat him on one of the benches in the changing room, where he curled up like a child and began to snore. Each sound he made incensed Adam further. His whole body was shaking. Anthony broke the silence.

"He do this a lot?"

"He used to, this is the first time in a while."

"Right." He shifted and looked at Adam, studying him. "Look, man, you're a good player and a nice lad but I can't have this sort of thing happening on my team. You're off the team. Sorry." To his credit, he did look genuinely sorry. The pity in his eyes was obvious. And that was that. Adam didn't even try to change his mind and Anthony walked off. He stared down at his pathetic excuse for a father and hoped they would lock him up and throw away the key.

The door to the changing room burst open and his uncle flew in. What was he doing here? thought Adam. He couldn't have got here so quickly. Could he? "I'm so sorry, Adam. I tried to stop him. He was there one minute and gone the next. I'm so sorry. Are you okay?"

"They kicked me off the team." His voice was relatively calm, considering the explosion of emotions that he was experiencing inside. A strange look, a bit like satisfaction, passed through his uncle's eyes, but then it was gone, replaced by a fury that matched Adam's. He must have imagined it.

"No! What dickheads! Do you want me to have a word?" But Adam knew there was nothing he could do. Reputation was everything around here. And his was in the trash.

# Chapter Seventeen

## Billie

A couple of months after the fight in the street with the Grimshaws, Billie and Eric were walking through the fields around the village. It was one of Billie's favourite things to do. This time, Eric was teaching her where to collect conkers and how to get them. They were standing in front of a magnificent green-leaved tree. It had clusters of lovely white flowers and its branches were so far-reaching, they made a sort of dome shape. It seemed impossible that its gnarly brown trunk should be able to support it. All around the tree, on the ground, there were green balls, like green golf balls, but with small, delicate spikes covering them. "This is a horse chestnut tree, and inside this green fruit are the conkers." He picked one up and broke it apart to reveal the richly coloured conker inside. "They only start to fall to the ground between September and October, so we are in perfect time. Did you know that they originate from Turkey?"

Billie snorted. "No, Mr History Man. You do realise you aren't a teacher and that stuff is boring?" He chucked his conker at her half-heartedly.

"Less of the cheek." She chuckled and began to gather up the conkers.

After a while she sat on the ground, her large pile of conkers between her legs.

"Are we really going to use these in a game? They look like they would hurt if we are going to start throwing them at each other." He half smiled at her.

"Just wait until we get back home." He walked towards her and then sat right next to her. He stared at her for a long time and she wriggled under his scrutiny. He reached out and lightly grazed his finger down the side of her face, but instead of stopping as usual, he carried on. Down her neck, down her T-shirt, until his finger lingered on her breast. His finger turned into a hand and he gently cupped her breast. Billie's heart was banging in her chest and she went cold all over. What was going on? This wasn't supposed to happen. Why was he touching her there? Her fear must have shown on her face. He moved his hand away from her and spoke to her quietly.

"Don't look so scared, I would never hurt you. I love you. Your mum and gran would not let you spend time with me if I was going to hurt you. They know you are here and they are fine with it. So, you should be too." He wrapped an arm around her and pulled her close to him. "I love you, sweet girl. You are my special girl, remember? Nothing is wrong." He looked sincere but she still felt conflicted.

Why was he doing this? More importantly, what was she supposed to do about it? She felt she should tell someone. Just so she could be sure. But would that mean she would not be allowed to spend any more time with him? Would her gran leave him and come back to live with them? She didn't want to be the reason that happened. She didn't want to lose Eric in her life. School was so hard and her parents didn't give her half the attention Eric and her gran did. Could she really lose that? She felt like crying. She hated how she had felt when he had touched her like that, she felt sick.

They got up off the ground and Eric threw a conker gently at her. "Got you," he smirked. She threw one back, unenthusiastically. But before she knew it she was shrieking and running for cover behind the trunk of the large tree, peeking out only to quickly hide again as she heard the sound of a conker whizzing past her. All the confusion and terror she felt before had vanished, as she was absorbed in a game of miniature dodge ball. She laughed, and threw conkers without looking in what she hoped was the right direction. She heard a small whack, and a groan from Eric, and giggled with delight. Her spirits lifted but, in the back of her mind, she was still wondering if what happened earlier was right.

Billie was helping her gran do the washing-up after dinner when she finally plucked up the courage to talk about what had happened in the conker field. Her heart was hammering in her chest and she was sure her gran could hear it.

"Gran, when I went to the field with Eric, he … he … erm …" she faltered, not wanting to finish the sentence. She lowered her voice to barely a whisper, "H-h-he touched me here." Billie motioned to her breasts. "And I … I'm not sure … if that's right. I mean, he basically said you'd said it was okay. But … but I just keep thinking it's not right." She was bright red; she could feel the heat spreading across her cheeks. She looked at the plate she was drying, desperately waiting for her gran to tell her what to do.

Her gran had stopped washing the pots; her hands were in the water but not moving. She was quiet for a very long time. It felt like hours had past before she started to wash the pots again. She didn't look at Billie, but her voice was strong and firm.

"Don't be so ridiculous, Billie, it's wrong to tell such lies. Eric would never do something like that to you. You are a silly little girl, he is a grown man. Don't you understand how awful it is for you to tell such nasty lies? After everything Eric has done for you, you turn around and make accusations like this? You must be mistaken. I don't want to hear you utter anything like this again." She was quiet for a minute, and then she said in a softer voice, "You're lucky it was me you said this to, if you'd said this to anyone else they would send you away. They would think there was something wrong with you." She paused, her eyes softened with her tone. "Now, sweetie, I understand that you've made a mistake, so I won't say anything, but you must swear to never ever say anything like this again, okay? I don't want my favourite granddaughter to be sent away."

# Chapter Eighteen

## Adam

Adam felt so awkward. His uncle had said on the phone that he needed a favour. The next minute he had walked through the door to Adam's house, half dragging a young girl with him. They took her straight upstairs to the box room, luckily the single bed in there was always made never used. After they had got her settled, his uncle explained what he needed. His friend's daughter was a druggie, and she'd been beaten up by her dealer because she couldn't pay. Mark didn't want his wife to see her like this, and the hospital had discharged her. Uncle Eric didn't have enough room at his house with Sylvia so had hoped she could stay with Adam. A question that didn't need an answer as she was already there.

Before he left, his uncle made Adam swear not to tell anyone that she was there, and if anyone called asking for him, to say that he'd not seen anybody today. Adam didn't understand, but he couldn't ignore the fear and worry in his uncle's blue eyes. Normally so confident and bright, it was strange to see him so vulnerable.

So, Adam was sat on the wooden kitchen chair watching over the girl. He was worried she might need to go back to hospital she was in such bad shape so he had decided to sit with her for a while. He fiddled with his phone as he guiltily studied the girl. It felt wrong to be staring at her when she didn't even know where she was. Her blonde hair fanned out on the pillow. That was the only evidence of her beauty as her face was covered in a patchwork of bruises in varying shades of purple and red. It looked so painful, no wonder she had barely been conscious when she'd arrived. Underneath the bruises he thought she might be younger than him. He doubted that she was more than sixteen. Suddenly, the girl jerked upright, like she'd been thrown into consciousness. Her breathing was ragged and her head whipped around, taking in the room, searching for anything familiar or for danger he couldn't tell. Her tawny-brown eyes focused on him.

"Who are you?" fear laced her voice. Adam didn't really know what to say.

"I'm Adam, you're at my home. Until you get better. My Uncle Eric brought you."

"Please help me," she whispered. Her eyes pleading with him. "Don't let him hurt me."

Adam felt compelled to comfort her so he placed a gentle hand on her arm. She winced as he realised he'd probably touched one of the many bruises littering her body.

"He can't hurt you. You're safe in my house. We will protect you."

"You don't understand." She shook her head in frustration, it must have cost her as she lay back down on the bed. She looked so weak and fragile. Adam was about to ask her what she meant when his uncle walked in the room.

"Is she awake? I heard voices." Adam looked at the girl, who appeared to have gone back to sleep.

"She was." His uncle looked at him sharply.

"Tell me exactly what she said, word for word."

"She was just scared. Asked me not to let him hurt her. Whoever 'him' is."

An emotion crossed over his uncle's face, but it was too quick for him recognise.

"Probably her dealer." He turned to leave. "Let me know if she wakes up again. Do not speak to her! She's off her head, so God knows what rubbish she'll be spouting."

# Chapter Nineteen
## 2007
### Billie

Billie was sitting in the front seat blasting Britney Spears from the car stereo. She was looking at the album, trying to decide which track she wanted on next, actively ignoring the groaning coming from the back seat. Holly had been moaning about the music since they'd set off. Billie was feeling very smug that she had been allowed to sit in the front and Holly was stuck in the back with Gran. Eric had never taken to Holly the way he had with Billie. It was refreshing that, for once, she was the favourite. Holly was witty and very quick with her jokes and sarcasm in a way people loved, and she was undoubtedly their mother's favourite.

Billie exercised her power of being in the front by putting on every song that Holly hated, and turning in her seat to smirk at her and check she was enjoying the view from the back. They were on their way to a caravan park in Scotland. Their parents were having a well-deserved break in their opinion. Billie was so excited; Eric and Gran would actually do things with them on this trip. Their parents were far too strict and didn't like to do a lot with them.

They finally arrived at the campsite and the holiday officially began. They went for a walk around; there was a small amusement park in the centre of the site. Billie headed straight for the dance machine. Her pockets were loaded with pound coins that Eric had happily handed over to her. She put her money in and began the arrow-choreographed dance that was scrolling up the screen. She had one of these at home granted not as big or as good as this one but with the same songs and instructions. She happily darted her feet between the four arrows, occasionally jumping quickly to keep up and switch her feet around. The song ended and she was given a grade A by the computer in the game. She smiled broadly and spun round to the applause behind her. Eric was standing close to the machine, a big smile on his face. He looked so proud of her. It was just a game, but she loved how he took an interest in the small things she did. He was always there, supporting her and encouraging her. She would watch him when they spoke and she could see that he was listening to every word she said. When she was at home, her mother was always busy and Billie was convinced she only listened to every other word. It had got to the stage where Billie had started to call her mother 'Megan', to try and get her attention.

Holly was in the driving seat of a racing game and Billie was putting her hands in front of her eyes so she couldn't see the screen to see where she was driving the car. Holly's angry protests were ignored by Eric, and Billie relished having the upper hand with her sister. Being so cute and little, Holly was always able to get Billie into trouble, so she was going to savour these moments. When they had spent all their money, they headed back to the caravan to get ready to go out to dinner.

Billie was at the kitchen table, rooting through her bag to get a change of clothes. Eric came over to her and picked out a top she had brought. "You should wear this, you look beautiful in this." Billie blushed uncomfortably and was grateful that Holly and Gran were in the bathroom washing Holly's hair because Holly always said she didn't know how to get the conditioner out. Since the day with the conkers, Eric had acted like nothing had happened and he hadn't done anything else to her. She felt sorry for telling her gran about it it had been nearly six months. Maybe her gran was right. She had made a mistake. It was too confusing to think about so she put it to the back of her mind. She was overreacting; there was nothing to worry about.

The bed in the caravan slept four. During the day it was the dining table and sofa, but it transformed into a large bed that they could all sleep in. Billie woke up to find Holly's arm wrapped around her head it was the lack of air that had woken her up. She tried to move but found that Holly's leg was flung over both her legs, trapping her underneath. Billie huffed. For a little person, she certainly had a strong grip and very heavy limbs. With some not so gentle nudging, she was able to push Holly enough to flip her over on to her side.

Eric's eyes looked black in the dim light of the caravan, but there was no mistaking the fact he was awake. He had been lying on the other side of her gran but he must have changed position at some point in the night. His body was close to hers, though thankfully not wrapped around it like Holly still was. He reached out and brushed some hair away from her face; her blood stilled and her heart stopped. She didn't like the intense way he was looking at her.

"Come here," he whispered. He was wheezing a bit as he spoke. She didn't move. She tried to convince herself that he probably just wanted a hug. He hugged her a lot and she had always loved being held by him. But something stopped her this time. Her intuition was screaming at her not to move. Fear must have shown on her face because he smirked at her and whispered to her again.

"It's okay if you don't want to come here. I will wake your sister instead and give her my attention. I'm sure she would like it." When she still didn't respond, he started to rise and move towards her sister. Instantly she went to stop him, before he could fully move, and grabbed his arm to pull him back down. She moved away from Holly and knee-walked across the bed to his side.

Eric turned her, so her back was pressed against his chest. Billie could hear his breath in her ear and it made her feel sick. He was huffing and wheezing as he reached down and moved her legs apart. She had no idea what he was going to do. She was so scared. She felt something hard rubbing against the material at the apex between her legs and her mind shattered. This wasn't right and there was nothing she could do. All her thoughts disappeared and she was floating. The sound of his fast breath against her ear and the feel of his hands, rubbing up and down her body, lessened; until those senses had shut down and no longer existed. She stared at her sister's face as she slept. She had her thumb in her mouth, blissfully dreaming. Billie wondered what she was dreaming about. She would love to know. The innocence of her sister's face filled her vision and mind, and that was all she thought of until she felt Eric go still. He patted her shoulder, then she felt him roll over to cuddle up to her Gran, and he didn't move again.

The next day, Billie was sat on the sofa in the caravan with her legs up to her chest and her arms wrapped around them. Eric walked up with a loving smile on his face and passed her a purse. It was hers, and after he'd left she looked inside and saw three twenty-pound notes in it. Billie didn't know what to think, what was the right response to this? Did this make her a prostitute? Why would he do this? What was she supposed to do? Her heart ached and her head hurt as she stared at the money with growing horror and disgust. What was she meant to do? She couldn't understand it, Eric was a good man. Everyone said so. He was so kind to her. But why would he do what he did last night? Was he allowed to do this? She felt so lonely. It was confusion that had made her intercept him last night when he had gone towards Holly. He'd had the same look in his eyes when they were by the conker tree. She would not let her sister be subjected to the same turmoil. She didn't know if what he was doing was supposed to happen or not, but she knew the way it made her feel and she never wanted her little sister to feel like that. She was the eldest and it was her job to protect Holly; whether she liked her or not.

Billie looked out of the window at her gran. She was spread out on the sun lounger. She had a happy smile on her face as she relaxed. She looked so elegant, she had the best and most expensive clothing. She always looked so stylish and sophisticated. She was wearing an exquisite diamond necklace with matching earrings that were glinting in the sun. She wanted to go out there and beg her to tell her what she should do. But she had already done that. Her gran had quite clearly explained that Billie would be sent away. Where would she go? She didn't want to never see her mum and sister again. As much as they weren't perfect, she loved them with all her heart. And who's to say Eric wouldn't start doing these things to her sister. She turned away from the window and sighed; took some deep breaths and resolved to not think about it. Like last night, she would focus on something else to fill her mind. If she didn't think about it, it hadn't happened. The worst part of the whole situation was that she couldn't hate Eric. Not even a little bit. She was scared of him, but she didn't hate him. He had become more important to her than anyone she knew. He would listen to her, console her; he was whatever she needed at that moment. The moments he scared her were very few and far between. The ways he made her life better outweighed the way he scared her.

As if he knew she was thinking about him, he came back into the caravan and sat next to her.

"Look, about last night," he said. "I'm sorry I reached over to your sister. That was unacceptable. I just wanted you to be close to me so much. I know how jealous you get of your sister, so I thought that would make you stop thinking so much and just come to me." He looked at her, put his arm around her and smiled warmly. "You are so beautiful; can't you understand why I would want to be close to you? I know that you are still young, but you will understand and learn to enjoy our close time. I won't push you again. I don't want to upset you. Your happiness means more to me than anything. I'm just trying to guide you, you are still learning, let me help you. I know what is right and what isn't. I won't do anything that isn't right." He stared at her so intensely she couldn't fail to see the sincerity in his eyes. She sighed.

No one ever spoke to her like he did. He always knew the right thing to say to her, what she wanted to hear. She was scared that he was right: she'd thought she was protecting her sister last night, but was she jealous? Was she too young to understand? Maybe she did need to let go and trust Eric. After all, he only ever treated her with love and kindness. Did she really want to lose him when he was the only person who gave her attention? Everyone at school disregarded her as a person and made her their target for cruel comments when they were bored. Her mother was a drama queen, wrapped up in her own world, and unable to tear herself away from her sister's little-girl charms long enough to spend much time with Billie. All she had was Eric.

# Chapter Twenty
## 2005

### Adam

It had been seven years since his mother had died and Adam hated the fact he could no longer remember her laughter. The time he had with her was always filled with her flowery laughter; she loved to laugh and be happy. It caused a pain in his chest, which he didn't think would ever heal, when he tried to recall the way her face had lit up when she saw him. The pictures he had of her didn't capture that, they were two-dimensional, dull and bland. They didn't show how warm her cuddles were, the sparkle in her eye when she laughed, the energy she'd buzzed with every day. The only thing that made him feel better was Elle. They were in the same year and he had finally plucked up the courage to ask her to be his girlfriend. Since they'd all grown up together, everyone had got used to the fact that Adam's dad was a drunk. It was normal and he was no longer ostracised from the other kids. But he had missed out on the formative years, when you make friends for life, so he only had acquaintances, not any real friends. However, he had a good enough social standing at school to be considered an adequate dating partner for Elle, so he'd been told. She had the same infectious laughter that his mum had had, and she was as vibrant and funny as her too. It made Adam want to be happy again. They were only fourteen but he was convinced she was the love of his life. In fact, he was ready to introduce her to his uncle as his official girlfriend. She'd met him at the zoo a couple of years back, but this was different.

Uncle Eric drove into the car park of a cafe and they all got out of the car. It was a lovely day; the wind was gently blowing Elle's shoulder-length brown hair. Adam couldn't believe his luck.

As a growing young man he thought they looked quite good together both slim and good looking. Well, that's what Elle said when they passed notes at school. They sat on the benches outside the River Café; it was picturesque, and relaxing to hear the bubbling of water beside them. It was Adam's favourite kind of day. Part of him always longed to be outside, walking around and exploring. The days his uncle wasn't there he found it easier to escape outside than deal with his dad's changing moods.

They had eventually managed to coexist together. If he stayed out of his dad's way, his father would sign forms that needed to be signed and give out dinner money. All the finances were sorted by his uncle because his dad had been signed off sick with depression, and didn't really care about anything apart from where his next pint was coming from.

Adam was lucky: he'd discovered, if you knew where to go, that there were some beautiful places in Worcester. He would take his bike and cycle anywhere and everywhere. He would sometimes talk to his mum, telling her how much she would love this tree or that flower. He felt more at home in the forests than indoors. There were so many animals and so much activity in the woods, it quelled some of his loneliness. If it wasn't for his Uncle Eric's visits, he would be tempted to live in the forest permanently. On a day like this, he longed to be out among the trees, watching animals basking in the sun. But Elle was making him happier and bringing him back into the world, encouraging him not to hide away. Plus, he would not miss his uncle's visit for the world.

The conversation flowed easily between all three of them, although Uncle Eric didn't seem to like Elle's endless questions about his life. She couldn't understand why he didn't bring his girlfriend, Sylvia, down with him sometimes.

"Surely she can't be working every weekend?" Each time she asked a question he didn't like, he just ignored her and changed the subject. Adam was disappointed because he'd really wanted his uncle to like Elle, but there was an inexplicable friction they both seemed to pick up on. Sure enough, once they had dropped Elle at home, Uncle Eric asked if they could go for a drink somewhere before they called it a night.

"Son, you know when you have any problems, you ring me and I give you my advice?" Adam nodded, resigned to where this was going: that he was too young for a girlfriend, blah blah blah. "Well, I want to give you some advice now. We haven't really had the 'girl talk', have we? And we both know that it is unlikely you'll get it from your dad. Well, what I've learnt from all my years is that there are certain girls that you should go for, and certain ones you need to watch out for. Now, listen up, son, this is the best advice you'll get. Elle is cute, don't get me wrong, she's nice to look at, she's confident and chatty, but she's the type of girl you need to watch out for. If you end up getting tied down to a girl like her, she'll have you trained up like her own personal pet before you know what's hit you. Does that make sense? The girls you want to go for are the vulnerable ones. The unpopular ones. Men like us, Adam, we aren't the sort of men who want to be made effeminate and controlled. We are men's men. We are strong and in control. We need women who respect that. We need women we can turn into who we want them to be. Look at your dad. No disrespect to your mum, she was an amazing woman, but she was one of those who train men to become who they want them to be, and now he can't exist without her; without someone to tell him what to do and how to be. You don't want that do you, son?" Adam shook his head.

His uncle's words filled his mind. It was obvious when you put it like that. Why hadn't he realised this before? Man, he was so lucky to have someone who was so honest and upfront with him. "I knew you'd get it. You're so smart and intelligent. We're similar you and me. So, when you go back to school, find a girl who is unpopular, a loser, and ask her out. She'll be so grateful for your attention that she'll do whatever you want. That's the sort of girl us Bondwells need. Isn't that right, son?"

As soon as school started on Monday, Adam told Elle the news. She was really upset and Adam felt terrible because he did like her. But his uncle was right. Everything he'd said made sense; he was only looking out for Adam's best interests and he had never steered him wrong before. He really wished he lived with his uncle, life would be so much simpler.

# Chapter Twenty-One
## 2008
### Billie

Billie had a boyfriend. It was awesome and she was so happy. But a small voice in the back of her head said she was living a lie. She'd barely seen Eric for a couple of weeks as he had been away a lot. Not that she ever knew why. But she worried about when he returned. From what she knew of boyfriends, they expected you to tell them everything and be faithful. She failed on both counts. She wanted so much to explain her circumstances to Carl, but she couldn't. How could she tell him that when she finished school, she had to go to her gran's house where Eric would make her let him touch her wherever he wanted using her sister as blackmail? When he was done with her, she would rush outside and find Carl and they would kiss and cuddle. He wouldn't understand. She didn't even understand. All she kept thinking about was what Eric had reminded her: she was protecting her sister and keeping her family together. Anyway, she had become exceptional at compartmentalising, she shoved her guilt and disgust in a box and locked it away. Instead, she focused on the glowing feeling she got when she thought of Carl. He was so handsome and lovely, she didn't know what he saw in her. She couldn't wait to tell their children how they became girlfriend and boyfriend; the edited version though, even Carl didn't know all the story.

Until she met him, her life had been a lonely existence, she was completely isolated. She went out to play in the village with Carl and his friends because she couldn't stand the look on her mum's face when she stayed inside and read. Without fail, her mum would appear at the bedroom door.

"I thought you would have been out with the other kids by now? Your sister has already gone." Her question was really an order. On the rare occasion she refused to go out because she was unwilling to stand and be ignored by the other girls. Her mother would look at her as if she had let her down. She wondered how she would react if she knew everyone ignored her at school. But now, she had to admit, something had come from hanging around outside, she had been able to make a connection with Carl.

He liked to skateboard and listen to Green Day and one day, unable to cope with being invisible, she told him she had every album they had released, and her mum was going to buy her a skateboard and ramp next week for her fifteenth birthday. From then on he would speak to her, and he said he didn't understand why everyone at school hated her. He had thought she was weird until he realised she liked Green Day and skateboarding. She knew buying that skateboard ramp would pay off. Since then he had talked to her; he made time to speak to her and she felt she could be herself.

A couple of months later they went on a walk. It was snowing, as it did most winter months in the Lake District. Having nothing much else to do they began walking, and they were so busy talking they just kept going. They had so much fun; they threw snowballs and talked and talked. For an avid skateboarder there was so much she could talk to him about despite the fact there was no trace of a Tony Hawk gene in her body, and the music he listened to made her want to cry. He was really funny as well. They were walking down a country lane where there would normally have been grass banks either side, but now there were mounds of snow. Carl was telling her something that had her in hysterics she couldn't remember exactly what, because what happened next had driven it from her mind. She'd bent over because she was laughing so much, and she realised with horror that she was about to pee. The urge was undeniable and panic flushed through her. In desperation, she launched to the side, into the snow, and started to make a snow angel. "What on earth are you doing?" chuckled Carl. She peed in the snow, as quickly as she could, and used the snow to cover the most humiliating thing her body had ever done to her. She laughed to cover her embarrassment and hoped he would think it was the cold air that was making her cheeks so red. She couldn't believe what was happening, and she hoped and prayed that when she stood up she had covered her … indiscretion with enough snow. She quickly got up, put her arm through Carl's and pulled him further down the lane.

"Making a snow angel of course, but now I'm too cold so let's hurry back." They walked down the road and Billie tried hard to continue as if nothing had happened. She regaled Carl with stories to distract him from looking too closely at her; she talked about her childhood, family, the girls at school. As she talked, she was furious with whichever god it was that hated her so much her body failed in front of the cutest boy in the world.

When she got home, Billie ran a bath to warm her body, which was shivering in protest at her escapades in the snow. She was about to get in when the house phone rang. She was the only one in the house so she ran to her mum's bedroom, hastily wrapping a towel around her. "Hello?"

"It's Carl."

"Oh, everything okay? You've only been gone ten minutes."

"Yeah, go outside."

"What? No thanks. My bath just said I'm not allowed to as that's rude, and it's too cold."

He laughed. "Well, could you please tell your bath that this is a matter of utmost importance?"

She giggled at the posh voice he put on. "Are *you* outside?" she questioned, she tried to remember where her clothes were and exactly how quickly she could get dressed.

"Nah, but I left something for you. Under your plant pot next to the bench."

"Okay." It showed in her voice how weird she found this request. "Can I have five minutes to change?"

"Go now, just put a dressing gown on or something." He was chuckling, she wished she knew what was so funny. She walked into her bedroom and put on her fluffy pink dressing gown it was the only one she owned and she crossed her fingers that this wasn't a trick and he wasn't stood outside the house.

She walked downstairs, still with the phone to her ear, through the front room, kitchen and into the hallway, and opened the back door. The red patio stones were freezing against her bare feet. She walked towards the bench, lifted up the small mahogany plant pot and found a scrap of paper. She darted back in the house, paper in hand.

"Got it," she said into the phone, but was met with the dial tone. How rude. Anticipation got the better of her and she unfolded the scrap of paper to read: *'will you go out with me?'* Her mouth broke into the biggest smile and she lit up from the inside. She had spent so much time longing to be with Carl. She had converted her music taste and bought a skateboard. She had changed herself into someone he could like. She knew if he really knew her, he would run away screaming. She had spent every waking minute picturing his perfect sandy hair, which hung in a slight curl towards the end, and what it would be like if she could run her hand through it. He was the coolest person she had ever met and she couldn't believe he was her friend, let alone his girlfriend. As one of the few kids their age in the village, she'd spent a lot of time with him. She wasn't modest, but she honestly couldn't work out what he saw in her. At school she was picked on in front of him. The school was full of perfect girls, they were tall and slim, and even in their school uniform they looked like models. She felt like a frumpy penguin with red hair.

Even though she couldn't work it out, she was still on top of the world. It was the best feeling; she couldn't stop smiling. She went upstairs in a daze and pondered the fact that one of the most romantic people in the world was going to be her boyfriend.

It had been an amazing few weeks with Carl, Eric had been away so she had been able to spend most weekends with him.

When they were at school he walked with her to the school bus they sat and waited together, writing messages to each other in their homework diaries saying what they loved best about each other. Then they would have their lunch together, sit together in lessons they shared and on the bus home. After tea, they would meet and go to the school field, climb up onto the roof of a sort of shipping container that you could access by climbing the fence built next to it, and they would kiss. She couldn't believe the kissing. It was sensational. She was so nervous when they had their first, she had no idea what to do, and hoped she could copy what he did. As it happened, she was a natural, according to Carl. He was so passionate, he would hold her face with both hands and his lips would meld to hers, moans escaping every now and then, making her hormones go wild. She was no longer alone. But that caused her a lot of conflicting emotions.

Billie found it really confusing that, despite what was happening to her in her secret life, she was still able to feel such passion and wanting for Carl. She'd thought she would be numb to sex and all it entailed. This confused Billie more; she knew inside that what Eric was doing was wrong, but maybe there was something wrong with her. It was hard because he hadn't hurt her. In fact, he treated her like a princess and smothered her with love and attention. It was only occasionally that he would do something like what had happened at the caravan. She had started to reduce the amount of time she spent there, because a few times she had woken up with no clothes on. Eric was nowhere to be found and her head was pounding. The third time this happened, she decided to have a break from seeing Eric. She loved his attention but she was freaked out.

She couldn't talk to anyone about what was happening and she didn't dare look it up on the computer because she shared it with Holly. The only information she had been able to glean about what was happening, was from an article she had read in one of those trashy magazines full of other people's stories. The one she had read, had the headline: 'Mother stole my husband

and my dog'. There was also an article about how a stepfather had abused his stepdaughter. The daughter had described how she felt dead inside and how she was unable to have a sex life now because she was so traumatised. Why wasn't Billie feeling like this? She deserved what was happening to her if she didn't react like that, maybe that's why it was going on because she wasn't an ordinary person. It was best not thinking about it. Besides, being with Carl had shrunk the target on her back to a certain extent at school. She was gradually being talked to and accepted. She didn't want her other life to ruin this. If she could keep Eric and Carl happy, she felt she had a chance to be happy as well.

# Chapter Twenty-Two
## 2008

### Adam

"I think Sylvia is cheating on me." Adam nearly choked on his sandwich. Stunned, he turned to look at his uncle to check he wasn't joking. His uncle never talked about Sylvia or his life up north with Adam, unless it was by accident or Adam had directly asked. He was always forthcoming with advice or help for Adam, but he never asked for any support in return. He'd always presumed it was a generational thing, stiff upper lip and all that. This gave a lot of weight to the revelation that his uncle needed help. He must really be desperate. Although Adam was like a fish out of water; he wanted to be supportive but he didn't have a clue what to say.

"Really? Why do you think that?"

His uncle barked a humourless laugh.

"The stupid bitch isn't very clever at hiding it. Parading all over the village with him." The viciousness in his uncle's voice was intimidating.

From the little he knew about affairs, people usually strove to keep them secret. "She was lucky to land me, and now she is throwing it back in my face. All the attention I've showered on her, all her whiny moans, and all the comfort I've provided her. I've spent these past four years looking after her and this is what I get in return." His mouth was drawn in anger and there was a surprising fury in his eyes. His uncle's sandwich was a bready-pulp in his hand. Realising what he'd done, he threw it on his plate.

Adam glanced around the beer garden, the outside benches beside them were empty as usual; his uncle's troubles wouldn't be witnessed, thankfully.

"Four years? You and Sylvia have been together for more than that I thought?"

"You're right, but not much longer. I'm getting old, son. Forget my head if it wasn't screwed on." His uncle sighed and his whole body deflated. It didn't last long, he seemed to remember what they had been talking about and his anger inflated him, his muscles tensed. "That's irrelevant anyway. The fact is, she is cheating on me, and I can't decide how to handle it."

"I take it you haven't spoken to her about it, then?"

"Oh no. I want to be able to control myself when I talk to her about it, right now I could kill her."

Adam could tell, his uncle looked so wound up. His body was shaking; he kept clenching his fists and his eyes blazed, ready to scorch anything that made eye contact.

"You definitely need to confront her. It's out of order what she did. You're the most amazing person I know. You don't deserve to be treated like this." Adam hoped his outrage would suffice as he had no advice, he was out of his depth. He kept his eyes on the remainder of his sandwich, not wanting his uncle to see how uncomfortable he was.

"I'm thinking I might confront her when she's next with him." His eyes sparked and narrowed as he enunciated 'him' with a snarl.

That didn't sound good, thought Adam, but what could he say? He didn't want to risk irritating his uncle. After all, he'd only had one girlfriend. Adam didn't need to answer, as his uncle continued. He seemed oblivious to Adam's presence. Lost in his own worries.

"That's what I'll do: I'll follow her and, when she's with him, I'll let her see me. I can just imagine the sick feeling she'll get when she sees me. When she realises that I know what she's doing. Of course, I'll forgive her in time, but for now, the power will be mine."

An involuntary shiver ran down his spine at his uncle's words he felt uneasy at his reaction. He sounded happy that Sylvia had screwed up. There must be a better way to handle all this.

"Don't take this the wrong way, but that sounds a bit me. I know she's done something bad, but why don't you talk to her. And why are you forgiving her anyway? She's broken your trust."

His uncle reached out and squeezed Adam's shoulder, laughing gently. "Son, I forget sometimes that you're still so young. What you need to understand is I've invested so much of my time, of myself, in this relationship. Yes, she has messed up, but she will know that, and realise her mistake; then we can move on. I think I may have confused you earlier when I said, 'I will have the power', what I meant was, I will have the power to bring us closer. To make sure that we are stronger than ever so she won't be tempted to stray again. When you make a commitment, son, you keep it. Like me, I've kept my commitment to you, haven't I? I'm a man of my word. Well, I made a promise to her that she would always be my number one, and she would always have me. I don't break my promises."

# Chapter Twenty-Three
## 2009
### Billie

When Eric learned that Billie had a boyfriend, the steady routine she had become used to blacking out the uncomfortable encounters with him was blown apart. She had been at Clatford's Jump with a group of kids from village. Billie and Carl had held hands as they raced towards the edge of the embankment and leapt, still holding hands, into the river below. The force of the water wrenched Billie's hand from Carl's. She surfaced, laughing from the adrenaline coursing through her body.

"That was awesome," she crowed, as hands wrapped around her waist. Carl's laughter sent shivers down her spine. She loved his laugh and the feel of his hands on her. His touch made her feel at peace in the crazy life she was living. She could focus on that and she felt normal.

"Again, my love?" he questioned with a smirk.

"I thought you'd never ask."

She pulled his arm to lead them out of the river and back up the embankment. There was a queue of children waiting to jump off the edge: this was the highest and safest spot to jump, so on a rare, warm summer's day, the kids all gravitated towards it. Carl sat down, waiting for the queue to get smaller; he pulled Billie down so her back was against his chest. She half turned so she could look up at him and his lips lowered to hers. A shiver of passion went through Billie. She wasn't even embarrassed that everyone could see. All she could feel was him and her, and the rest of the world shrank away. *What do you know!* The films and books weren't exaggerating, love was as amazing as they portrayed it. A cold splash of water broke them apart and the sound of raucous laughter surrounded them.

"Thought you needed cooling down," one of the lads quipped. Billie got up, wiping the water from her face she was soaking wet from their first jump so it was futile. Carl's arms took their usual place around her waist, and his nose nuzzled her neck. The wind had picked up and it blew her hair into her face.

As she shook her head to get rid of it, she caught sight of a figure on the opposite side of the embankment where there were lots of trees and plants. There was also a small pathway that was part of a long nature walk and it followed the river for a while. The path eventually veered of toward the village and it was here she could make out the slim figure of a man. His balding head, customary blue jeans and designer black raincoat let her know exactly who it was. He was stood rigid, from what she could see from the opposite side of the river. As she felt her legs give way, he turned around and started to walk towards the village. Carl's arm held her firm and he glanced at her, puzzled.

"Sorry," she said. "I just went a little dizzy."

"Maybe you should sit down for a bit?" he suggested. The look of concern in his eyes nearly caused her to cry, but she knew if she did, she would end up confessing to him, and that would be the end of their love. She wasn't stupid, boys don't like liars. This whole side of her life was a lie.

"Actually, I think I will head home," she replied. "I'm not feeling so great."

"I'll walk you," he insisted. She shook her head.

"No need. You stay. Please. It's only five minutes up the road. I will call you later." Before he could protest, she kissed him and began to walk around to the bridge.

Once over the bridge, she followed the path along the opposite side of the river. She hurried after Eric; she knew it was better to speak to him now. She had angered him once before when she had refused to let him put a twenty-pound note in her knickers, and she had stayed away, thinking he would be less angry once he'd had time to cool off. Instead, he had taken it upon himself to convince Billie's mum to let him take her to her a violin lesson. He had driven her in silence and suddenly pulled over at the side of the road and cried. He was so distressed she had stayed away from him, he had missed her so much and he only wanted to talk to her. When something was wrong he liked to sort it out. He didn't play games.

She hadn't told him about Carl because she knew how much it would upset him and she was wary of his reaction. It was so frustrating, some days she hated him for all the things he was doing to her. But other days, Eric was so nice to her, it made her brain hurt trying to understand how someone, so kind and caring, could force her to do things like pose with her pants around her ankles while he took photographs. She had learnt that when she complied with everything he wanted her to do there were no threats to her sister. He was nicer to her whole family when she did what he asked. She hoped that he wasn't too upset. He must have realised she would be interested in boys? She felt nervous. She didn't know what she would do if he cried again. It was awkward and she didn't like seeing a grown man cry. God, why did her life have to be so complicated? He was an elderly, caring monster that somehow managed to make her upset if he cried.

She caught up with him quickly. It was as if he knew she would come straight away. He leant against a fence and looked at her, his eyes were flashing and intense. When she was close enough he strode towards her, he had something in his hand, but she didn't have time to work out what it was because he had his lips pressed hard against hers. She tried not to grimace. She hated doing this. He stopped just as suddenly.

"Let's go home," he growled at her. At least he wasn't crying, she thought. He motioned for her to walk in front of him; she sighed and then began to lead the way up the path. She was working out what she could say to him when she felt a blow to her back. She fell on her knees, crying out in pain and shock. Waves of agony swept through her, it felt as if her back was on fire. She turned around on her knees to work out what was going on. She saw his arm lower towards her and the small, thick branch he was holding smacked against her side. The force of his attack knocked her down on her side, gasping for breath. She had never felt pain like it. She curled up, waiting for another blow.

Instead, she sensed him kneeling and coming close to her head. She could feel his hot breath on her cheeks as he moved his lips to her ear.

"You stupid little whore. How could you let a boy touch you like that?" His voice was soft but laced with an anger so fierce she was too scared to open her eyes. "You are a slut. Is that what you want people to say about you? Why do you think he is touching you like that?" He paused, reached his hand down to her face. He cupped it with his fingers and forced her to meet his blue eyes, they were narrowed in anger. "Do you think he loves you like I do? NO!" He roared at her. She cowered against his hard grip on her face. "I love you so much, and for you to go and let another person lay hands on you like that ... do you understand nothing? You are so stupid; can't you see that he is just using you for sex? He won't treat you the way I do. He will never understand you the way I do." He stopped shouting and just stared at her.

She felt her tears sliding down her face but she didn't dare move.

His eyes softened. "I'm sorry, sweetie, I shouldn't have hurt you. I was just so mad at you. Do you understand what it is like to have all these feelings for you, and then see you with that boy? There isn't anything I wouldn't do for you, but I won't share you." He sighed, releasing her face. "Maybe I chose the wrong sister. Maybe your sister is more deserving of the love and attention I give you." He got up from his position next to her and began to slowly walk away. She fought through the pain that was radiating from her side and up her back. She hobbled after him and cried out.

"Stop!"

He slowly turned around to look at her. She caught a glimpse of the knowing smile on his face before he was able to straighten it. At that moment, she saw him for what he really was. She knew the truth. He could wrap up what he was doing to her, as love and affection, but that smile revealed this was all just a massive manipulation. Her anger swept through her body. She had been taken in by the gifts and the love he had lavished on her. She had almost begun to think this was normal. She had been convinced that he loved her and he just couldn't control himself sometimes. But now she knew. After four years, the cloud of confusion that had plagued her was blown away by the sight of that manipulative smirk that he hadn't been able to hide. Before she saw his smile, she had believed that he was in love with her and that he had every right to be mad at her. She had even felt a twinge of jealousy that he would choose Holly over her. She was about to grovel and beg so he wouldn't leave her.

For the past four years she had relied on him, even though at times she didn't understand what he was doing. The love and attention he gave her, the support when she felt she had no one, was worth so much to her. But it had all been a lie. Those moments she had put down to him loving her too much; they were what he was doing this for, not the other way around. He was every bit like the men he had warned her about. He had made her feel so special, but she wasn't. Just like the kids at school had told her, she was nothing. She thought of Carl and realised he was probably playing the same trick on her as Eric had. Lavishing her with attention until he could get what he wanted. Well, she wasn't going to stand for it any more. She pulled herself up, the adrenaline from knowing she was going to stand up for herself quelled the pain in her back.

"You don't love me." She paused, breathing through the spasms of pain. "You just want to do those awful things to me to satisfy yourself!" She knew what she wanted to ask next but she was afraid of the answer. She sucked in a deep breath and carried on. She'd got this far.

"What I don't understand, is why you had to spend so much time making me feel special? Why lie?" She could feel tears welling in her eyes. She had trusted him. But she was as worthless as when she had first met him.

He had stilled when she began, but as she faltered, trying to hold back the sobs, he recovered and moved towards her. Looming over her.

"It is easier if you are compliant," he said. "It saves me from worrying about you telling anyone what we are up to." His tone was so matter of fact it hurt even more than if he had screamed at her. "If I made you love me, then you wouldn't leave me. I do love you. At first I saw what everyone else saw: a dull, ugly, fat little girl. But I have made you better. Without me, you are nothing. Just a whore. As I am sure your boy down there will soon show you." He motioned towards the river, a cruel smile on his face.

"I didn't have to spend all this time and money on you, but I felt sorry for you. No one will ever want you, Billie. You aren't funny. You aren't intelligent. You aren't pretty. You aren't wanted. You aren't special. The only people that will ever love you are your family, and that's only because they have to. You will just be sex to any man you meet. But I am willing to overlook that. Why do you think you have no friends? You need me. That's what I figured when I saw you. I knew, if I made you feel loved, that you would be mine. You should be thanking me. I am the only one who will ever want you. I have forced myself to love you. If you stick with me, I will make sure you want for nothing. I am your only chance in life to be happy." He was so eloquent. Even when confessing how he had tricked her into believing she was special. Even when insulting the very nature of her being, his wording was elegant and to the point. And worse still, he was convincing. Everything he said was like a knife in her back, and it seemed like he was the only one who could stop the bleeding.

Her spirit felt crushed, and the anger she felt earlier had fled as if it knew it was an unrighteous anger. She had known from a very young age that she was not special. Her dad had abandoned her before she could even talk. Her mother was more concerned with her own relationships and her own world. She wasn't the apple of her mum's eye, the way that she knew other daughters were. She was never met with the same love and adoration that Holly experienced from their mum. At school, she dreaded PE; she wasn't top set for anything. She remembered Eric's wonderful pep talk about how she was the best at being herself. But now, here he was telling her it had all been a lie. She felt broken inside. She moved to walk past him. She needed to lie down. The pain in her side was slowly returning as her mind shut down, as she absorbed the truth about herself.

He stopped her from getting past him. A light rain was starting to fall and she was already shivering from jumping into the river and then standing still for so long. She felt his hard grip on her arm, made even more painful by the cold. The rain exacerbated the chill that was numbing her body.

"Now, look," his tone was authoritative and made her look up at him. Didn't he know he had done enough? What more could he possibly want from her?

"We both know where we stand, there is no reason this still can't work. I'm happy to keep treating you exactly the same. Maybe you will be a bit more receptive now you know what I have had to put myself through for you. I expect no more refusals. And if you even think about telling anyone what has happened between us, I will be infuriated. I just hope your sister won't be nearby when I feel angry. And yes, I will be able to get to her, because if you do tell anyone, no one will believe you. We have already established your worth, so it isn't hard to see whose word people would take. I am a respectable member of this neighbourhood." He moved his other hand so he was holding both her arms under her shoulders. He glared at her. "Do you understand me?" he asked.

She realised as she nodded that her life was never going to be the same again.

# Chapter Twenty-Four
## 2009

### Adam

Adam walked into school with his head held high, feeling confident. A man with a mission. It was Monday and he'd just spent one of the best weekends of his life with his uncle. On this trip, his uncle had told him exactly what to do when he saw Sophie today. When he spotted her at one of the tables in the library, reading something, he took a deep breath and recalled the conversation with his uncle, trying to commit every word of his advice into his head. They had gone on a road trip and it was awesome. They took his uncle's motorbike and drove wherever Adam had wanted. They played the left and right game. At each crossroads, Adam would tap his uncle's left shoulder if they were to turn left, or right shoulder to turn right. Some of the views they saw were stunning. The power of the bike and the feel of the wind pressing on him from all sides was exhilarating. After hours of driving, his uncle stopped at a pub. Adam wasn't sure where they were, and neither was his uncle. It was a strange feeling but made the sense of adventure even better.

Adam was a little nervous when they walked into the pub. It felt like everyone turned around to stare as the door opened. He'd never been one who liked to be the centre of attention. It didn't seem to bother his uncle, though. He shot the barmaid a charming smile and ordered drinks, oblivious to the stares of the locals who were taking in his and Adam's leathers. His uncle started chatting with the barmaid and told Adam to go and find a seat and he'd get them some food.

Adam walked past a family of four on his way to the booths in the corner. As he sat down, he felt the familiar slice through his heart when he thought of his mother. Last week it had been the anniversary of her death. Sometimes it felt like she had died yesterday, his mind would fill up with her shining hair and her sparkling eyes and he'd relive the laughter that had surrounded her; the force of nature she'd been, the gentle touch of her hands running through his hair. Other times, though, he felt like he was losing his memories of her. When he tried to picture her face, he could see her hair and her eyes, but the rest of her face was blurry. Then he would feel the weight of every day he had been without her; it made it difficult to get out of bed. That was what this trip was about. His uncle had called and heard Adam's voice and knew that he was struggling with the anniversary.

His uncle came over, even his walk boasted confidence. Adam hoped he would grow up to be exactly like him. He was cool, he could talk to anyone and, most of all, he was kind. Everyone could see it. All his teachers at school loved Eric. They all thought Uncle Eric lived with Adam and his dad. He was Adam's emergency contact. He was the one Adam brought to school events. The mums and teachers were bowled over by his uncle's generous nature. He would volunteer for anything and he was always donating money for this and that. Last month, he had come down for the bake sale the school was holding to raise funds for a new sports centre. Adam had panicked because it was a weekend, and the school had said everyone had to have a grown-up with them and a selection of cakes. His father would either refuse to go, or he'd go, but only after some 'Dutch courage', which would end up with him being asked to leave. Luckily, Uncle Eric was free that weekend after he'd heard the fear in Adam's voice. His uncle was Adam's guiding light in the darkness that had filled his life the day his mum died.

"Smile, son." His uncle was so perceptive, he knew exactly when Adam was sad or when he needed to be cheered up. "You know what you need, you need a girl."

"But I only broke it off with Elle a couple of weeks ago. It wouldn't be right."

"Son, you're only young. You can do what you want. It's not like you and Elle were married. Now come on, think. I had a look when we were at the bake sale. You've got quite a few options in your year. I was talking to a lovely young lady called Sophie?"

"You didn't talk to her about me? That's so embarrassing; why would you do that? Anyway, my mates would all ditch me if I went out with her. She's a nerd." Adam's foot started shaking up and down. What if Sophie told everyone at school that his uncle was trying to set them up? He'd never live it down. His uncle didn't understand; there were people you could go out with and people you couldn't even talk to.

"Calm down, son. I didn't say anything about you. I just asked her about herself. I was sizing her up for you. What are uncles for?" he said as he rubbed his knuckles on Adam's head. "She's perfect. I only had to give her a couple of compliments and she opened right up."

"But I don't like Sophie."

"Oh Adam, you do disappoint me." Adam felt like he'd been hit over the head. His uncle had never said anything like that to him. He'd only ever shown Adam kindness. To think that he was disappointed with him made him feel sick, although he didn't really understand how disagreeing with him was wrong.

"Don't say that, I don't get it," said Adam, trying not to let distress show in his voice.

"I'm sorry, son, I didn't mean to upset you. What I mean is, we have already talked about this. You said that you understood the advice I was giving you. I thought you saw the bigger picture. I thought you were a smart boy who made clever decisions. I thought you wanted my help and guidance," Eric sighed heavily, deflating with what looked like sadness. "I'm sorry, I was just trying to help you, without your mother around to guide you I thought you might want me to help you with things like this. Don't worry, I'll keep my mouth shut from now on. You do as you like. I'm an old man, what do I know about young lads and their troubles?"

The words tumbled out of Adam's mouth as he tried to placate him. He couldn't have him thinking that Adam didn't value his advice or support. He was the only person who cared about Adam. He didn't have anyone else. He couldn't lose him.

"No, no, I do want your advice. You're the best uncle in the world. I do want your advice, please explain more about Sophie. I just wasn't thinking before. Please go on, tell me what you thought." Eric was silent, he examined him intently. Adam squirmed under his gaze. Whatever he was assessing Adam needed to pass. The consequence of failure would be unbearable.

Adam was about to explode from the tension when Eric began to speak. "All right, son, listen up. This is what you need to do."

# Chapter Twenty-Five
## 2010
### Billie

The only way Billie was going to escape was through her exams. She had chosen the university she wanted to go to. She knew the course she thought she might like to do. She knew the grades she needed to get. She had achieved relatively good GCSE grades so she was confident that she would be able to escape by going to the furthermost university from the Lake District. She wanted to run away now, but she was a coward, and she had nowhere to go. All she needed to do was get through the next few weeks. She had made expert revision cards that she was rather proud of. Her bedroom was covered in spider diagrams that she had spent hours painstakingly colouring in, trying to find any way to make the information absorb into her brain and stay there.

Since the day at the river, her life over the past year had settled into a routine. In the beginning she had tried to avoid ever being alone with Eric. She was terrified that, now the bandage had been ripped off so to speak, there would be no limit to what he would make her do. But that had lasted for only one month before he had shown her there was no way she could avoid him.

She had been walking back from the bus stop and he had been waiting down one of the many alleys that crisscrossed the village. It was the perfect movie-like scenario: he had grabbed her, put his hand over her mouth and dragged her into the darkness of the alley. The smell of rotting food wafted from somewhere but the large trees, which lined the alley, stopped her from seeing where the smell may have been coming from.

"I thought we had a deal," he'd whispered into her ear. The other kids were still walking home, she could hear their shouted conversations, and through the trees she could see patches of colour as they walked past.

"Let go of me!" she tried to scream through his hand, struggling to be free.

"Did you think that you could avoid me? Did I not make myself clear? You will do as I say." He shook her slightly, as if for emphasis. "Your sister has still been coming around but I haven't seen you. It's been making me terribly angry. I may not be able to resist taking it out on that sister of yours. Or maybe I will start coming over to see you." He paused as if this was a new thought. "Hmm … that sounds like a better plan. I still have the spare key from when you all went away to America. Maybe next time when you wake up I will be there. I will be watching. You will never know if I'm coming to you or not. I could even be going to your sister's room. You are leaving me with no choice. If you won't come and see me, then I will be forced to come and see you. But I might not be as nice." With that, he released her and thrust her out of the alley.

Billie took the warning seriously. She figured out a routine that kept Eric happy but allowed her to spend as little time with him as possible. Her only respite was when he went away at weekends. She would go over straight after school. Her gran was normally at work, and even if she was at home Eric found a way around it. He didn't want to do sexual things every day. Some days he would be the old Eric: he would make her laugh and for a moment, despite everything, she would forget who he really was. It made it hard to hate him; if he just used her for her body every day, then she would be able to harden towards him. But he wasn't like that. Despite all the violence and lies, he was able to get under her skin and make her briefly forget what he really wanted from her. She knew it was his way of keeping her under control but she couldn't help it. She could tell from his body language whether he would be nice or horrible when he opened the door to her each day.

Her body would sag with relief when she saw there was no wicked gleam in his eyes that meant he had been thinking about what he wanted to do to her. She would go inside and he would soon be poking her until she was laughing, albeit reluctantly. He would tell her jokes and play pranks on her. Some days he would play games or take her out for dinner. It was these days that made Billie feel guilty. As if she was encouraging him. She should hate him for what he was doing to her, but she still went for dinner with him.

It didn't make any sense. When he wasn't nice to her, she was terrified of him, when he wanted *that* from her, it filled her with fear that he was going to, one day, go from touching to actual sex. She hated the fact that she could still fall for his charm when she spent most of her time terrified of him.

Eventually, she stopped trying to figure it out. At the end of the day, this was her life now. No one would believe her if she told them what he was doing; how could they when they were always being seen together? Going to dinner, playing tennis; it wouldn't make sense. How could anyone take her seriously when she laughed and smiled in his presence? Even if she wanted to tell someone, she was far too scared. Whenever she was with him, when he was in *that* mood, she would shake with fear. He was aggressive and sometimes violent with her when she refused him. She had been on the receiving end of his violent outbursts so many times and she couldn't bear to imagine what he would do to her if she told anyone. His threats on her sister still rang in her head as clear as day. Could she really be so selfish? Condemn her sister to his fists of anger and his wandering fingers of lust to save herself? No, she was the elder sister, it was her job to keep Holly safe. This was her life now. If she could keep her head down and study, and find a way to save her sister, maybe she could escape to university. If Eric didn't ruin that too.

# Chapter Twenty-Six
## 2009

### Adam

The cluttered table full of university brochures mirrored the chaos in his mind. He had a big decision ahead of him. Inside, he was desperate to move away; to escape his drunken father by leaving for a university far away from Worcester. He dreamed of moving somewhere new, St Andrews, Preston, Lancaster. But like his Uncle Eric had pointed out, what would become of his dad if Adam was to move away? At the moment, when his father came in rolling drunk, Adam would put him to bed in the recovery position in an effort to stop him from swallowing his tongue again. Adam was the one who hid the car keys so he would no longer be able to drink-drive. Adam was the one who locked him in the house when he tried to go drinking for seventh day in a row. It was Adam who held him and wiped away his tears when the grief he refused to deal with broke the surface. Adam was finally making some progress with his dad. His influence had stopped him from drinking every day, it was now only a two or three-day occurrence. Two days were spent at a part-time job working in a friend's garage. His high-powered London job was a thing of the past. Adam cooked the food, cleaned the house and made sure all the bills were paid. He didn't really like his dad. Their communication was limited to essential exchanges. They never spent any time together, unless his father was unconscious or they were passing each other on the stairs.

In the early days after his mother's passing, he had tried to become close with his father, thinking it was what his mother would have wanted. But no matter what he did, it never worked.

He'd even tried to find things in common to start a conversation, perhaps even bond over a shared interest. But it was as if his mum had taken his dad's soul with her when she died. His reason for living had gone. This also meant he had lost any desire for a relationship with his son. Adam remembered finding a stash of car magazines in the corner of his parent's room. Excitement ran through him as he realised this could be the thing to get his dad to talk to him. He had spent ages reading up on cars, memorising the makes and models and how the mechanics worked. He had been trembling with happiness as he waited impatiently until his father was at his most calm, after his first drink of the evening. Eventually he went ahead and tried to engage him in a conversation about the benefit of manual transition over automatic, and asked what his dad's favourite car was. Adam gave a pre-prepared speech on what his favourite car was and anxiously waited for his father's reply. He was met with a wall of silence. His father was staring into the can of beer he'd just opened. "Dad, are you listening?" He watched as his dad seemed to blink himself back into life. His eyes focused on Adam, cold and uncaring.

"Will you shut up yapping in my ear? Don't you get it? It should have been you!" The can of beer flew across the room before Adam realised. The shock numbed the pain in his head. The beer had arched across the room, covering him and half the room. The stench of alcohol made him feel sick. His father stood and, without looking over at Adam, he grabbed his keys off the mantelpiece and slammed the front door behind him so hard the house vibrated. He didn't even look back when he said he was going to the pub. That was the last time he tried to connect with his dad. He hoped his mum would understand. He would never be able to erase the hatred in his dad's eyes as he'd told Adam he should be the one who was dead. The hole in his life where his mum had been, was now filled with a devastating guilt that he knew would never leave. He had tried to do everything he could to make it up to him. Tried to make amends for the fact that he was alive, and his mother wasn't. But nothing worked. At least now he understood why he didn't want him. He vowed to try and make life as easy as he could for his dad. So many times, he had hated himself for being alive when his mother was dead. And now he knew his own father shared that feeling, guilt consumed him and it resolved him to being the perfect son.

As a result, the thought of leaving him to move away caused his guilt to flare. Would his mum approve of him moving away, or would she want him to stay? He picked up the University of Worcester brochure and flicked through the pages, the campus was only fifteen minutes away so there would be no need to move out. He'd been to it when he was at school for different events and it looked like a good campus. It was always getting renovated and the new Hive building meant the library facilities would be good. But, in his heart, it wasn't as exciting as moving to a campus he had never been to before. To explore a new place, somewhere he didn't know. If only his uncle thought he should move away. With his support Adam knew he could fight the guilt of leaving his dad. But even Uncle Eric thought staying in Worcester was the best thing.

On his last visit, Adam had mentioned his conflict, desperate for the ever-constant advice he knew his uncle would have. Deep down, Adam was hoping that his uncle would soothe his fears about leaving his dad, and tell him to go wherever he wanted. That he would look after his dad, and that Adam needed to get away.

"I've been looking at different universities and there are some great journalism courses, I really like the sound of the one in Manchester, but I don't know if I should leave Dad. Is it fair to abandon him? I need your help, what do you think I should do?" His uncle finished his turn on the chess board, ruthlessly taking another one of Adam's Bishops. It was their new favourite game, they were playing with the sparkling glass set his uncle had just given him as a surprise present. His brow was creased as he thought, and Adam wasn't sure if it was his question or the game that his uncle was considering. Eventually, he looked up and spoke.

"You know I always give you my honest opinion. I only want the best for you, son, so, if you want my advice, I think you are better off staying where you are. If you stay here, you know what the university is like, you know what to expect and, best of all, we can still see each other. If you go to a different university somewhere else, I might not get to see you as much. You'll be too busy with all your flatmates and socialising. If you stay here, you'll save money as you can live at home, and I will be able to pop over here knowing where you'll be. That's if you still want to see me?"

"But if I went to Manchester I'd be closer to you; I even looked at Preston University which is even closer. I'd get to see you loads if I moved there because I wouldn't be four hours away."

"Son, I'm an old man. I'm not up to traipsing over to a university campus. There wouldn't be a spare room for me at your accommodation and I wouldn't feel comfortable. I may be being selfish but you need to think of your family. Look, I didn't want to tell you this yet, but me and Sylvia have been looking at places to move to down here. To be closer to you. She knows how much I wish I could see you more so she's agreed to have a look. If you move away, she won't let me move to be near you. Wouldn't it be better if we were in the same city?"

Adam quickly assured his uncle that he would stay where he was. There was a moment where he felt sceptical; Uncle Eric had never mentioned this before, but he dismissed it. At the end of the day he was the most honourable man he knew and he only wanted the best for him. His advice, company and support since his mother's death had proved it.

With these thoughts in mind, Adam realised that he stood to gain much more by staying where he was. If he moved away, he'd be even more alone than he was now. He needed to take a leaf out of his uncle's book, he needed to put his family first. His dad had been devastated and broken by the loss of his wife, he was to be pitied, not abandoned. And Uncle Eric was dead set against Adam moving away, so that was that. He had been there for Adam when no one else was; Adam needed to make sure he knew how grateful he was. It was his turn to do something for him, to demonstrate his loyalty and respect. Apart from the one for Worcester with a heavy heart he threw all the brochures in the bin. He had made his decision. He was sure it was the right one.

# Chapter Twenty-Seven
## 2010
### Billie

Billie sat on the windowsill of her bedroom. She was exhausted with living a double life. One where Eric tormented her, and basically did whatever he pleased to her before she went home, and the other where she had to go to school and pretend that everything was fine. In her bedroom, the pink walls were covered with Green Day posters.

She'd had to tell Carl she could no longer be his girlfriend because she didn't love him any more. He took it surprisingly well. Apparently, he wasn't as okay with just kissing like he'd promised. He didn't try and persuade her otherwise, but instead began dating Nicola one of the 'plastic fantastic' girls who she'd known all along he should be with who, he said, 'wasn't frigid'. Before he'd said that she hadn't wanted to end it. She had known all along that Carl would never stay with her because he had been pushing her into being intimate, but each time he'd tried to put his hand up her shirt she had been unable to hold back her tears. While she was officially his girlfriend she could pretend that she would be able to have a future, that everything Eric had said was a lie. His daily references on how she was ugly, and no one could ever love her, were awful to hear, but having Carl in her life made it bearable.

She almost didn't do it, but then she looked at the bandage around her fingers and thought back to the previous night when Eric had followed her into his garage she was going to get a can of Pepsi. He slammed the door shut and locked it and all she could think was 'what now?' She didn't have the strength to put up a fight. She almost considered just taking her clothes off so he would hurry up, but then if she did that it would encourage him to do more, sometimes she got off lightly with just a bit of touching and kissing. She looked up at him and immediately moved backwards until she hit the caravan that had residence in the garage. His eyes were smouldering with anger. She was sure she had been careful and not done anything that could anger him.

"Don't look at me like that," he demanded as he walked towards her. "Did you really think I wouldn't find out that you are still with that dickhead?" When she didn't answer, and merely hung her head while cursing her own stupidity, he continued.

"I saw the two of you ... fondling." He spat at her. "Don't I give you enough of that? Am I not doing enough for you?" He grabbed her by her hair and began to move her towards the locked door. "You are mine," he breathed into her ear. He slightly opened the garage door. He released her hair and put a hand tight over her mouth. With his other hand, he shoved her fingers into the gap under the hinge on the door. When she didn't move her fingers from where he'd left them she knew better than that he slammed the garage door shut, and a cracking sound was audible, accompanying the bang of the door latch against the frame. Pain erupted in her fingers and she almost fell to the floor, but his hand on her mouth, silencing her screams, held her up. He promised that he would do it to the other hand, or to her sister's hand, unless she swore to break it off with Carl.

They went back into the house, Billie pitifully holding her fingers to her chest. All her fight left her with each throb of pain. Her gran looked up from her tapestry when they walked in; she looked at Billie and sighed.

"What have you done this time?" She was referring to the previous month when Billie had decided to try once again to stand up to Eric, and not let him do what he wanted. They had been alone in the house and she was 'invited' over by Eric, under the guise of needing her help setting up his new video camera. She had set it up for him and he had decided he wanted to film her. He said she should get used to stripping in front of men because that was all she was good for. She just couldn't do it. It was bad enough having to submit to whatever sexual need he had, but to have it recorded on camera was just too much. She wouldn't do it. She'd refused and Eric had walked over to her and smashed the camera into her face. She had fallen back with the force of it. It was at that moment they heard her gran coming into the house through the back door. Eric had thrown the broken camera onto Billie, and knelt down, cooing, "Don't worry, you'll be okay, it was only a silly camera, sweetheart." He was stroking her face as her gran had come into the room. Eric explained how Billie had been running around with the camera and tripped over, hitting her face and the camera into the edge of the display cabinet in the corner of the room. She watched him lie effortlessly. If she hadn't been there, she would have believed him too. So, she knew this time there was no point trying to cause trouble by saying that Eric had hurt her fingers, because she was not as good a liar as him. She just told her gran that she wanted to go home.

All the way home she was terrified that her mother would work out what had happened. She was a nurse before she'd changed careers, and she didn't know if Eric's lie about him trapping her fingers in the door by accident was going to work. Although a tiny part of her hoped she worked it out. She needn't have worried. Her mother didn't even undo the bandage Eric had given her.

Billie knew she was protecting her sister and stopping her family from breaking apart, and most of the time she could bear it, but she really loved Carl. He was the only solace she had, but when she broke up with him, she had no illusion or way of pretending that she had a normal life. One that she could use to drown out the memories and experiences she had with Eric. Despite her anger and disgust, deep down, she missed Eric. Not this new Eric, but the one he had been when she first met him. He was different now, no longer supporting her and making her feel special. Instead, he was using every tool in his belt to make sure she submitted to whatever he wanted. He was obsessed with her, and controlling her seemed to be his life's work. He certainly spent enough time at it.

Their house was at the end of a terrace, and on the other side there were lots of fields. She could see them from her bedroom and she knew that Eric could see her bedroom from the fields. He had a perfect vantage point from a cluster of trees at the edge of one of the fields. She hadn't even noticed until he had told her that he loved seeing her sitting on her windowsill, looking deep in thought, and that next time she should wear some of the lingerie he had bought her. He was everywhere she went, apart from school, and it was slowly dragging her down. He was an omnipotent presence in her life that she knew wasn't going to leave her alone. But she had to live life as if nothing was happening. She knew what would happen to her sister if she didn't. Eric reminded her that she would ruin her mother's life if she were to talk about what he did. He taunted her, saying her mum probably knew and let it go on because she also knew that Billie would never amount to anything more than a hooker.

The only way Billie was going to escape was through her exams. Her AS levels were just around the corner and then it would only be one more year until she could leave and never come back. She worried that she was leaving her sister unprotected, but her mum was insistent that she go to university so she didn't really have a choice. Eric couldn't blame her, could he? She was protecting her sister as much as she could for the moment. Eric didn't have the same sort of relationship with Holly because Billie had made sure that she never spent time alone with him. It would be harder for him to get close to her. She was also their mother's favourite so that would protect her too, at least Billie prayed it would. She pushed it to the back of her mind. Instead, she thought about the university she wanted to go to. She wanted to leave now. Get as far away as she could. But with no where to go she wasn't brave enough to follow through. Instead, she needed to get the best results she possibly could so she could escape from Windermere, to Hereford College of Arts and study photography.

The next week, Billie walked into her room, still cradling her hand, but she stopped at the doorway; she knew at once something was wrong. Her eyes jumped immediately to her desk. It was empty apart from one solitary piece of paper. A feeling of foreboding swept through her as she crossed her room to the desk. 'Try and leave me now' it said. She dashed around her room, trying to find the stack of books, the revision that was plastered on her wall and the neat pile of revision cards that were on her bedside table. She frantically searched everywhere, checking under the bed, her wardrobe, starting what she knew was a futile search. If she could find something he'd left behind, then maybe this feeling of hopelessness would recede and she would not feel like going to her window and jumping out head first. After turning everything upside down, including her bed, it was obvious he was too smart to leave anything behind. She leaned against her bed, brought her knees up and rested her head on them.

This was all her fault. She had snapped and lost her temper with him the day before he had put something in her drink, she was sure of it. He liked her to go over after school every day, he said that the school uniform even on someone as ugly as her really turned him on. So, one minute she was sitting on the sofa watching TV with him and the next she was in his bedroom, naked. She should have expected something as it was Thursday, the day her gran always worked late. She shuddered and forced away the thoughts of what he'd done. When she had found her clothes and gone downstairs, he had winked at her and asked if she had slept well. She was normally numb after anything he did to her. This had been going on for as long as she could remember and she knew there was nothing she could do to stop it; that she had let herself fall for his grandfatherly charm. Even her sister had seen through him, she had never wanted anything to do with him. That day she was so fed-up of feeling out of control that her temper, which was typically non-existent, reared its head like a bear coming out of hibernation, long enough for her to shout at him:

"You think you are so clever, don't you? Drugging me? But you've actually done me a favour, now I don't have to remember your disgusting, old, wrinkly body anywhere near mine! Anyway, don't get used to it. Your days are numbered doing this to me. After my exams next week, I only have one year left and then I will be going to the furthest university away from here, and you will never see me again. I've suffered this for seven years, what is one more?"

Her anger spent, she raced out of the house and back home before he could execute any retribution. She knew she would pay for that, but what could he do to her that he hadn't already done? Well, she knew now, this was what he could do. How she was going to explain this at school, she didn't know. She thought about telling the truth, just to spite him. But she knew that no one would believe her. He had thought this out too well. He had planned for every eventuality and this brazen intrusion demonstrated that. That was when her fear of him became all consuming. She was never going to get away from him. This was how the rest of her life was going to be.

# Chapter Twenty-Eight
## 2010
### Adam

Uncle Eric walked into Adam's bedroom and tipped him off the mattress as if he weighed nothing. "Get up, you lazy arse, we are going out." Adam's uncle had decided they needed to be more selfless with their time. He said his home life was perfect, everything was exactly how he wanted, so it was time to give back. He marched Adam down to the homeless shelter and it was becoming a routine for them.

The first couple of times they had helped to prepare lunch. As ever, Uncle Eric made the most mundane tasks fun. They bantered back and forth while peeling vegetables and washing pots. It felt good, and Adam felt his heart swell with happiness at the simple pleasure of spending time with him. He felt a pang of sadness as he again wished that Eric was his actual father. This weekend they had been asked to mentor some of the service users to the centre. Adam was standing at the entrance, too nervous to approach anyone, but Eric was revelling in the opportunity. He was sat with two scruffy looking girls, laughing and joking with them, when only an hour ago they had slinked in, pale and nervous. He had an effortless charm, it was something Adam envied. He had tried to emulate his cool attitude at school, but his relationship with Sophie had petered out much to his uncle's disappointment. Adam just couldn't see her appeal. Uncle Eric believed he needed a girl he could shape to be who he wanted, but when he spent time with Sophie he got bored. She was too nervous to speak to him and he lacked an easy manner to make her feel less awkward. He had persevered with these uneasy encounters at his uncle's behest but after a while it became simpler to tell him the truth.

It was hard knowing he was going against his advice, but it didn't feel right. Luckily, after a couple of weekends of tense silence, their relationship went back to normal.

They left the shelter feeling high from doing something selfless. His uncle, in his typical kind and selfless nature, had given some money and his number to the two girls. Unwilling to end the day, they stopped at a local cafe in a bookshop they both liked. His uncle brought the tray over to their table and Adam was surprised to see a sombre expression on his face. He sat down with a sigh and looked at Adam as if to make sure he definitely had his attention.

"Right, as you've probably guessed, I need to talk to you, son. I've got a problem back home and I need to spend more time there, sorting it out. I know I promised you that I would come at least once a month, but would it be okay if I didn't for a while?"

"I suppose so, what's wrong?"

"Well, I guess I may as well tell you. You know that Sylv has granddaughters? Well, one of them, Billie, she's becoming a bit of a handful. Not doing as she's told. Rebelling. It's upsetting all the family. She used to be such a well-behaved and loving girl, but something has changed. She's just getting out of hand. No one seems to be able to control her but she responds well to me. So, I need to be around more. Do you understand?"

Adam assured his uncle it was okay and it didn't matter, but deep down he was raging at this girl, Billie. Didn't she know he didn't have anyone else? That his uncle's visits were the only happy times in his life? He was so lonely. Uncle Eric had told him that men shouldn't show their emotions, they are meant to be stoic and strong. Each day he woke up in the same room, with the same useless father and the same echoing silence, it began to feel more like his own personal prison. When he came home the house was usually empty, and he would have to clear up either his father, or the mess he had created. Most of the time he would make a meal for one and sit at the breakfast bar in the kitchen. Some days he would imagine his mother sitting on the seat opposite. He would tell her about his day. He longed to hear one of her silly stories that she would create just for him. Even his imagined image of her lit up the dreary kitchen. Any time he got to escape the draining solitude with his uncle, made his life worth living again. Each visit gave him the strength to fight his daily sadness and gave him hope for the future. Uncle Eric was more than a relation. He was someone he could aspire to, someone he could emulate when he wasn't sure who he was. He was always at the end of the phone, and he didn't know what his life would be like without him. He wished he could say all of this to him so he would know that even missing one month was going to be awful.

However, he had always wanted to be like his uncle, so this was his perfect opportunity. Adam had seen him act selflessly so many times, and he knew first hand how much difference having his uncle around would make to a person's life. He hoped this girl knew how lucky she was. To have someone who was so kind and thoughtful taking care of her, and trying to get her life back on track. He wished he could help. She was so lucky to have an entire family around her.

As his uncle dropped him at home and set off for his four-hour drive back home, Adam wondered, not for the first time, why he refused to let him visit up there. Adam had met Sylvia once, but not any of her family. He often thought that, if his uncle would let him visit, he might be able to become part of the family. But Eric was adamant and he always had a reason why he couldn't go. He didn't push it because he didn't want to risk angering him. He was all he had. This Billie had better appreciate everything his uncle was doing for her.

# Chapter Twenty-Nine
## 2010
### Billie

**B**illie sat on her bed and stared at her feet in pure misery. Even though she had closed the curtains she knew he was out there. Watching for a glimpse of her. She had seen him today when her mum had driven round to pick up Gran for work. She was going with them as she didn't need to be in school until later. She had sat in the back and, as her mum pulled away, Eric had caught her eye and winked at her with a knowing look. She'd shrunk down in the seat and tried to push the image to the back of her mind. When would this ever end? Every time she saw him she felt sick. No matter how hard she scrubbed her body, she could never be clean. He had ruined her life. How could she ever hope to get married and escape him? She was terrified of men. Her brief fling with Carl would be the only relationship she would ever have. She would never have sex without thinking about the awful things Eric had done to her. She knew from reading and movies that sex was a requirement in marriage, and she was broken. Eric had taken something that most people consider special and he had made it crude and disgusting; he had made her fear it. She had no friends to turn to because they were now indifferent to her presence. She would never be one of them and she didn't have the courage to try and build relationships. She only had enough energy to get through school, get through the torment that was Eric, and then go home.

That day, she walked around school like a zombie and relied completely on autopilot to get her to the right classroom. She managed to get through school only hitting a few walls because she wasn't watching where she was going. One of the nicer teachers had asked if there was something wrong as she looked so listless and pale. But there wasn't anything wrong; there was just nothing. She wasn't overwhelmed by her thoughts; she was empty. Trying to live a normal life while stamping out the memories of her time with Eric, and dealing with the foreboding that flooded her when she wasn't with him, was just too much. She couldn't do it any more but there was no way out. If she didn't play along he might go for her sister, she knew this wasn't very likely but could she take that chance? She went home on the bus and sat on her bed, staring at her feet, trying to will away the hopelessness that was coursing through her.

She could try explaining to her mum again, but she had understood the subtext last time she tried: her mum wasn't in a position to help right now. She should grin and bear it. She had told her something minor that Eric had done, as a test. She couldn't tell her anything else because she wouldn't even know how to put it into words. She felt dirty and disgusted with herself just thinking about what happened. She couldn't imagine having to say the words. So, she settled on one of the many times that Eric had offered her money in exchange for sexual favours; one of the least traumatic that meant she would not have to mention any specific body parts or acts. She had given her mother the quick notes version, but she remembered every detail.

They had been stood in the kitchen and her gran was, of course, sewing.

"You can have this money, but you have to let me put it down there for you." He'd leered at her private parts and pointed to her jeans. She hadn't known what to say: saying no angered him and that was never wise, so she had just ignored him and made some non-committal noises. "Come on; it's not like I'm making you do it for free." He'd eventually given up; Gran being in the next room had meant he couldn't do anything else. Not that she'd notice.

She had sat at the end of her mum's bed and poured out the story while she was putting on her nightly creams. She'd stopped rubbing in the cream for a second, when Billie mentioned 'private parts', but continued again. It was the only sign that she was listening. When Billie had finished, her mum was so quiet she wondered if she was going to say anything. Billie got up to leave, but as she was about to move her mum spoke.

"Look, that sounds awful, but I can't afford to lose your gran from the firm at the moment, we are in the midst of a massive case and I can't afford to lose anyone. It would tear this family apart. He might not even have done it; he could have been drunk; he could have been joking. I don't know, Billie. It seems too trivial a thing to create such an uproar. I tell you what, if he does something worse we will go to the police. In the meantime, why don't you go to counselling? Get your head straight."

Billie had agreed and left the room.

Her mum had said the exact words that Eric had been saying. *She would rip the family apart if she said anything.* As soon as her mum had said that, her worst fear had come to life. She couldn't stop thinking; *what if everything else Eric had said was right; what if her mum had known all along and didn't mind?* The scenario she had hoped for involving her mum becoming outraged and storming over to their house, trying to beat up Eric and get him arrested was destroyed by the knowledge that Eric was right. She shouldn't have been surprised; after all, her gran had had near enough the same reaction. Billie couldn't even cry in disappointment. She was just grateful she wasn't going to be taken away like her gran had said. So, she continued ignoring the problem and it was never mentioned again.

Now, sat on her bed, that conversation a distant memory, her heart hurt. She wanted to be able to tell someone, and for them to pick her up and take her away from this awful situation. He was everywhere she looked. She couldn't escape him and he knew it. There was one way he couldn't get to her … She had thought about killing herself before, but truth be told she was scared about what would happen once she had.

She believed in heaven and hell and she was convinced that she would be going to hell. She had told so many lies in her life.

She knew this was all her fault. There was no doubt that, in some way, she had led Eric on; she had let him think that she wanted whatever he was doing. Then, when she changed her mind, he got nasty. So what right did she have to tear the family apart by going to the police and telling them what had happened? Tonight, though, she was more scared of living than she was of going to hell. She had no fight left in her to keep on living a normal life for her family's benefit. The confusion and debates in her head were constant and she couldn't handle it any more. She couldn't imagine a future without him leering at her. His face was everywhere; he had infested her life and there wasn't anyone to help her be rid of him. The only way he would not be able to control her, was if she were dead. It was the only way she could be free. The thought gave her hope, and she was sure that this return of feeling meant she was doing the right thing.

She jumped off the bed and slowly walked downstairs. Matthew was in the living room with two friends he had known since school. She had already greeted them when she got back from school so she walked quickly through to the kitchen. She was glad her mum was still at work, as she would have insisted that she 'come down and be sociable'. With the breakfast bar in the way, she was confident no one would see her empty the medicine cabinet of anything that looked like painkillers; she took lots of ibuprofen as it seemed more harmful than the paracetamol. She wasn't doing things by half measures, she would do this properly, it had to work. She stuffed the pills in her jumper pocket and returned to her room. Billie sat on her bed with her dirty white teddy, that she'd always had, on her knee. She always had it near her and guarded it as her mum had threatened numerous times to wash it. She began popping one pill at a time from the packets; she took them one at a time in the beginning, but the more she took, the more confident she felt that she was making the right decision. She took more and more in one go. Soon there were no tablets left. She lay on the bed and smiled. She couldn't wait to be free. No more living under the threat of Eric. No more pretending to be normal when inside she was breaking. She was so relieved her ordeal would be over she didn't feel guilty about what her death would do to her family.

Billie felt dizzy and lethargic, but she didn't feel like she was dying. It had been an hour and she was still conscious; she couldn't sleep because she could hear her pulse thumping away in her head. She was distraught. Why wasn't it working? Billie looked at the empty packets; there were over forty. Why on earth was it not working? Why couldn't she escape? It wasn't fair! She couldn't even die when she wanted to. She stumbled out of her room and down the stairs. Instead of going through to the living room, she went out of the front door. She could hear disjointed laughter coming from behind her. Why wouldn't they go away? Didn't they understand she needed this? Tears poured down her face as she lurched up the road, away from her house. Her vision was blurry from the tears and dizziness. She fell to her knees but kept picking herself up. This would end today. She would find a way.

"Billie? Oh my God, Billie!" a voice shouted at her as she attempted to pick herself off the ground again. Hands came around her face, directing her head up. Through her fuzzy vision she could make out the face of Gillian, her mother's friend, who lived on the same street as them.

"Are you drunk?" she questioned Billie. At the sound of the concern in her voice, Billie split open. She was unable to keep it in any more. She'd had enough.

"Why isn't it working? I took all those pills and it's not working … I want it to work … I can't … do … it any more." She heaved, emotion steam-rolling her, making it hard for her to get her words out. Gillian's hands came under her armpits, bringing her on to her feet.

"Billie, sweetheart, I need you to walk for me, just a few steps, my house is right there." Billie pushed at her hands and screeched in what she hoped was Gillian's direction; she couldn't make anything out any more, her vision was getting black around the edges.

"I need to die! I need to be free!" The desperation she felt inside made her collapse with more tears. She was swept up, presumably by Gillian, and a few minutes later she was sat down.

"Drink this, Billie. I need you to drink this, now!" Gillian was shouting at her. A glass bumped against her teeth and she tasted salt water. She tried to spit it out but her head was forced back and the drink poured down her throat. Once it was empty, the glass was taken away. Billie tried to curl up in a ball, but Gillian's firm hands stopped her, she took Billie's face and forced her to look at her. The dizziness was getting worse and she could just make out the look of terror in Gillian's eyes. She tried to put a hand on Gillian's face, to let her know it was okay, that this was the only way, but her hands were heavy and she was struggling to breathe.

"Roger has called your mum, she will be here in seconds; the office isn't far. Hang on, sweetie; you need to stay awake. I need to make you sick, can you put your fingers down your throat?" Billie could barely understand what she was saying. She heard the odd word but they weren't making any sense. She wanted to go to sleep. Her body and soul were exhausted; weary of the life she'd been living; ready to move on. But her head was pounding with the beat of her heart and it was so loud it was preventing any thoughts of rest. Billie felt fingers going down her throat and couldn't work out if they were hers or not. She felt like a floppy rag doll: like her mind and body were nearly unconnected. It was only the sound of her pounding heart that kept her from floating away.

Fingers wrapped around her hand and she would know their touch anywhere. She was a baby again and here was her mother, come to wipe away her tears with her soft fingers on her face. She tried to move towards where she thought her mother was, but she had no strength to open her eyes, and instead felt herself falling. The world went black around her but she could still feel her mother's hand. Why does she keep hurting me? Every few seconds her mother would pinch her hand, but then she would kiss it. She couldn't remember the last time her mother had kissed her hand. It was nice. She knew there was something she was supposed to be doing, but right now her mother's soft hand in hers was all she could think about.

She thought she could hear a siren, why would Gillian set the fire alarm off? What was going on? Billie was scared. She couldn't open her eyes. She couldn't feel anything except her mum's hand. Sleep was calling to her, but each time she tried to go to sleep her mother would pinch her again and she was unable to drift off. She was exhausted, she couldn't stave it off any more; she couldn't feel her mother's hand any more. Why would she let go, didn't she want her? Didn't she know Billie was scared and needed her?

# Chapter Thirty
## 2010
### Billie

Billie opened her eyes as pain coursed through her body. The nurse who had rudely prodded her into consciousness had told her she had been so close to dying that her life had been on a knife-edge and she was a 'silly girl'. She also said she had probably done lasting damage to her stomach lining and it would be a lengthy road to recovery. After this heart-warming speech, her mother came into the room. She looked dreadful. Black mascara streamed down her face, marking the path her tears had taken. Someone cleared their throat at the back of the room. Her mum's sister, Aunty Susan, took a few steps forward and appeared from the darkness. Her mum said the police would be coming to speak to her soon and she would have to tell them everything. They had been to Gran's house to persuade her to leave Eric, now that everything was going to come out, but she had refused; she'd called Billie a liar and insisted that she wanted nothing to do with any of them. Billie's heart sank, the very reason she had kept quiet for all these years was because she wanted to avoid this. Her family was now fractured because she was weak and a coward. She was also really scared. All those warnings from Eric about no one believing her were playing in her head. What if the police didn't believe her? Everyone would think she was a liar and she would have no one. What had she done? The fear was all consuming. She felt so ill. She closed her eyes to the world and prayed for sleep.

She woke in the night to her body purging the tablets she had taken; she had been sick constantly since she'd arrived at the hospital. As she was seventeen, not quite an adult but not a young child, they had put her in the locked gynaecology ward. She couldn't understand how the nurse knew what she had been through as she couldn't remember telling anyone. Maybe her mum had. But wouldn't that mean her mum would have admitted that she knew what Eric had been doing? She looked around the room. Normally her mother was there, holding out the weird looking cardboard bowl for her, each time she was ripped from sleep by the awful pain of needing to be sick, but she couldn't see her and she started to panic. She yelled out while being sick all over the floor. She knew this would happen. Eric had got to her mum and killed her, just like he'd promised he would if she ever told anyone. She screamed, "Mum!" as loud as she could, while trying desperately to get the wires out of her body so she could go and find her. Someone opened the door, but her relief was short lived when she realised it was a nurse.

"Where is my mum? Please help me! I've got to find her! Please!" she begged the nurse. She couldn't tell if she recognised the nurse or not in the weak moonlight that was coming through the window; all she could see was her blue uniform. The nurse didn't answer, but quickly came over to the bed and stopped her from pulling out the needle and tube which were firmly lodged in her hand.

"Calm down," she said sternly. "Your mother has just gone to the bathroom."

"Are you sure? Did you see her go? Did she leave the ward? How long ago did she go?" Her heart and head were pounding with fear and adrenalin. If the nurse hadn't been holding both her hands, pushing her down into the bed, she would have been shaking her by the shoulders to make her answer faster. But it wasn't necessary, as her mother walked into the room at that moment.

"Billie, what's wrong?" her mum asked, with a tenderness she hadn't heard in a long time. She walked straight over to the bed and put her arms around Billie to stop her shaking and her tears. Billie didn't answer. She nestled as close as she could to her mum and breathed in her smell. Relief slowly trickled through her veins, calming her heartbeat and quenching the fire of fear that had consumed her. Most of the time Billie thought her mum was frustrating and she spent a lot of time wishing she would change. But tonight, she couldn't bear to think about losing her. For the first time since she was a little girl, she fell asleep with her mum's arms wrapped around her, and wasn't plagued with nightmares.

The police came the next morning and at first Billie refused to tell them anything. The officer who sat right next to her, was tall and quite round with long, curly black hair, that she had tamed into a side ponytail. When she'd first walked in she had seemed imposing, but when she sat down and started to ask Billie questions it was possible to see her kind eyes and hear her gentle tone. She introduced herself as Lisa and she said she didn't buy Billie's story, that she had taken the pills by accident, for one minute. Instead, she took her hand and asked her to tell her what had 'really' happened.

Billie had never spoken about what had happened and she didn't know how to start. She said her step-grandad had 'done things he shouldn't have', and it had been happening since she was twelve. After a while, Lisa asked Billie why she had never mentioned anything to her mother. Billie quickly realised that her mum must have told them she didn't know anything about it. At first she was annoyed with her mum; *why wouldn't she back me up?* But then Billie reasoned she had caused enough trouble for her mum, so she told them that she couldn't, because of all the violent threats that Eric had made which was the truth with just a bit missing.

The more she spoke with the police, the less hopeful she felt. She knew they would not believe her because she had no evidence. Lisa kept asking if she could think of any evidence she might have, but everything he had done had been when they were alone. She knew he had pictures and videos of her as he had brought them out to show her once, when she was refusing to cooperate. He had told her he was going to distribute them on posters. When she was older, and she had threatened to tell the police about the videos, he had calmly informed her that he kept everything incriminating at his sister's house. She told this to Lisa but they said that the police couldn't get a warrant on Billie's say so. She had gone to the doctors with injuries over the past two years when she'd had to, but each time she had lied. Billie felt so frustrated. She knew he was clever, but it was becoming clear exactly how clever. His manipulations and threats had allowed him to make sure he could never get caught. She expected no less, to be honest. He was such a clever, well-spoken man. He had fooled her into believing that he loved her for four years. When that went up in smoke, he had bullied, tortured and forced her into cooperating, all the while covering his tracks; never hitting her in a way that could look like abuse, always in a way that could be explained as an accident. Aunty Susan left the room just as the police looked ready to leave. She gave her a look that Billie couldn't decipher but it made her heart sink. She would later find out that her aunty had never believed her anyway, and had gone to Gran's house and told her everything Billie had said.

When Billie was released from hospital she was filled with terror. Eric lived in the village and she was no longer in a locked ward. She knew he had keys to their house from when they had gone on holiday and he would cat-sit. It was only a matter of time until he got his revenge. The worst part was that her mother was capitalising on the whole thing to gain sympathy from everyone. She'd arrived home to a gathering of her mother's friends, most of whom she'd never met. Her mother had friends in the village who took her side, whereas Billie had none. No one spoke to her or offered their sympathies, but they were happy to drop by and gossip about who had seen her gran, and where.

Her gran was proclaiming Eric's innocence to anyone who would listen, and the fact Eric had lived in Windermere all his life, pretty much guaranteed him supporters. "No one from around here would do something like that", they said. For Billie, it was humiliating. Her mother was spouting all the cruel things he had done to gain attention and was loving every aspect of the drama. It was as if she had no idea about the fear and revulsion Billie felt on a daily basis. Not only was she waiting for Eric's visit, but she also didn't want everyone to know the intimate details of the worst moments in her entire life. The ones who believed her must be thinking how stupid she was. When people looked at her, she felt like they were imagining her doing all those things with Eric. It was unbearable. From all angles, the situation was untenable.

Her family was broken. Jealousy consumed her sister because of the attention Billie was getting and their relationship was strained at best. Matthew didn't know what to do, so he threw himself into his work. She didn't know how to deal with all the pain and suffering she was causing. She couldn't pretend it wasn't happening like she had before. Everyone told her to take comfort from the fact that Eric could no longer get to her, but they were all so wrong. She felt his presence wherever she went. The door locks hadn't even been changed because her parents were sure that he wouldn't do anything, now he was so notorious, and it was such a 'bother' to change them. So, Billie barely slept, waiting for him to come for her.

Little did she know that it would get worse. The police interviews were torturous. It felt like they were her punishment, not Eric's. Lisa kept telling Billie that Eric was the one who was in the wrong, but she was the one who had to sit in a room and explain in graphic detail the things he had done to her. She had to use terms like 'penis' and 'ejaculation'. She had to discuss intimate areas of her body with Lisa, knowing that people were watching and video recording them. Didn't they understand that this had been going on since she was twelve? She was now seventeen, and had spent all those years locking away every disgusting action of his. When she told them the things he had done, she cringed. She felt sick. She wanted to kill herself all over again. They hadn't been there. She would never be able to stress to them that Eric had become the most important person in her life. How could anyone understand that, in the beginning, he was the nicest, kindest person she had ever met, and she'd wanted to spend every minute of the day with him? She was in too deep when he'd showed who he really was, and she was too scared and alone. Everyone in the family had always said how close they were, and that she and Eric had a 'special bond'. He had wrapped her up so she was isolated from everyone, and by then she could never run. She would have no one to turn to. Every time she tried to explain this in the interviews, she floundered. It was too hard. The room she was interviewed in was barren, and Lisa couldn't help her say anything so it was up to her. Her surroundings made her feel like a criminal. Lisa's silence felt like a judgement. When her voice echoed back to her, she felt that her words sounded pathetic so she clammed up, desperate for it to be over.

There was so much that had happened to her. How on earth was she supposed to tell them every little thing? If she could force herself to remember, she would likely be doing three years' worth of interviews. She felt sick after every interview, and sometimes she was physically sick during the them. Frequently she ran out of the room into her mum's arms, crying hysterically, when she was made to relive the most traumatic ways he had touched her. She had to recount waking up with his mouth on her breasts which made her dry-heave and unable to breathe. Her mother was great in the interviews. She wasn't allowed in because they were recorded, but whenever Billie broke down, her mum would rush to the door and sweep her into her arms, calming and reassuring her until she felt a little better. Gone was the selfish, gossip-driven woman. Instead, she smoothed Billie's hair; whispered that she was proud of her strong, brave girl, and she needed to do this. The video interviews made her feel so disgusting, and she hated every minute.

When she found out that she would have to have a physical examination, she looked for the nearest cliff. The intrusion of it, and having her body examined like a lab rat, made her feel like the lowest of the low. She was disgusted with herself and everything that was happening. The worst part was that Eric had told her, if she ever told anyone, it would be the worst thing she ever did. She should have just kept quiet. What was Eric having to do, just sit and be asked questions? Did he have to go and have his body examined? He only had to listen to others asking him what he had done. He didn't have to do anything; he didn't have to prove anything. He just had to sit there. When Lisa told Billie, time and time again, that she was so brave, and that Eric was the person in the wrong, it was this thought that ran around her mind, taunting her. If Eric was in the wrong, why was she the only one suffering?

# Chapter Thirty-One
## 2010

### Adam

Adam walked into the living room, bleary eyed from sleep. His father had called him downstairs. That had him worried and he quickly made his way downstairs; it was rare for his dad to even speak to him, let alone request his presence. Both Uncle Eric and his dad were sat on the sofa so he took the seat across from them. His father kept crossing and uncrossing his legs, shifting in his seat, while Uncle Eric just sat on the edge, his head bowed in his hands. Adam thought someone might have died, but there wasn't really anyone left.

Finally, his father found his voice. "Now son, we've got something to tell you. I know you're a bit young so if you don't understand that's okay." Adam hid his balled fists under his legs. *I'm twenty, not twelve!* he wanted to yell. He bit down his retort and nodded at his father, who was staring, waiting for a response. "Your Uncle Eric is in a spot of bother."

"What kind of bother? Is it serious? Are you going to be okay? What's happened?" Adam fired questions at his father and then at his uncle. Fear clogged his chest making breathing difficult. He couldn't lose his uncle. The one person who was always there for him, who didn't treat him like a child. Uncle Eric didn't even look up when Adam asked his questions. His shoulders were slumped down, his head was hanging in his hands as if his fight had left him. Adam was scared. This person in front of him was unrecognisable, an old man with nothing left to live for. His uncle was usually vibrant, clever and brave, not like this.

"Calm down, boy. Let me finish," growled his father, giving him his signature scowl before continuing. "The thing is, you know Sylvia, the woman your uncle has been knocking about with? Well, she has a granddaughter." His father stopped as if that explained it all, but Adam could not see where this was going. Realising this, he cleared his throat a few times while he struggled for words. He kept looking at the door as if gearing up to sleep. "Well, this girl, she's about your age. She's got it in her head that Eric has been doing stuff to her, like." A red tinge crept across his father's cheeks and he leaned away from his brother. They had never had the sex talk in the handful of conversations they'd had as father and son. It was Uncle Eric who had explained all of that to him. Aside from scolding him and giving him chores, his father kept all conversation to a bare minimum.

Adam was bewildered, *what stuff?* When he asked his father this, he began to tap his heel on the floor and he frowned at Adam. "Well, you know, sex stuff; it's bad stuff. She is underage so it looks really bad on your uncle." As if he felt that was explanation enough, his father got up and announced he was going to the pub. "You'll be all right, won't you, Eric lad?" he said to the front door, not waiting for a response. Adam walked over to his uncle and sat next to him. The silence was deafening and uncomfortable.

"Uncle Eric, tell me what happened."

"It's all lies," whispered his uncle. He slowly raised his head and looked at Adam, his eyes pleading for him to believe him. "All I ever did was love that girl as if she were my own. I spent time with her when no one else would. Her own mother couldn't be bothered with her and I just felt sorry for her, no kid should go unloved like that. So, I stuck around. I tried to make a go of it with her gran and be a real family. All I did was love her." His eyes were watery with tears but they flashed with anger as he said, "This is the thanks I get."

Adam was furious. How could anyone think his Uncle Eric would hurt a girl? He was so kind and generous. It was only a couple of months ago that he had stopped seeing Adam so he could concentrate on helping one of Sylvia's granddaughters. *Wait, was this the same one?*

"Was it Billie? The one you were trying to help?"

At her name, his uncle's eyes burned with fierce anger. Adam felt an irrational desire to back away to a safe distance, away from the sparks flying from Eric's eyes.

As he struggled to compose himself, Adam felt his own anger rise, matching that of his uncle's. This man would do anything for Adam. He'd given him advice, and guided him through difficult things in his life, while his father had lain snoring on the sofa. He imagined his uncle could not have resisted helping this girl, if she was ignored like he'd said. It was in his nature to help anyone. Adam had witnessed his kind heart so many times.

He remembered how they had been out for a pub lunch and a young brunette girl, who couldn't have been more than fourteen, had sat at the booth next to them with an older guy. He'd looked about eighteen, although it was hard to tell under his Adidas cap. They hadn't been able to avoid noticing that the guy was shamelessly groping the young girl and she was pushing him away. In the end, he had stormed off in frustration, shouting that she was a 'frigid cow'. The girl had stayed where she was, sobbing her heart out. She looked lost and afraid. Adam didn't have time to feel appalled, as Uncle Eric was straight over to her, comforting her, and offering to take her home. Luckily for Adam they weren't too far from his house, because there was only room for two in his uncle's old Frogeye Sprite. He had watched him drive off with the girl and his heart had swelled with pride that he was such a good Samaritan. His father would have just slagged the girl off, saying she was stupid to have gone with the boy in the first place. He was one of those who would not even think to help a woman who was overburdened with shopping, or help an old lady carry her drinks tray over to a table. He walked around, in an alcohol fuelled haze, never sparing a thought for the people he shared the world with unless he had to.

Adam sometimes thought Eric had a 'good deeds radar' as he was always helping someone, and no one more than Adam. After his mother had died, all the good qualities his father had possessed died with her. On the anniversary of her death, he wasn't just crying for his mother, but also for the father he lost too. If it wasn't for Uncle Eric's visits, Adam would be raising himself. It was Uncle Eric who helped Adam sort out his father's accounts so they would not be without electric again. It was Uncle Eric who kicked Adam's father all the way to the doctors to be officially signed off with depression so they would have some money coming in after Adam had collected his drunken father from underneath his desk at his fourth job that year.

Adam felt physically sick looking at the distress in his uncle's eyes. Who could do something like this?

"What exactly is she accusing you of? Has she called the police?"

Eric took a deep breath, considering his words. "What you need to understand is she's not a well girl. She's been starved of attention her whole life. She gets picked on at school because she is what they call 'short and fat'. Well, I could see going through all that was hard for her, she was struggling to cope. I was just doing what I could to help, giving her hugs and attention when she wanted it. I said nice things about her hair, trying to build her confidence, you see. But the damage must be worse than anyone could know because of the things she has said." He closed his eyes as if physically wounded. He continued weakly "She tried to kill herself. I was distraught when I found out. I'd really come to care for her. But then when they asked her why, apparently, she told them it was because of me. I'd …" He cradled his head in his hands. As if his spirit was broken, unable to face the world. Adam ground his teeth and his nostrils flared as he tried to breathe through the flame of fury flickering around his body. This was unacceptable, his uncle didn't deserve to be hurt like this. He wanted to punch the wall and throw things around the room. The unfairness of the situation was frustrating. His uncle's good nature was being taken advantage of. He was being vilified and he of all people did not deserve that. Adam felt impotent. He could do nothing but listen to the rest of the story.

In a small voice, Eric told Adam how this girl, Billie, had told the police he had been sexually abusing her since she was twelve. He was about to leave the house when he'd been taken in by the police and asked when it was that he'd started grooming Billie for sex.

Adam was horrified. He didn't know what to say. Uncle Eric looked up and must have seen the expression on his face. He seemed to pull some strength back into his body and became more like the person Adam knew and loved.

"Don't worry, Adam, it will all be cleared up, she's got no proof. I've just got to get through this rough patch until they realise they have got it wrong."

"What does Sylvia make of it?" Adam asked.

"Well that's the thing, she doesn't believe a word of it; she says she wants nothing more to do with any of them." Adam felt better after hearing that the fact the girl's own gran didn't believe her showed how ridiculous the whole thing was. For the rest of the weekend, Adam comforted his uncle as he swung from sadness at the suffering Billie must have experienced to make up such lies, to anger at how she had taken advantage of his help and repaid him this way. Adam thought it was lucky Billie lived hundreds of miles away, because he wanted to kill her for the pain she was causing his uncle.

# Chapter Thirty-Two
## 2010
### Billie

When she finally saw Eric again, he was at her front door. She hadn't been expecting it, with them both being the talk of the village, she was constantly being told he would never do that. But he did. He forced his way in and slammed the door behind him. She couldn't move from the shock. She hadn't realised till that moment how much she had enjoyed not seeing him, and had got used to it even. Her brain couldn't process that he had just walked in through the front door. He turned on her immediately, pressing his lips against hers. Restraining her with his hands, one on each of her arms, gripping tightly. She was pretty sure he was gripping hard enough to leave her bruised again.

"You need to stop this, Billie. You are never going to win. I will never leave you alone. I'm not going to prison. I've been too clever and you are too stupid."

"You shouldn't be here," was all she could get out. Her voice betrayed how scared she was.

"If you stop this now, everything will die down, and then, in a little while, things can go back to how they were … I can see how you are suffering. I told you this would happen. You need to trust me when I say there is nothing you can do that will keep me away from you. I will keep coming for you. If you don't do as I say, your family will suffer and hate you, and eventually I'll have to hurt one or all of them too." He stopped. Letting his words sink in.

When he could see they weren't having the desired effect, he pulled back his fist and punched her with all of his force. She realised at the last second what he was doing and she managed to twist her body. His fist landed on her arm. She felt an explosion of pain rocket through her body. She fell towards the door. Leaning on it, she pushed off it at the last minute, attempting to get around him, stumbling to get away from him. When she heard a metal thud, and felt another wave of pain more excruciating than the last time she registered her mistake. Why the hell had she turned her back on him? She went down hard and couldn't get back up. Her body was completely unresponsive; no longer allowing her control in case she caused it more pain. She could tell, from the dark shadow that cast across her, Eric was standing over her.

"Take this as my final warning. Withdraw your statement. Stop this stupid investigation."

He stopped speaking, stepped over her and knelt by her head. Grasping her hair, he pulled her head up until she was face to face with him.

"I know you thought you had got rid of me, but I have been watching, waiting for my perfect moment. I know everything about your family: I know where Matthew is, and I know that your mum and sister have gone to the shops to buy a birthday present for your cousin. I know you didn't want to go because you said you had a headache. I laughed when I heard that, we both know you hate being second best when your sister is around. I thought about killing you. I have considered how easy it would be. But, then I realised I'm not done with you yet. I need this investigation to stop, Billie. You are going to do that for me, or I will kill your sister, then your mother, and anyone else I want. And it will all be your fault."

He released her hair, and her head fell to the floor. "It's funny, the one person you are the most jealous of, is the person I have been able to use to get what I want. It's a powerful thing love. I wonder if your sister knows how much you have done for her. Oh well, not my problem. I'll be getting off. Just remember what you need to do, Billie, and everything will be fine. You can stop all this heartache and do the right thing for everyone."

She heard the front door slam and she just lay there on the floor. She was still there when her mum and Holly came home, they both ran to her prone body and they hefted her up between the two of them. They were shouting questions at Billie, not even waiting for her to reply. She wasn't even sure she had one. She didn't know what to do for the best. She wanted to tell them what had happened, but maybe Eric was right. She was just going to cause more heartache and she was the only one who could fix it.

In the end, she didn't need to tell them because they worked out what had happened for themselves. She supposed it was obvious that there was only one person who would leave her, a broken mess, lying on the floor. Eric must have been really angry; he was normally smart enough to only leave bruises in places she could easily hide, but there was no hiding from the fingerprint bruises around her wrists.

When Billie refused to make a statement to the police, she could see the doubts begin to flare in her parents' and sister's eyes. They couldn't understand why she wouldn't do one more video interview.

She'd walked in on them talking. Before they'd realised she was there, she heard her mother say, "I feel awful because she's my daughter, but honestly, some of it is a bit far-fetched. And she's no proof. You don't think she could have beat herself up, do you?" They either didn't realise she'd heard, or they didn't care, as they changed the subject and began to coerce her into giving a statement.

In the end they tried to trick her into it. They arranged for Lisa to turn up at their house without her knowing. But as soon as she saw the car, Billie was up and running across the fields out of sight. One advantage to living in the countryside was being able to hide. They didn't understand. She didn't blame them. But she couldn't do it. She felt sick at the thought of entering that room where all her memories of Eric were. When he'd attacked her, he had beaten every last bit of fight out of her and she couldn't do it. She was broken. Like the straw that broke the camel's back, she was done. She knew if she gave a statement, Eric would be back. But this time it might be her family he went after.

She tried to do as he had asked, but the police would not drop the investigation after her mother had told them about the attack. They said it was coercion and she didn't have the strength to argue. She didn't have the strength for anything any more. Convincing herself to exist was hard enough. Billie knew this was an indicator she was getting really low, but she couldn't try and kill herself again; mainly because she didn't know how. Her parents had ensured that the house was Billie-might-kill-herself-with-this proofed. To combat these feelings, she read. She lost herself in different lands and different places. Living out a new life, where misery was turned into joy by the end; something she couldn't ever visualise happening to her, especially knowing she had to go back to school the following week.

# Chapter Thirty-Three
## 2010
### Adam

A dam felt torn. He was disgusted by the accusations made against his uncle, but a small part of him was relishing the amount of time he was getting to spend with him. The trauma of the situation seemed to have brought them even closer, as if they really were father and son. While the police scrambled to build their case against him, Adam reassured him everything would be fine. He called him every day, he even tried to go up and visit, but Uncle Eric wouldn't let him. He would have got the train but he wouldn't have him wasting the little money he had. There was no defying him when he had made his mind up, so Adam had to do what he could over the phone.

To his delight, his uncle was coming over today. It would be nice to support him in person. It reduced his frustrations at being useless in his uncle's time of need. Adam's father would not dream of going over to support his brother, so it was his responsibility to help when he could. When he arrived, Adam gave him the longest hug they'd ever shared. They weren't really a touchy-feely family, so Adam hoped it would demonstrate how much he meant to him as he couldn't find the right words. Eric laughed it off, pushing him away gently, and asked if they could go for a walk. They set off along the river; it was always nice in autumn and, as Adam later found out, it offered the privacy his uncle wanted. Apparently, the orchestra of his father's snores was not the backdrop he'd wanted for their conversation.

Even though they were walking, Adam could tell his uncle was uncomfortable. His shifting eyes and his stilted conversation had Adam really concerned. Adam tried to wait patiently for him to get to the point. He breathed in the heady scent of nature, enjoying the melody of songs coming from the birds. The colours around him glistened brightly from a gentle shower earlier that day. It was one of those days where everything looked so stunning, it made you feel lucky to be alive, but Adam doubted his uncle knew where he was. Frown lines creased his face making him look old and worn.

Eventually his uncle led them to a bench, his leg began to shake uncontrollably, and he finally met Adam's eyes. "I need to ask you the biggest favour I could ever ask of you. I love you as if you were my own son, and it pains me that I have to put you in this position, but I don't have a choice." Emotion choked his words, stopping him from saying any more. He smoothed the tops of his legs as if trying to calm the shaking.

For the last ten years, Adam had drunk in the confident, charming and kind nature of his uncle. In the last few months he'd seen so much sadness and unhappiness in him; he didn't deserve it. Adam was beginning to get seriously worried as each time his uncle visited, a piece of him seemed to have gone. He was used to him being the strong one, the one that Adam could rely on, but now it seemed the roles were reversing. As much as it unnerved him, he would do anything for him. It was sad his uncle felt it was a burden, when, in fact, the more he thought about it, it felt good to be able to give him something back.

"What is it? You know I'd do anything for you."

"Thanks, son, I knew I could count on you. Okay, well, I'll just say it, and then we can be done with this conversation. I'm having some problems with the investigation. I need to provide evidence of where I was on certain dates so I can refute the claims that are being made. Sylvia was with me for most of them, but there are a few dates when I was alone, and I can't prove where I was. Do you think you would be able to say that I was with you? If I give you the dates? I know it's a lot to ask but I'm desperate, son. I'm already guilty in the eyes of the police, I can tell by the way they treat me. But, if I can say I was with you, it will put it all to bed and I can get on with my life. Before you answer, know this: my life has been hell since this started. I was escorted to the station in a police car. Everyone in my village saw me. I've had pervert sprayed on my car, I've been spat at in the street, no one believes me. No one believes Sylvia either. We've had to move to a new house to escape the abuse I've been suffering. It's awful, Adam."

He grabbed Adam's arm and shook it a little, his eyes were fearful and watery. "No one believes me. They've known me all my life and they think I could hurt a small girl who was in my care. I wouldn't do it. I swear. You've got to help me, Adam. If these allegations aren't disproved, I don't know how I will cope. I beg of you. Please help your old uncle, it's what your mum would want."

It was a passionate speech and Adam wanted to tell him that it was completely unnecessary. He would do anything to help him, and he knew these allegations were false, but he didn't really want to lie. Of all the things he remembered about his mother, it was how much she hated lies.

He had a hazy memory of himself as a boy; he had sneaked in and greedily eaten a chocolate bar from the cupboard too hungry to wait for his tea. When his mum had asked him if he had done it, he'd lied; not realising his cheek had a chocolate stain on it. When confronted again he'd crumbled, and his mother's disappointed eyes had held his as she'd told him how much she hated liars. It showed how little his uncle had known his mother. He was wrong about her, she hated people who lied and she'd be sad that Adam would lie to the police. He was sure, if she were alive, she would tell him not to. But she wasn't alive. She had left him, and the only one who had cared for him was Uncle Eric. So, he had to help. Even if it meant going against his principles. How could he not, when his uncle was being made to suffer because of someone else's lies. Hopefully, his lie would cancel out Billie's.

"Don't worry; of course I will help you. Tell me the dates and what you need me to say."

# Chapter Thirty-Four
## 2010
### Billie

Billie walked through the front doors of her school with her head down, face pale, and her heart full of dread. She could tell when people had noticed her because the entrance hall grew quiet. Normally it sounded like a zoo: all the animals screeching to see who could make the most noise. She kept her head down and continued walking. It was such a small school, she knew everyone would know.

The police would not normally make it public knowledge if they weren't able to bring a case to court, but her gran had put it in the paper. The village paper. That everyone read. Her gran had given Eric an alibi for everything Billie had accused him of. She hadn't even been there but she knew all the details thanks to Aunty Susan. She couldn't understand why people weren't making that connection. But, as she had known from the start, Eric was too clever. There was no evidence, she had no one backing her and lying for her, so he'd won; just like he'd told her he would.

She had been told not to take anything to heart. She walked to the door that led to the sixth form corridor and breathed a sigh of relief, but it was short lived. A voice broke out from the silence, and as she opened the door she heard it say, "My grandad is free if you want a go … he isn't loaded, though." A cacophony of laughter broke out behind her as she closed the door. She leant against the wall, grateful that no one was in the corridor. She took deep breaths, trying to hold in the hysteria that wanted to break free from her. Didn't they know that her entire family was being ripped apart by this? Didn't they know she was still struggling to eat due to the agony in her stomach? Didn't they know she watched her mother cry herself to sleep because she could never again speak to *her* mother, all the while knowing that the pain her mum felt was her fault?

She counted to ten in her head and took matching deep breaths. She had caused this mess, it was her own fault, and she must deal with the consequences. She needed to study hard to get away from this place. She saw university as her salvation, her new escape plan, that would hopefully rid her of the indescribable pain her stomach. She knew that, at some point, Eric would find a way to get to her again. She just had to get through the next year, then she could go to university.

Billie stopped reading the notes that landed on her desk. They were all the same: how much money would she charge someone without wrinkles? Did dads do it for her or just old men? There wasn't a single person in the school who believed that she hadn't wanted any part of what had happened to her. No one spoke to her unless it was to stick the knife in further. This isolation was nothing new to her. The only thing that had changed was that the target on her back was now visible to everyone. She even heard Carl saying to his friends as she walked past, "She asked me to have a three-way with him, but I told her I don't do old men like she does." She didn't know what to do with herself, why did the school day have to have so many break times? It was as if the school was giving her ample opportunity to truly appreciate how alone she was.

Billie studied as much as she could, trying not to stare longingly at the girls on the other side of the room as they happily talked about the next party they were going to; preening their already perfect hair and makeup. She wanted to fit in so badly and to be normal. She shook her head and focused on the work in front of her; she began to write about President Kennedy's welfare policies, reminding herself that this was her ticket out. She would finally be free.

# Chapter Thirty-Five
## 2011

### Adam

Adam put his phone down on the table and allowed his relief to flow through his body. Its journey resolved a tension and stress he hadn't realised he had been carrying around with him. Finally, the nightmare was over, his uncle could start to rebuild his life. He could return to being the strong and happy man Adam enjoyed spending his time with. It was going to be a long road though. Adam knew his uncle was suffering more abuse than he'd let on. From what he had said, he was a pariah in his neighbourhood; he couldn't get any part-time work to support his pension and he'd lost all his friends. He'd also said he might lose his house. It was remarkable that words, even when proved false, had the power to destroy someone's life. What had been said couldn't be unsaid. All Adam could do was help his uncle try to put the pieces back together. He would do everything he could to help him.

Adam thought a lot about this girl, Billie. His uncle would not tell him much about her. He tried to do some digging of his own but, as she was still a minor, there wasn't much about her online. She had no social profiles, unlike most girls her age, so he was unable to even find a picture of her. It was hard to hate someone you'd never met, but he saw the damage that had been done to his uncle and he managed to hate Billie. He didn't understand why she had done it. If it wasn't for the lack of evidence, the case would have gone to court. How could someone get up on the stand, in front of people, and say all those lies? Maybe she was ill? But his uncle had said that she wasn't; she was just evil and vindictive, lashing out because of her poor home life. It made him feel better about the fact that he had lied, knowing he was fighting her nasty lies and not letting her get away with it. Still, he couldn't understand it. He knew there were evil people out there, but this crime was less obvious than killing someone. He wondered if she knew that the stories she had concocted had affected so many people. Him, his uncle, Sylvia, her family. To have convinced the police to investigate, she must have been a fantastic actress. It made him so angry and frustrated when he thought of her because he couldn't get the answers he needed. Why had this horrid girl turned her calculating and malicious nature on his uncle, one of the kindest people in the world?

# Chapter Thirty-Six
## 2011
### Billie

When Billie left her village in Windermere behind, to move to Worcester University, she also left her parents. She got on the train with as much of her stuff as she could manage, and promised herself that, once she got off at Worcester, she would not think about anything or anyone from her past. It was going to be hard; eighteen years of her life had been spent with her mum. But, as it turned out, it had only taken one act of betrayal to ruin an eighteen-year relationship. One conversation.

Billie's mum had sat her down, on a typical rainy day in August, a month before she was due to leave for Worcester. Billie had been blissfully reading her way through her last summer holidays in Windermere. She was too scared to leave the house. It wasn't worth it. She wasn't going to let anyone, or anything, stop her from leaving. Before she had overdosed, every time she had mentioned leaving she'd seen a fire light up in Eric's eyes, and she had believed there was no way he would ever let her leave. So, she was staying behind closed doors until she left for Worcester. Only then would she be safe.

When her mum had shouted for her to come downstairs to talk, it had made her very nervous. Her mother, until that day, had been happy to let Billie stay upstairs. She seemed to prefer it that way though she would never admit it.

She'd walked downstairs with trepidation, stopped behind the glass door to the kitchen, and her heart had sunk. Her mother was pacing up and down. Her normally stylish blonde hair was dishevelled. That was never a good sign. It meant her mum had done something and needed to tell someone. Billie had hoped it wasn't another affair, and thought back to the previous summer when she'd had to spend most of it covering for her mother by waiting in a coffee shop until she had returned.

"Listen, Billie," began her mum. She could feel her mum's leg shaking the table. "I've got two things I need to tell you. I've felt so sick keeping things from you, I can't do it any more." Her mum had paused, and stared intently at Billie's face but was unable to meet her eyes. "I'm leaving Matthew." The weight of those words had hung in the air between them. Billie hadn't really known what she was supposed to say. She loved Matthew, he had been in their lives for ten years  nine years and eight months longer than her own dad had lasted. She knew her mum was a flirt, but to leave Matthew? How could she do that after so long? What was the point of those ten years if she was just going to throw it away? With tears running down her face, her mum had told her how her new man was getting a house, ready for them to move in, just as soon as he'd left his wife.

Billie had felt selfish, but all she could think was, what about me? Where am I going to live? What if I don't like this new man? Billie didn't like change at the best of times, but this would mean a complete transformation of her life. No longer would she live in this house that she'd seen when it was just foundations. She would not have the sanctuary of her bedroom any more. What about her books? Where would they go? Would she have a room in this house? Would she be welcome? All these unsettling questions had whirled through her mind but she'd seen that her mum had desperately needed her approval and support. She had leaned forward and her eyes had pleaded with Billie's funny, she was able to look her in the eye then.

Billie had taken her mum's hand and said everything she knew her mum wanted to hear. "Of course I don't mind."

As her mum had swallowed each lie, her smile had grown and her tears stopped falling. Billie was about to get up, desperate to be alone, when her mum had stopped her with a hand on her shoulder.

Her mum spoke to her knees, refusing to look at Billie. "There's something else. I don't really know how to tell you this, but I know I have to. The thing is …" Billie couldn't remember ever seeing her mum so lost for words. What else could be worse than uprooting her whole family and leaving the man Billie had considered a father figure? "I've been seeing your gran again."

The pain in her chest at those words had been immense. She'd honestly thought it must be a physical wound. She'd looked down at her chest. Nope, no holes or bleeding. She'd tried to breathe through her panic, worried that this was it: he had found a way back in. Billie had listened as her mum the woman who had sat by her bedside in hospital after her overdose, and had promised that she would protect her no matter the cost explained how she'd run into her gran, quite by chance, and they had been unable to deny how much they had missed each other. Billie's mum had then gone over to her Gran's house "Don't worry *he* was upstairs" and they'd talked and talked and decided to put the whole mess behind them because, after all, they were mother and daughter. Billie's fingernails had created bloody holes in her hands she had clenched them so hard. She'd stared as a trickle of blood made its way from her hand to the black material of the kitchen chair cushion.

"Billie, look at me." Billie had looked up, ever the dutiful daughter, doing what she was told. "Do you understand, Billie? I miss my mum. She's my mum. You get that don't you? We don't have much family, Billie, and I've lost my mum and my sister over this mess. I've supported you through this, but you're about to go to university and I will be here with just your sister and Marcus."

*Who's Marcus? Oh yes, keep up, brain, Mum's affair.* "I love my mum and I've missed her so much. Do you understand?"

Billie had wanted to stand up and scream at her mum. "No, I don't understand! We are mother and daughter too! What about all the promises you have made? You said you hated her. You said what she had done was unforgivable. I already forgave you for not doing something about Eric when I told you before I overdosed.

Why are you doing this to me? You promised you would never hurt me again. You promised you would always choose me. Aren't parents supposed to love their child more than anyone else? Why don't you love me enough to be on my side? Am I not enough for you? What does Gran have that I don't? She's a liar. She lied to the police. She shamed us to anyone who would listen. How could you?" But she didn't, she hadn't said anything. Instead, she had taken a deep breath, and locked all her real feelings in that box they now belonged in. "Yes, of course I understand. Let's just get you through this divorce first."

From that day, Billie's relationship with her mum was broken, irreparably. She couldn't say anything to her mum because she knew it would not make any difference. It wouldn't make any to Billie either. The damage was done. Billie's mum had broken them when she had decided to enter the house of the man who was responsible for destroying what should have been the most innocent and happy years of her life.

The train pulled into Worcester; Billie had put her foot down when her mum had offered to drive her. She wasn't having it. She hadn't told her mum but, from that moment on, she had no intention of seeing or speaking to her or Holly ever again. Her sister was just as bad as their mum. She had quite happily had tea and biscuits in their new home with Marcus and their gran. They were all one big happy family and she was no longer part of it. It hurt so much. Especially when she considered that the reason she had put up with Eric for as long as she had was to save Holly from the same fate and for her mum not to lose her mother. What was the point?

She let that anger force her pain and memories of them away, and she stepped off the train into her new life. Life as an orphan. A life without family. But, most importantly, a life without Eric. She truly believed that was possible now. The entire time she had studied at home she had been convinced that he would come and destroy her escape plan, but she hadn't seen or heard from him in nine months, twenty-eight days and eleven hours. She was free and safe. She meant to keep it that way.

Billie made her way to her halls. She tried not to be intimidated by the massive blocks of flats that formed the campus village. She was excited but terrified. She saw danger around every corner. She was trying to find 'Flat One' but she wasn't sure which building it was. She was standing outside what she thought was the right one when a raven-haired girl came out of the door she'd been hovering outside. Her curvy figure and beaming smile looked Billie over.

"You looking for Flat One, babe?" she asked. Billie could only nod. The reality of her new life hit her like a ton of bricks. This was her life now, she would have to interact with people. Make her own way in the world. The gravity of what she'd done was crippling her. Luckily, this girl seemed oblivious to Billie's internal anguish and was happy doing all the talking. She looped her arm through Billie's and dragged her into the flat, firing questions at her without waiting for the answers.

Billie sat in her room breathing deeply. When her new roommate Helen had dragged her in the flat, she had thrust her into the kitchen to face the other flatmates Steve, James, Hannah, Kate and Harriet only waiting long enough for names to be exchanged. She had then unceremoniously yanked Billie from the room and guided her down the corridor to a hallway lined with doors. They walked, to the end of the hallway, to the last grubby green door on the right.

"This is yours. They aren't much, but then we will be partying, won't we?" said Helen. Again, Billie just nodded, wondering what the polite way to get rid of Helen was.

"Helen, come look at this!" shouted an excited voice from the kitchen.

"Well, see you later, neighbour, mine's that one if you need anything," said Helen, pointing at the door next to Billie's as she walked away.

Billie knew she needed to unpack but she couldn't move from the bed. Her room was empty and it made her sad to think she didn't really have anything to furnish it with. The barren room echoed her new life, she was completely alone in the world now.

She'd left behind as many reminders as she could of her old life. She had her books, though; those favourite ten books she couldn't be without. The thought of them cramped up in her travel bag was enough to get her off the bed.

She emptied them onto her bed, stopping to inhale their smell of imagination and escapism. As she put the last one, *Jane Eyre*, on the small bookcase, a white piece of paper dropped from between the pages. Call it intuition, or sixth sense, but her heart nearly stopped. Gingerly, she picked up the folded piece of paper. It read: *My dearest Billie, I hope you enjoy your time in Room C, Flat 1, Bromsgrove Hall, at the University of Worcester. Please know that I will be thinking of you and, though you can't see me, I will always see you. It pains me that we can't be together right now, but I will always be thinking of you and I look forward to the day that we are finally reunited. Who can say when that day will be? It could be days, months or years. Just know that where you go, I go. I will always be with you. Eternally Yours. E.*

# Part Three
# Present Day

*"I am not what happened to me, I am what I choose to become."*
Carl Jung

# Chapter Thirty-Seven

## Diary Entry

I've had enough now. I have had my fill of being patient. I've watched her from afar since she left me. I've revelled in her suffering and the pointless existence she has led since then. I've spent years waiting for her to trip up and lead me to the evidence she has on me. I was so careless, leaving that camera in her room. I wanted to scare her into dropping the case, but it didn't strike me that I was handing her evidence. It was so unlike me not to think things through. I guess I was just getting desperate, thinking I would end up getting charged. Well, my work isn't done. She obviously doesn't know she has it, but it is getting more dangerous now that she is with Adam.

I don't mind admitting, in the privacy of my own writing, that I have been getting jealous. She belongs to me. At first, it was fun watching Adam woo her using tips that I gave him. Watching the whole thing and knowing he was using her to expose what she did to me. Of course, he hasn't told me this but I know. He is the man I made him, I know everything about him. But now it is starting to leave a bitter taste in my mouth.

I watch them together and I've noticed the confusion behind Adam's eyes. She is undoing all my hard work, but, more importantly, she is becoming happier than I've ever seen her. Once she walked around, oblivious to the world, her fear weighing her down like rocks in her pockets, but now I see her smiling. It burns my eyes to see this. She left me. She doesn't get to be happy. She needs to remember that she is in my control. And she needs to hand over that bloody camera. It rankles, knowing that she has the power to bring me down. But I know I have the power to bring her back to me. I am her master after all.

# Adam

He screeched to a halt outside the only food shop Billie ever went to. He understood her fears now, and why she had constructed a set routine that made her feel safe. So much about her was starting to make sense.

As he jumped out of the car he had to beat down the guilt and disgust he felt at what had happened to her; the knowledge that it was his uncle who had done it. He had to concentrate on getting to her and making sure she was safe. He had seen his uncle in her flat, which meant that he was waiting for her. He burst through the door of the shop like a tornado. His eyes darted around looking for her. There was no one in the shop, not even a shop assistant. When he spotted the top of her head a couple of aisles down, he nearly sank to his knees in relief. He didn't know if his uncle would hurt Billie, or what he planned to do, but he was sure that he did not know who his uncle really was. Unwanted images from the walls of Eric's study danced before his eyes: a young Billie tied up, her face red raw from crying, rope burns and bruises lining her naked body. Nausea rose within him and he shook his head to dislodge them.

He needed to get Billie away. Her safety was his main concern. It was the least he could do, considering. He felt a stabbing pain in his chest when he realised he was going to have to tell Billie that he was related to the person who had made her life hell the man who had made her live in fear of the world. Adam had got through her barriers, and it scared him to think she might recede even further into herself once she found out the truth. If he couldn't convince her that he was another victim of his uncle's staggering manipulation, he would lose her.

He raced over to her and, when she recognised him, her face brightened, her body relaxed. In that moment it hit him. He loved her. Pure and simple. But he was going to lose her because of the one person he had trusted most of his life.

He tried to grab her arm and hustle her out of the shop but she wasn't stupid. She wanted to know what was wrong. As he was about to explain, he saw the colour drain from her face. He felt her body shaking where his hand gripped her arm. The terror on her face filled him with dread. She wasn't looking at him but at something behind him.

# Billie

As Billie looked at Eric she felt like the ground had disappeared and she was falling indefinitely. Her stomach rebelled inside her as if it was trying to escape from her body and get as far away from Eric as it could. Seeing him unleashed suppressed memories, and images of his cruel face and the awful things he made her do floated into her vision. She felt sick. She was terrified. How was she going to explain to Adam who this was? What if Eric convinced Adam of his innocence? What if Adam didn't believe her like everyone else? On countless occasions Eric had demonstrated his powerful ability to manipulate anyone. Everyone he met dissolved under the force of his charm, then he put them back together how he wanted them his loyal puppets. She wasn't stupid, she knew she would see him again one day, but the reality was more debilitating than she had anticipated. Her fear of this moment had caused her to live a shadow of a life. These last few months, because of Adam, she had begun to crawl out and live again. As she looked at Eric, she realised she would pay the price for that. She was going to die. He had promised her that, the next time he saw her, he would kill her once he was done tormenting her. She had never forgotten finding his note when she'd unpacked her books; his promise to her.

She wondered what it was that had made him wait five years. Until she had met Adam, she had always felt his presence lurking in the background. The feeling of being watched permeated her entire life. Had he always been watching? Was he angry that she was starting to be happy and come to destroy it? All these thoughts swirled through her mind as she looked at him. He looked older than the last time she had seen him. His skin was as white and creased as a used tea towel. But his eyes still belied his evil nature; that would never age. He was completely unremarkable in a simple black coat, black jeans and shoes. Blending into the background just like she used to do. The one thing that stopped her from crumbling to the floor and submitting to whatever he wanted, was Adam. She had to explain. More than that, she had to keep him safe. Get him out. She was about to move when Adam turned and shielded her with his body. He began to speak to Eric, but it wasn't to ask who he was. It was to tell him to leave. Why would he do that? Did he sense the evil within this man?

# Adam

Adam took a deep breath, and slowly turned to see the person he knew would be there. As he turned, he moved Billie so she was behind him. He would not let anyone hurt her. As he looked at his uncle, he realised with horror that he barely recognised him. His eyes were cold and hard, and his stance was that of a predator. Not the kindly, ageing uncle Adam had known. The evil glint in his eye, and the confident swagger he had were so unlike the man Adam had relied on all these years. He realised that that man had been one of his uncle's many faces.

"Hello, son. Fancy meeting you here," smiled his uncle, chuckling. A joke? Adam couldn't believe it. It seemed he was happy that Adam knew the truth. Why wasn't he ashamed? More importantly, what did he want? What game was he playing? Whatever it was, Adam would not let him win. Not this time.

"I think you should leave," said Adam. His voice sounded much stronger than he felt inside.

"Leave? Why on earth would I do that? The party's just getting started," replied his uncle as stepped closer towards them.

As he moved, a flash of light reflected off the knife he had in his hand. Adam's heart stopped. He had spent his whole life worshipping this man, and now he was threatening him. It felt ridiculous. Like a nightmare that had been so vivid, when he woke, he was disorientated for the whole day. In this case he was waking up from the manipulations of his uncle, realising what he really was.

It was Billie's small gasp of terror, and the feel of her hands on his arm tightening their grip, that brought him back to reality. He had to concentrate. This man in front of him was as good as a stranger. Adam had no idea how he was going to get them both out of there safely. Could he really hurt his uncle? Could his uncle really hurt him? Had it all been a lie? He hoped his survival instinct could overcome his emotions. He wouldn't let Billie suffer any more than she already had. This time, he let the images of her suffuse his mind and strengthen his resolve, hardening his heart against his uncle.

"Now, son. All I want is the girl. I don't want to hurt you, but she is my property. I've let you play around with her for long enough, now I want her back."

"No."

"Look, boy, do what your uncle says, like you always do, and get out of here. Now. I won't tell you again!"

# Billie

'His uncle?' screamed her brain. It pierced the fear that had encased Billie since she had laid eyes on Eric. It couldn't be. Adam was related to the man who had almost cost her her life. Adam had invaded her carefully built defences, but all along he was playing her just like his uncle had. *His uncle.* She had never felt so betrayed. It was like when she had seen the real side of Eric all those years ago, but worse. She had fallen in love with Adam. She'd thought he was her happy ever after. She had loved Eric, but in a father-cum-grandfather sort of way. She hadn't loved him as deeply as you love the person you want to give your life to that's a stronger and more powerful type of love. Even though she hadn't known Adam long, she knew she loved him. Unequivocally. He made her a better person. He had blasted away the crippling fears she'd had with the force of his vibrant, energetic and loving personality. He had patiently pulled her from her solitary existence and shown her there was so much that life had to offer if you just had a little faith.

Well, look where faith had got her. He had lied to her. Played her even better than his uncle had. With Eric, she had been confused by what he was doing, even though deep down she had known it wasn't right, but she had never thought that about Adam. She had initially been wary, because of Eric, but she could never have imagined that he was related to him and that he was toying with her. Now the bracelet made sense. Bloody hell, he was one of the best actors she'd ever met. She'd apologised to him. He'd bought her that bracelet, knowing how she'd react. Knowing his uncle had bought a similar bracelet for her years ago. Oh, my God. She couldn't believe it. She had thought she knew him. The times they had talked, late into the night, he had even told her about his uncle. He had opened up to her on their first date and told her how his mother had died, and how he'd only had his uncle to help him throughout his life. He hadn't held anything back when he'd described his 'useless drunk' father, and if it wasn't for his uncle, he'd be completely alone in the world. Since then, when they'd talked, his uncle was always mentioned. Without any parents, it was clear he had played an important role in Adam's life and he loved him very much. From Adam's description, Billie had thought he was a saint, and couldn't wait to meet him. He'd sounded lovely.

How could he have done that? He made his uncle sound like such an amazing person. None of the anecdotes he had told her had sounded fake or made up; the wistful look on his face and the attention to detail in each story had made her feel like she had been there with him. How could all that be lies? If Adam was working with his uncle to fool her, then she was more of a mug than she'd thought.

Looking back over their time together, there was nothing, no clues, that would make her think he was anything but a genuinely lovely man. How wrong had she been? She didn't think she could survive this. The revelation about Adam was slowly crushing her. She wished he would stop the charade. Loud voices drew her back to the present. She tuned in to their conversation that had become background noise while she was digesting Adam's betrayal. She heard Eric mention something about puppets.

# Adam

"Look, boy, do what your uncle says, like you always do, and get out of here. Now. I won't tell you again!" At his words, Adam heard Billie crumple to the floor behind him. Shit. This was not the way he'd wanted her to find out. She would not understand. She'd think he had known what his uncle had done; that he had played a role in it; that he had been seducing her as a game with his uncle. She would think only bad of him. The truth was, he loved her, and he had no idea what his uncle was capable of. He couldn't turn his back on him to comfort her, so he raised his voice so she would hear.

"Billie, it's not what it sounds like. Yes, he's my uncle, but I had no idea what he had done to you. He told me you had made it all up and I believed him. But I know the truth now. You've got to believe me." Even he could hear the desperation in his voice. He couldn't risk looking at her to see if she believed him, not with the knife being so close to him.

His uncle moved a step closer, a lazy smile spreading across his face. He knew exactly what he had done by revealing their relationship to Billie. Adam had to get her out of there. He looked around the shop and realised there was no one to help him. His uncle must have guessed his thoughts because he spoke up.

"No one is going to help you, son. It's amazing what people will do for money, isn't it? I've had the shop owner here on my payroll for ages. Pretty much as soon as the girl moved here."

"What do you mean? I don't understand. What's happening?" He hoped to keep his uncle talking until he figured out a plan.

"I told you, she is mine." His uncle looked over Adam's shoulder at Billie and directed his words at her. "Did you really think I would just let you go, Billie? No, no, I invested so much time and effort into making you mine, I'm not just going to give that up. I couldn't believe my luck when you moved to Worcester, of all places. It was like fate. I knew then that you would always be mine."

Adam could hear that Billie was losing control, lost in her fear. He didn't even know if she could hear them anymore. Her gasping breaths were getting louder and more desperate. He hoped to God that she wouldn't pass out in the shop. He needed to distract his uncle from her. *Think, Adam, think.*

"If you've been following her, then you must have known I had started seeing her, why didn't you say anything to me? Why would you let me see her if she is, as you say, 'your property'?"

"Oh, Adam, of course I knew it was her you were seeing, but I know you. I knew you were doing it to get retribution for me. I saw you guzzling down all those bullshit stories I fed you about losing my house and my money. I saw how angry you were at what you *thought* my life had become because of her. Why else would you have approached her in that cafe? You aren't the first-move type too scared of losing someone just like you lost your mother. Nothing happens to Billie that I don't know about. It was fun watching you both. A little more entertaining than watching her mope around. Not that that's boring." His uncle stopped talking. His exuberance shone and he exuded pride and happiness.

Adam felt a wave of revulsion sweep through him as he realised his uncle was enjoying himself. He was practically bouncing on his toes, his eyes bright with equal parts of glee and menace. This side of him made him look younger than he was.

"Son, when you gave her that bracelet I couldn't stop laughing. Her face! You had no idea you'd bought her under my instruction nearly the exact bracelet I once bought her. It was hysterical, better than I could have imagined. Mind, your face was a picture too. You were so angry and confused. It really was fantastic entertainment. I felt like a puppet master watching his puppets dance. Your entire relationship was orchestrated by me. I got her beaten up by those lads so you could sweep in and be her knight in shining armour. I know you so well, Adam. I may as well have built you myself. But, now, alas, the game is over."

Adam couldn't see exactly where Billie was. All he could hear was her hysterical breathing somewhere behind him. He kept all his focus on his uncle, assessing whether he could grapple the knife from him before he could use it. His uncle was nearing his sixties, surely Adam could overpower him? He just had to be brave.

As Adam was about to move, his uncle closed the gap between them and tried to grab Billie from behind Adam. He had the knife pointed towards Adam. His other hand was grasping the air, trying to reach Billie. Adam lunged at him. He grabbed the arm that was holding the knife with both hands. He tried shaking it from his uncle's grip but his strength surprised him and he ripped free of Adam's hold. He turned back to Billie, as if he didn't register Adam as a threat.

"You're coming with me," he said as he grabbed her.

Rage burned through Adam. He tackled his uncle and forced Billie from his grip. They both crashed to the floor; Adam landed on top of his uncle. At the last minute he realised he didn't know where the knife was. Too late he saw his uncle's arm arc towards him. Pain erupted in his side but he refused to acknowledge it. He yanked at his uncle's arm and slammed his hand that held the knife, hard on the floor. The knife clattered and Adam kicked it away. It slid across the aisle with a menacing sound, coming to a stop under one of the shelves. His uncle seemed startled to have Adam's weight lying on top of him. Adam took advantage and punched him in the face. Once. Twice. He was about to hit him a third time, when dizziness struck him and he felt his vision darken. Eric took advantage of Adam's weakened state and pushed him hard so he could scramble from underneath him. Adam fell back against the shelves, breathless with pain. Once again, his uncle went for Billie. He was like a magnet that was inextricably drawn to her.

# Billie

Billie watched in horror as Eric stabbed Adam. She had cried out to warn him but was too late; the knife sliced into his side. Adam carried on, as if he couldn't feel it, and managed to wrestle the knife from Eric. Billie was terrified and confused. If Adam and Eric were working together, why the hell did Adam get stabbed? When Adam tackled his uncle, his mouth was set in determination, but she thought she had seen fear in his eyes. She was so confused. She'd thought for a moment that it was a fake knife, but she saw a dark patch staining Adam's dark blue jumper. There was blood on the knife as it clattered to the floor. Adam kicked it away and she thought she might be able to reach it. But, just as she was about to lunge for it, Eric lurched from under Adam. He came towards her, wild, with fury blazing in his eyes. He was going to kill her.

The fear of dying froze her; she felt every inch a pitiful girl, crouched up against the shelves of bread. For a second she considered throwing some bread at Eric. A crazed giggle left her mouth. She was about to die, and her only defence was bread. What the hell was wrong with her? Her breath died in her lungs as Eric came closer. He grabbed her hair. The pain woke her breath and she let out a gasp as her hair was almost ripped from her scalp. She rose, trying to alleviate the agony, as a blurred shape crashed into them.

# Adam

Getting to his feet was taking all his energy. The pain in his side was excrutiating, and he didn't know how much time he had before it rendered him useless. He turned, and was horrified to see Eric dragging Billie up from the floor by her hair. Adam looked for the knife, but he couldn't find it.

"Leave her alone!" he yelled, trying to distract his uncle. He crashed into him once more. It sent them both sprawling on the floor. Adam knew, this time, he would not be able to get up. He'd fallen on his side and he could feel blood trickling down it. As he moved his hand to put pressure on it, he realised he'd fallen next to Billie. He could see her white, drawn face, and her terrified, shaking body.

"Run, Billie," he whispered. The effort of talking drained him, and he was powerless to prevent his eyes from closing and his mind shutting down.

# Chapter Thirty-Eight

## Billie

Adam lay in front of her. Whispering for her to run. His voice reconnected her senses and she was up and running before she even registered that she'd moved. She burst through the door and ran out to the street. It was deserted apart from Adam's car. She wished she could drive. A few cars drove past but they were going too fast, and their drivers were too self-absorbed to notice the terrified girl who was in danger.

Billie ran towards her flat. She made it to the building within minutes fear giving her speed.

The door was unlocked.

She didn't pause to wonder why. Instead, she ran inside and, grappling with her bag, found her keys and locked it. Satisfied it was secure, she slumped against the door. Her breaths came frequent and fast. Her body was shaking violently. What the hell had just happened? How had her quiet, normal life been blasted apart to resemble something out of a movie? Her mind's eye filled with the look that Eric had given her; a promise of suffering. It couldn't be true. Not even her nightmares were as horrifying as what had just happened. She couldn't process it. Her mind flashed with Eric's face. Weak and terrified, her body was shutting down in protest. She didn't know what to think about Adam. She couldn't believe she had just left him there. Was this all part of a master plan that she hadn't discovered yet?

An echoing knock on the door reawakened her panic. She stopped breathing. *Don't breathe. They won't know you are here if they can't hear you.* She put her hand over her mouth. Her lungs burned and protested. Billie backed away from the door silently. She moved towards the window, she would jump if she had to.

Just as she turned to look out of it, she heard a key in the lock. The noises of the entire world stopped. She heard each pin lining up as the key slid into the door. The sound of the key turning echoed around the room.

Billie couldn't have breathed if she'd wanted to. She was immobilised by fear. Her horror grew as the door handle was pressed down and the door began to open. She briefly thought of hiding but she was rooted to the spot. Eric walked in. His presence filled the room and she inwardly cringed away. His gaze was hungry. Like the predator who knows he has won and is about to make his kill. Even though one of his eyes was swollen, the fire still burned brightly. There was no mask hiding his true self. He leisurely walked towards her, taking his time. Basking in the anticipation. This was who he really was. A hunter who feeds on fear and power.

"Have you missed me, Billie?" he asked, taunting her. Billie refused to look at him. He reached out a hand, and gently brushed a finger down her cheek. She swallowed the bile that had risen to her mouth. He pulled away with a tear on his finger and put it in his mouth. "I love the taste of fear in the evening."

Without warning, the back of his hand smashed into her face, the force knocked her to the floor. She landed hard on her side. She barely had time to draw breath before his foot connected with her stomach. This was it, the beginning of her death. She would die a terrified, shaking mess in the corner. In the past he had said he couldn't wait to kill her. Each time he threatened her into silence: "if you leave, I'll hunt you down and kill you". It was his favourite promise.

He stood over her for a moment and then, as if satisfied she wasn't going to move, she saw his feet move towards the kitchen. She could hear kitchen drawers being opened and shut and then his menacing footsteps prowling back over to her.

His foot connected with her ribs; he kicked her again and again until she was lying on her back. Through her tears, she saw him kneel. He loomed over her, his breathing fast but not out of terror. He grabbed her shirt and ripped it open, her stomach and her black bra on show.

"I see you've been overeating since we last met. Getting quite chubby, aren't we?" She paled at the sight of the small kitchen knife in his hand. He brought the sharp point to her stomach. She felt it pierce her skin and the blood trickle down her side. "Hold still or you'll make it worse."

She knew he would feed off her reactions, so she closed her eyes tight. She'd been through worse; she went to her safe place. Despite the fact she could feel the knife slicing her skin, in her mind she was surrounded by oak trees; the wind breathed life into the leaves and toyed with her hair as she ran happy and free around the forest. A sharp pain broke her concentration and she looked down to see a mess of cuts, some deep and some shallow, over her stomach. She closed her eyes, trying to retreat from the horror.

"There, I've got my name on you now, you'll always be mine." He must have seen that her eyes were closed as she felt him grab a fist full of hair to hold her head up by it, then he smashed it back down on the floor. "Open your eyes," he growled. She did, desperate to avoid any more pain. She thought she had felt the worst of his wrath in the past, but this was a new level.

"If you want the pain to stop, I need to know where you put that camera I gave you."

Through the fog of pain, she tried to remember what he was talking about. *What camera? Oh wait, that camera.* The camera he had left her with pictures of her family and her room on it, and even ones of her asleep, when she had lived in Windermere and he was trying to convince her to drop the case.

A few fields away from her house there was a field that had a strange rock formation. There were four large black rocks that circled together, the rain had smoothed their surfaces. The rocks were slanted towards some water, which was the size of small pond, at the bottom. It was one of her favourite places to go, she didn't think anyone knew about it as there were no paths to it, and she had never seen anyone there. She had taken the camera and thrown it into the water. Then, she'd sat on one of the slanted rocks, staring down at it, wondering if there was enough water for her to drown as well.

This memory played in her head and it distracted her from the pain coursing through her body. She didn't know what to do. Of course, he was worried that the camera could be used as evidence. Why the hell had she thrown it away? She hadn't thought about the camera since that day. It was part of her coping mechanism. But now she was faced with the gravity of her actions. She'd been so stupid. That was probably what had kept Eric away: the fact he thought she had the camera and could use it against him. One of the most damning photos flashed into her mind. In it, she was asleep in her bed and Eric's face was right next to hers, barely a millimetre away. The malice in his smile had stayed with her for days after she'd seen that photo. Should she tell him she'd thrown it away? Oh God! What was the right thing to do? Her mind was firing scenarios in her head, trying to figure out how she could get out of this alive. This thought shocked her, as before she had met Adam she would have happily welcomed death.

# Adam

The pain in his side pulled Adam back into consciousness. Flashbacks of what had happened had him anxiously lifting his top, fearing the worst. He'd never seen a knife wound before. It had stopped bleeding so he took that as a good sign, but it was extremely painful.

He tentatively got up and managed a couple of steps without passing out again. As he straightened up, a voice in his brain yelled, Billie! She must have run away. Or been taken by his uncle. God, his uncle.

His head hurt more than his side when he thought about the monster that his uncle really was. If he wasn't so scared for Billie's safety, he would have laid back down and considered what impact this was going to have on his life. What would he do without his uncle's guiding influence? He winced as he realised it was pure manipulation. He had to help Billie. His blood began to boil at the thought of what his uncle might be doing to her. She didn't deserve this. He needed to protect her.

He looked around the shop. He couldn't believe the owner had just upped and left for a pay-off. He tried to run but it made him feel light-headed. He staggered, grateful for the walls along the way that were helping him. He felt faint and dizzy but his desire to protect Billie kept him going. With his uncle's betrayal threatening to tear him apart inside, she was all he had left. Even if she chose to never see him again, he had to make sure she got to make her choice somewhere safe and free from danger.

He pushed through the door to the building and made his way up the grey concrete steps. He expected to find her green door closed and stopped dead when it was wide open. He could hear voices from inside and was tempted to rush straight in but the logical part of his brain stopped him. His uncle had already proved that he was happy to resort to violence, and he could end up putting Billie in more danger rather than helping her. He needed to be clever. He was already struggling, his breathing laboured, and he felt that any minute he would lose his balance. He silently edged towards the doorway, thanking God for soundless, concrete flooring. He heard his uncle's voice.

"I've got all night, my dear. Give me the camera."

He peered around the corner. His heart nearly failed when he saw his uncle kneeling over Billie with a knife poised over her stomach. He could see blood pooling on her skin from various cuts across her torso. Her face was gaunt and the fear in her eyes was gut-wrenching. Suddenly, her bright-green eyes locked with his, and his uncle turned to see what she was looking at. Damn. He didn't have time to be smart. He had to act. He launched into the room and hurled himself at his uncle third time lucky, he might be able to keep him down this time he managed to get him flat on his back. Adam held him down, by his arms, using his own weight to stop himself from being bucked off by his uncle's flailing body. No longer sure what his uncle was capable of, he used every ounce of the strength he had left to keep him on the floor. He turned to Billie.

"You need to get out of here. Go!"

# Billie

Billie stared at Adam. Her brain had stopped working and she could only see his mouth moving; she couldn't take in what he was saying. One minute, Eric had been leaning over her, promising to cause her no end of pain if she didn't give him what he wanted, the next minute, Adam was there. Once again wrestling his uncle to the ground. Was this part of the ploy? Use her feelings for Adam to make her give them the camera? Some weird kind of good cop/bad cop thing? Did they think she would be so grateful to Adam that she would lead them to the camera? She looked closer at Adam and saw sweat dripping off his forehead, his eyes were creased, and his mouth was grimacing in pain. It was costing him a lot to keep Eric down. She could see drops of blood creating a puddle on the floor. Could they really be pretending?

She didn't know what to think. Her heart didn't want to believe that the man she'd thought she knew was as evil as Eric. But she knew what Eric was capable of. Waves of pain throbbed her head, her confusion causing her mind to protest. *What the hell was going on?* She was so scared Adam was working with Eric, she didn't know what to think. Should she run like Adam said? A part of her wanted to run away and just keep running for the rest of her life. She was so scared of Eric. Even with him pinned down under Adam she couldn't stop shaking in fear of him. This man had tormented her for so long. She had experienced his cruelty and the depths of his depravity.

# Adam

Tears were pouring down Billie's face, and he sensed that she was close to breaking down completely. Kicking himself for not doing it earlier, he knew they needed to call the police. What did he think he was, some sort of superhero? This was real life, not a movie. He wasn't qualified to keep Billie safe. They needed help. He refocused on Billie. Trying to keep the worry from his voice, he spoke to Billie in a reassuring tone.

"Billie, I need you to get my phone. It's in my back pocket. Get my phone, sweetie. You can do it." When he first started to ask her she wouldn't move, her fear held her prisoner on the floor, but his voice must have wormed its way past her fear as he saw her shoulders drop and she slowly moved towards him. As she got closer to his uncle, Adam was able to appreciate how terrified Billie was of him. She was acting like he had asked her to enter the cage of a man-eating animal that would surely kill her.

She kept her eyes on his uncle, needing to know where he was all the time. As she reached into the back pocket of Adam's jeans, his uncle began to thrash wildly. Billie shrank back in fear, phone clutched in her hand. Adam continued to resist his uncle's attempts to escape with as much force as he could muster. Seeing Billie's reaction to him made it easier; fierce anger rushed through his body, strengthening his muscles so they could hold the older man down. Eric seemed to realise that he wasn't getting away as the struggling lessened.

Adam saw beads of sweat on his uncle's wrinkled brow and was reminded how old he was. How could this old man be capable of such malice? Turning away from his thoughts, and his uncle, he looked over at Billie. She was curled up in the foetal position, hands covering her head to protect herself from an attack. He only had his voice to soothe her, he longed to go to her, he wanted to wrap her in his arms and hold her tightly until she realised that he would never let anyone hurt her.

"Billie, it's okay. I've got him. He's not going anywhere."

No response. He tried again. "Billie, look at me!"

He used his most authoritative voice, and it worked. She looked up straight away. Adam didn't dare let himself think why she responded to that tone. He bet it was his uncle's doing.

"I've got him. He is not getting away. But I can't hold him forever. You need to call the police." At the word police, Billie began to moan and shake her head.

"They'll let him out again. He'll just come back. Please don't make me call them. They will just let him go."

"Billie! Calm down! I promise you, if you call the police they will not let him go. I promise."

"Why should I trust you? You've lied to me this whole time. He is your uncle."

"Billie, if I wanted to hurt you I wouldn't be holding him down. I wouldn't have got hurt trying to protect you."

"It could be an act. He likes to play games. You both could be trying to trick me into giving him the evidence he thinks I have."

This was exactly what Adam was afraid of. He knew how it would look to her. He didn't know what he could say to make her realise he'd had no idea what a monster his uncle was. But he had to try.

"Listen to me, Billie. Yes, he is my uncle. But I had no idea what he was. I only found out today when I saw the proof. Everything I've ever told you about him was the truth, I had no idea what he was capable of. As far as I was concerned, he has been the only person in my life who I could rely on. He told me you were a liar and I believed him. I didn't know who he really was and I am wracked with guilt that he did all those things to you."

Adam felt a tear trickle down his face. His guilt was ready to consume him. He needed to hold it at bay long enough to get Billie out of there.

"I didn't know what he was really like, I swear it. When I met you I wanted to get the truth from you. To clear my uncle's name. But, instead, I ended up falling in love with you. I am in love with you. I need you to believe that. My uncle had me under his spell, but my feelings for you broke it. The more my feelings grew for you, the more I began to see the cracks in his story. Today, I went to confront him, but instead I found the evidence of what he had done; what he did to you. I feel sick. I can't believe I loved a man who could do that." As he spoke, he searched her face, her eyes, desperate for a clue to how she was feeling. Her eyes were glued to his, tears poured down her face. He couldn't tell if she had accepted that he was telling the truth, all he saw was confusion and fear.

No matter what happened, or what anyone else thought, he loved this woman. She was kind, funny and incredibly brave. And more than anything, he wanted her to be his. "I will do whatever it takes to keep you safe. You may think I was playing a game, something my uncle orchestrated, but I assure you, right here, right now, I am no longer his puppet. I may have fallen for his lies, but I know what he is now. He does not control me, and I will do whatever it takes to get you out of here. I will protect you from him for the rest of my life. If you don't believe me, come and look at my side. Touch it; you'll see I'm not faking it. My uncle stabbed me while trying to get to you. I swear to you, Billie, I am the man you've got to know. I may not have had a genuine motive for getting close to you, but I promise, I would never hurt you."

# Chapter Thirty-Nine

## Billie

Adam's words fell on her ears and she tried to fight her heart; her heart was focused on the tears that slid down his face. Her heart looked at his expressive pale-green eyes and saw the desperate need he had for her to believe him. Her brain was berating her heart. If she hadn't let down her guard with Adam, she would not be in this position now. She would be safe. Despite everything, she ached to believe him. Against all logic and fact, she couldn't believe that Adam was capable of such deception. Not the man she knew. But her brain was willing to fight dirty. It whispered: even if she believed him, could she really love, and be with, a blood relation of the man who had abused her most of her life? Could she trust him ever again? She ignored the thought and forced herself to focus on the present. She needed to get away from Eric, and Adam was offering her the simplest way. With trembling fingers, she dialled 999.

While they waited for the police and ambulance, Billie couldn't help herself but go to Adam. Once again, as she got close to him, Eric thrashed and bucked, trying to get to her. This time, she only flinched; she didn't retreat Adam had held him down this long. She could see Adam following her with his eyes, she could see the pleading in them from the corner of her own. She lifted his coat out of the way; some of his blood getting on her fingers. As she lifted his top, she saw Adam inhale and he let out a hiss of agony. There was a wound where the knife had stabbed him. There was nothing fake about that. She looked around in panic. From the little she knew about injuries like that, she knew she needed to get something pressed on it to stem the bleeding. She thought it was a good sign that he wasn't bleeding too heavily, but it was still a large and deep wound.

# Adam

Billie was looking at his wound, touching him. He had to stare at his uncle to remind himself why he couldn't gather her in his arms. She touched the wound and his body flinched away from her, he hissed in pain. That distraction was all his uncle needed; the next minute Adam was thrown across the room.

Adam landed hard against the wall, the breath knocked out of him. Eric lunged at Billie and grabbed her hair and her arms; he twisted one of them behind her back and began to drag her out of the room. Without thinking, Adam scrambled to his feet and wrapped his arm around his uncle's neck. He was trying to bring him to the floor and pull him off Billie. His choke-hold was working, as his uncle let go of Billie to pry Adam's hands away. He elbowed Adam in the side where the knife had got him and he went down hard, the pain causing his vision to flicker. Eric must have been fed up with Adam's interfering as, instead of returning to Billie, he kicked Adam hard in the back.

He was on the verge of unconsciousness; all he could do was try to defend his body with his arms. Suddenly, a loud gurgle came from above him, followed by the thud of something large falling to the floor. Adam wasn't sure he had the strength to open his eyes. He was just relieved that the kicking had stopped. He felt cold, gentle hands stroking his face, but the blackness was enveloping him and he couldn't move or speak.

# Billie

I killed him.

# Chapter Forty

## Billie

When Billie was told that Eric was not dead, she had to hide her disappointment and fear. She had answered all the questions the police had asked, but couldn't shake her sense of hopelessness. She had been down this road before. She knew how it would go. Eric would come up with another way of evading the law. He'd twist it so she was the one being arrested and sent to prison. Unable to fight any more, she was honest and told the police everything, but there was no conviction in her voice. She just wanted to go home and carry on with her life. She knew she needed to move away quickly, because when Eric got out of wherever they had taken him he was bound to come looking for her again.

Before she left, they told her that Adam had backed up her story and that he had provided them with evidence of what had happened to her in the past. Eric had kept a hidden room containing photographs and surveillance equipment, and diaries spanning back to when she had met Eric for the first time. It was also revealed that she was not the first girl he had abused, or the last. They'd found pictures of other girls, along with evidence of what he had done to them. The police had assured her that this time Eric would be going to court, with the full weight of bullet-proof evidence to secure a conviction. She was told that they were already tracking down the other girls. He would not get away with it again.

She tried to feel the happiness she was sure she should be feeling but, she wanted to tell the policeman who seemed so pleased with himself, until Eric was officially locked away, she would not believe it. She couldn't afford to get her hopes up that he would no longer be able to hurt her. She knew what it felt like to have your feelings of safety shattered. In fact, it had only been six hours since that very thing had happened: six hours since she'd learnt that Adam was Eric's nephew; six hours since she'd found out that Eric had still been pulling the strings of her life in the background; six hours since the police had prised her blood stained hands off Adam's face. Twenty-four hours ago, she was so happy. She was in love and picturing a future with Adam. Now, she was in a police station, reliving the horror of seeing Eric.

It was the early hours of the next day when she was driven back to her flat. She had stood in the flat, listening to the promises of the young police officers. She surveyed the room. What had once been her sanctuary, was now a scene of terror. No one had cleared up the blood, hers, Adam's and Eric's. It was pretty much exactly how she'd left it. Just without Eric. The gravity of what could have happened to her sank in, and she lost her ability to stand. She dropped to the floor.

Wracking sobs left her, and she could barely hold herself together. It felt like she was crumbling under the weight of what had happened. She lay on the floor, crying out all the emotion she had bottled up. Expunging herself of the feelings she had denied. She cried about how scared she had felt, sobbed about her gran and Adam's betrayal, and the undeniable fact that Adam had saved her. He may have betrayed her, but he had also put his life at risk to save her. She felt so desperately sad and alone. She should never have come back to this flat, but she had nowhere else to go. She had no one.

# Adam

A quiet, repetitive beep roused Adam from his sleep. He was certain his alarm didn't make that noise. Maybe Billie had changed it. He smiled thinking about her face. She was so beautiful, more so because she didn't realise it. She had told him that she hated her fire-red hair, but he loved it. She was so different to anyone he'd ever met and her hair matched that. In fact, he needed to get up and seek her out. If only he didn't need to sleep, he could be around her all the time. Man, he was lame. He tried to force his eyes open, it took all his strength to do so. He couldn't remember ever feeling this tired.

He blinked twice when he saw the white walls around him; the unfamiliar white blanket and several monitors on either side of him. He tried to sit up to see more but a bursting pain rocketed from his side, forcing him to lie back down. He was in hospital. Why was he in hospital? As he asked himself that question, his brain unlocked the memories. His heart sank and he felt sick as he remembered he had lost both his uncle and Billie.

# Billie

Billie couldn't settle. She knew she had to go to court and once that was over she would finally be free. But until that happened she was living a nightmare; every bump in the night was Eric. She wanted to move, she longed to escape the flat but her mental exhaustion and the constant fear that followed her around held her prisoner. She couldn't move away. She didn't have the energy.

The police had advised her to stay put for the moment. She was only just holding on to her job by the skin of her teeth. Her boss had coldly reminded her that unexplained absences were not acceptable and she was on her final warning. They had given her some compassionate leave but she didn't know how long she would be allowed to take it. She had no friends or family to turn to; she felt lost.

It was more isolating than when she had self-imposed her seclusion from the world. Each day she worried and wondered about what the future might hold. Did she even have one? She felt as if Eric was still watching. Now she knew he had been watching her all that time, the feeling would never go away. She hadn't known then she was being watched, so how would she know now? Eventually her desolation led her to Adam's hospital bed.

When she arrived at the hospital, an over-friendly nurse informed her that Adam was sleeping. The nurse must have seen the alarm on her face as she assured her that he was doing fine, and his body just needed time to heal from his wound. She insisted that Billie should go through and see him, he'd had no visitors and the nurse said she felt sorry for him.

So, Billie found herself at Adam's bedside, holding his hand as he slept peacefully. With the blanket over him it looked like he was just having a good night's sleep. She stared hungrily at his face. Relaxed in sleep, he looked even more handsome than she had got used to.

When she had first discovered that Adam was related to Eric, she had thought the worst: that he had duped her into falling in love with him. But, she knew now without a doubt, Adam had been as much a victim as she had. His passionate speech, as he'd held his uncle down, played in her mind. His face was glistening with tears when he'd told her how he had learnt what his uncle was really like. She realised what she had seen in his eyes was pain. She remembered, from their first date, that Adam had worshipped his uncle because without him he would have been alone. But it was hard every time she thought of Adam, she automatically pictured him with Eric, laughing and loving each other. The man who had made her suffer and the man she loved were related, she just couldn't take it in.

She was feeling so lonely, she desperately wanted to wake Adam and tell him that, if he would have her, she would be his, but could she really be with him knowing that he was close to and had loved the man she despised. What if they reconnected? Could Adam really break the bond that had been nurtured over such a long time? Was it fair to ask him to give up the only family he had, monster or not? How could she live with him, knowing that he had a blood tie to the man who had caused her insides to try and escape from her body in fear?

She looked at Adam's hand. It took both of her small pale hands to hold his large one. She absently caressed her fingers across his palm. The movement and feel of his hand centred her. For the first time since the chaos of Eric's attack, she felt calm. Safe. She looked at Adam and checked he was sleeping. She moved her hand and caressed his face. Even his face was strong.

"I love you," she whispered. When he didn't answer back she felt emboldened; she wanted to unburden herself of the stormy thoughts that were thundering around in her mind.

"I want so much for you to wake up and hold me." She felt silly for talking to herself, but she couldn't stop now. "Do you love me, too? I know you told the police about your uncle. You gave them enough evidence that they think they are going to be able to put him away for the rest of his life. They got the camera from where I'd thrown it, so that will help too. If only I'd known; I could have used it last time."

She stroked her fingers through the blond curls that brushed his ears.

"You have no idea what it was like; he was so good at controlling me. I thought he loved me. I loved him more than anyone; I thought he could replace my dad, but in the end he replaced all my dreams and became my inescapable nightmare. It is so hard to keep control of my thoughts; any little thing can set off flashbacks. The memories of his breath on my body and his fingers touching me, they lurk in the dark parts of my brain. If I give them the slightest chance, they crush my defences and force me to relive it all. Until I met you, I thought I'd never be normal again. Within a few weeks of having you in my life, you had forced those memories further and further back into the recesses of my mind. I was so lonely before I met you.

"He cost me my family, but then I had you. Yes, I still have panic attacks and struggle, but it was getting so much easier. I could feel myself stepping away from the remnants of his control. I wasn't even around him and he still manipulated me until I met you. You were the antidote. I want that again, but how?"

She looked at his face. She would be mortified if he had heard her deepest thoughts, but part of her wanted him to wake up, look at her with those loving pale-green eyes and tell her the solution. Tell her that he could see the way.

"How could I ever trust you? I want to. Every fibre of me wants to trust you. I know you are disgusted by what your uncle did, but one day, in the future, what's to say that you won't regret cutting off your family. I know how hard that is. He reaches out to you … and you start to see him again. I can't be around that. M-m-y own mother …"

Her voice broke; she hadn't said that word in five years. Her mum's face floated into her mind's eye. "My own mother knew what he had done, but didn't help me, she let me suffer. Then she forgave my gran and was happy to be in the same house as him. Even after she knew about everything he had done. If my own mother could betray me, then why wouldn't you? My whole life has been defined by him. But I don't want that any more. If we stayed together, we would always been bound by it, wouldn't we?"

It was helping to sort through her thoughts. She loved Adam. The sight of him tackling his uncle to the ground to protect her flashed through her mind and she felt a tingling fill up her chest. Her heart expanded as she realised that Adam was everything she would ever want. She had always dreamed of finding someone who could protect her. Not only had Adam done that, twice, he had also protected her from the very man who was the reason she desired a protector.

But, she needed to protect herself, she couldn't get hurt again. When Eric had called himself Adam's uncle, it was the worst pain she had ever felt. Even worse than when she stopped talking to her mother and realised she was alone in the world. When she had let her guard down with Adam, she'd thought she was going to get her happy ever after. When it was taken away, she felt she was being destroyed from the inside. It was almost worse than anything Eric had done to her. She couldn't go through that pain again. Adam would break her trust; he may not have been in league with his uncle but he had lied to her. The fact he had started their relationship with the intention of making her confess that she had lied, was something she couldn't forget. When her heart tried to convince her to give in, and be with Adam, her brain would remind her of that. She told this to his sleeping form.

She lovingly stroked his face, trying to convince her heart that this was goodbye and the right thing to do, but it reminded her that, without her, Adam would have nobody. He had his friends but he had no family, and no one as close as they had been.

Could she really abandon him? He had put his life at risk to save her from his uncle, was this how she would repay him?

She sighed, the brief relief she had felt at voicing her feelings was short-lived. The familiar sickness in her stomach returned, along with a headache, caused by the conflict that was tearing her apart inside. What had she done to have to go through this? First Eric, now this; would she ever get a break, a chance to be happy?

# Adam

Adam smelled her scent before he even opened his eyes. He was about to open them, ready to drink in the sight of her, when he felt her fingers on his face. He didn't want to spoil the moment, so he concentrated on staying still. He wanted to enjoy her caress before reality tore them apart forever. He knew his relationship with his uncle had destroyed any chance he'd had with her. To his surprise, she began to talk. He thought for a moment that she knew he was awake, but he quickly realised she was talking to herself. He felt bad deceiving her, but she had never opened up to him like this. He sensed she was going to say things that she would struggle to say to him when he was awake. When she started talking to him about her mum, pretending to sleep became so hard. He wanted to ball his fists to express his anger. Billie was so strong and brave; to suffer the way she had, to still function and not give in to misery or lose herself. He wanted to find Billie's mum and shake her until she regained her senses.

Poor Billie, little did she know that he knew exactly how it felt to feel the gap in your life where your mum should be. He had a sudden urge to take Billie in his arms and heal the emotional wounds she had suffered. He wanted to right all the wrongs. He knew, if she would give him the chance, he would do whatever it took to make her happy. He didn't have anyone else in the world who cared for him, and neither did Billie. He could hear the echo of isolation and depression in her words. When she said that she could never trust him again, it hurt more than the knife wound in his side. He'd rather be stabbed all over than never have Billie in his life. They hadn't been together long but the feelings he had for her were powerful. They had been through so much together and they were connected in ways he hadn't even known. He had to come up with a way to regain her trust and make her see that he would never want anything to do with the man who used to be his uncle. He would find a way. He had nothing else to do with his life.

# Chapter Forty-One

## Twelve Months Later

*Worcester Times,* May 2016

### My Confession by Adam Bondwell

Twelve months ago, I was writing a column about the interesting things to do around the West Midlands. I was just an average guy; working and trying to find my way in this crazy, crazy world. Now, my life has been shattered in more ways than one and I am left picking up the pieces. Pieces that won't go back to how they were, so I'm creating a new picture.

I am hoping this confession will help me with that. For you to understand, I need to give you some background information, so forgive me for that.

I lost my mother at a very young age. I was left with a drunken father, desperately wondering how I was supposed to survive without the woman who was the axis my world spun around. Enter Uncle Eric.

The first day he walked into my life, he took the spot where my mother had been. We had never had a big family: no grandparents, no one except Uncle Eric. From the day my mother got ill, it was Adam and Eric against the world. He was kind, gentle and honest and I worshipped him. He taught me everything I needed to know to exist in this big wide world. His visits healed the ache of loneliness I suffered when he wasn't around. He was my world. He was my surrogate mother and father rolled into one.

What I didn't realise, the day my uncle came into my life, was that he'd planted a seed that he would nurture my entire life. Yes, he took care of me and helped me, but these good deeds were the water to make his seed of manipulation grow. He made sure that he was the sun; that I would gravitate and grow only to him. I was his creation. My world centred around him. I would, and did, do anything he asked.

Now, you might be thinking, so what? He used you. What are you crying about? Well, I'll tell you. My uncle is a paedophile. His manipulation of me enabled him to have inappropriate relationships with more than fifteen underage girls. Those visits to see me, they gave him an excuse to get close to girls. He used me as bait to gain people's trust. I didn't realise the extent to which I was a pawn in his games until I saw a girl at his trial from a homeless shelter we had volunteered at.

She had come forward to give evidence. At the time I'd thought my uncle was amazing, taking time to get to know girls who had no place to go. It sickens me now to know I was witnessing my uncle prey on a vulnerable girl. How could I not know? This is a question that will plague me for the rest of my life. This is my first confession.

The other half of my confession concerns my soulmate, my one true love. The woman I betrayed because I fell for my uncle's lies. I swallowed them and, because of that, I made the woman I grew to love, suffer unimaginable pain. I won't name her, but I hope to God she reads this; she will know it is her I am writing about.

I met this wonderful beauty when I was still my uncle's puppet. Little did I know, so was she. I saw her, and I believed that she had spread lies about my uncle. He almost went to prison because of her. She'd had the guts to press charges against him, but he was too smart to leave any evidence.

The most sickening part of this story is that I gave him an alibi for his crimes against her. After reading that, I know you will be judging me. *How could you, Adam?* Believe me, no one could judge me and be as disgusted with me as I am. All I can say is, I was a young man with no one in his life apart from an uncle.

An uncle who ensured that I worshipped him and would do anything for him. I will never forget what I've done, but I've had to forgive myself (or so my therapist tells me).

I struck up a relationship with one of my uncle's 'victims', intending to charm a confession out of her. Hoping to clear his name and make my career. Who'd have thought it would be him who would give me a boost up the career ladder?

Reader, I'm sure you see where this is going; I fulfilled every cliché, and fell in love with the woman I was supposed to hate for ruining my uncle's life. I thought she was evil and conniving but soon I discovered she was brave, beautiful, kind and selfless. The pain behind every smile, and the sadness in her movements, made me realise that something wasn't ringing true with my uncle's accounts of her. I went to visit him and discovered that he was only pretending to live in poverty. By doing that I kicked off a chain of events I both regret and am grateful for. Yes, I'm a walking contradiction.

My uncle took off his mask and showed me the magnificence of his role as puppet master, the master manipulator, the devil in a kindly old man's skin. He tried to take the woman I love from me I was injured protecting her but I was able to apprehend him until the police arrived. He is now in prison serving time for the crimes he committed.

I am pleased I could cut the puppet strings he had bound me with, and play a role in sending him to prison, but in doing so I lost the woman I love. She could no longer trust me I hadn't told her about my uncle. She came to visit me in hospital and told me that she couldn't stand knowing I was related to the man who had tormented her for years, there would always be a chance I may reconnect with him and shatter her life all over again I'd already done that to her once.

So, here I am confessing to the world that yes, I am related to the most calculating and evil person I've ever known, but his reign of power is over.

I was scared to be alone in the world, so I relied on him and that gave him power. But I am not afraid any more. I have learnt what real love is. I know men are supposed to be macho and emotionless, but we aren't immune to the might of true love when it hits us.

Before I lost her, I was happy; colours were brighter, the world was beautiful. I didn't feel alone. The woman I love didn't tell me how to live my life. She didn't use me. She made me laugh. She made me ache inside when I wasn't with her. She made me a better person. I was content and safe because I had her love. I could appreciate life and not feel like I was treading water. I could swim into the ocean of life, her love would be the lifeline tied around my waist.

So, woman I treasure, if you are reading this, please know that I too was a victim, under the control of my uncle. I didn't suffer the way you did, but I was still under his control.

There aren't enough words in the world to tell you how sorry I am for the pain my family and I have caused you. I want you to know that you can trust me. I have publicly denounced my uncle. I will never be part of his life again; I will give him nothing. If you will let me, I will give you everything. Yes, I am related to the man who nearly destroyed you, but I am not him. I may have only had my mother for eight years, but I am everything she taught me I am a good man. I have learnt from this experience and I will never be controlled again.

My uncle took great delight in telling you about our relationship, knowing what it would do to you. I don't want to let him win. I don't want you to come back to me just to stick it to him, you should come back to me because I understand you and the life that you've had. We've both been dealt a difficult hand in life. We've both suffered because of the same man; there are no two people better suited. I may have met you intending to trick you, but I couldn't help being myself around you. I spent ages trying to break through your barriers and the whole time you had sailed through mine. Everything you know about me is the truth, you know who I really am, you know these words I have written are the truth.

Readers, thank you for reading my story. If you get time, send up a prayer that the woman I love will find the courage to take a leap of faith and come back to me.

Although this was intended to send a message to one person, I also have a message for everyone. Never let yourself become a puppet; don't live your life based on other people's expectations or opinions. Be your own person. Be whatever you want to be. Every single person on this earth deserves to be happy and respected. So, look around you, think about the important people in your life. Do they make you happy? Do they let you be you? Or do they seek to run your life because they aren't happy with their own?

Never be afraid to let go of negative people. I let my uncle take advantage of me because I feared being alone. Don't let fear rule your life. Take a leap of faith. Have faith in yourself. It is better to be alone rather than a pawn in someone else's game. Maybe if I had realised that earlier, my uncle would never have been able to hurt all the girls he did.

Once again, thank you for reading; I wish you a happy life, full of decisions that you have made to make *you* happy.

# Chapter Forty-Two

## Billie

Billie had read Adam's article over, and over again. She had to venture out and buy another copy because her tears had smudged the print and ruined her first. Her heart was furious with her because she was still in her flat and not with Adam, holding him until they moulded into one person.

She looked at her suitcases, packed and by her front door. The court case was over and she hadn't even gone to the sentencing. She'd thought that hearing Eric had been found guilty would cause a reaction within her, but it turns out, she didn't care. She was numb to Eric and all that had happened to her. She had retreated into her shell, life was exactly as it had been before she had met Adam. But everything was duller, and it was harder.

She had tried to work after her compassionate leave had ended. The first time she had arrived at the building, she'd felt exposed by the large glass windows that opened up one side of the building. It had felt like everyone on each level was looking down on her, ready to attack and take advantage.

It had taken all her strength to convince herself to walk through the doors of the building. As she had pushed open the door to the office, she'd batted away the trickle of sweat making its way down the side of her face. Her breathing was laboured and a horrible thought had struck her. Would people know? Since that awful day with Eric and Adam she had been immune to the outside world. She didn't notice anyone or anything; as if there were a screen around her and the outside world. Of course people knew. Oh God. She had made a mistake. Her fear had risen and the panic attack took control of her body. She had only reached the door to the office and could see her manager coming over, concern on his face. He had his hands in front of him and she saw he was going to touch her. Just squeezing air through her constricted airway had been difficult; she'd had no way to scream at him to not touch her. His hand had landed on her shoulder just as she'd felt the ground race up towards her.

She was now officially 'let go'.

On the up side, she and Bobby had become inseparable. She lay on the bed, clutching the newspaper even though she knew each word by rote. Bobby was sat on her chest as if trying to heal the pain in her heart with his presence.

Adam's article was the most powerful piece of writing she had ever read. It was like she could see his heart and soul on the page. She couldn't believe he would expose himself like this. His brutal honesty and his unflinching assessments of himself were astounding. There was no way she would ever be able to articulate her feelings like this, let alone to the whole world like he had. She wished she could stand back, as he had, to analyse herself and what had happened. This was what she missed about him, he was so calm and logical. Each word exuded Adam's personality. She felt like she was right there with him, it was his voice she heard in her head.

There was no doubt that she wanted to go to him, but she had said goodbye at the hospital. She had got a new phone and saved Adam's number in it, although she had never given him the number. After she'd seen him in hospital, she had sent him a message from her old phone and asked him not to come to the flat. He had respected her wishes but had bombarded her with letters and text messages. Hence the new phone.

She looked at her packed bags. Two measly suitcases represented all her worldly possessions; one of them was full of books.

She was moving to Devon. She'd answered an advertisement to be a live-in carer for an elderly lady who had no family. The advert had been so full of the lady's loneliness that she couldn't help but respond. She knew how the lady was feeling. After a long phone call their mutual loneliness created an instant connection Billie was due to leave in a week. She was ready to start afresh. If she did go back to Adam, she would never escape her past. She needed to move on.

Billie was about to read the article again when there was a knock at the door. Her breathing stopped and she began to shake. The new door had not been knocked on since it had been fitted.

"Who is it?" she questioned in a shaky voice.

"It's Mum."

# Chapter Forty-Three

## Billie

B illie worried that she was dreaming. Her mother? It was her voice. Billie almost felt for her pulse because her heart seemed to have stopped. How had she found her? What was she doing here? She'd never made the effort to find her before. It had been nearly six years.

On unsteady legs, Billie walked towards the door. She didn't really want to open it; she couldn't help but be worried; she hoped that no one had died. She undid all six of the locks she'd had put on the door and opened it.

Her mother looked old. The wrinkles had invaded her face, burrowing into her youthful skin, making way for old age. Her hair was still the same dyed colour, but instead of the sophisticated work attire she'd always worn, she was in a pair of jeans and a jumper. She'd never seen her mother so underdressed, it made her even more uncomfortable; like a stranger had walked into the room.

The flat was never intended to have more than her in it and she gestured to the only chair in the room. As soon as her mum sat down, Bobby jumped up on her knee demanding some fuss. Billie gave him an evil look. Traitor.

Her mother stroked him absently and her eyes darted around, taking in the room. Billie was ashamed. When she had left home, she'd envisioned that if she were to ever see her mother again, she would be successful and rich. Not living in a dingy flat, barely more than a bedsit, with only one chair. She didn't know what to say. She sat on the floor next to the coffee table, and waited for her mother to explain why she was there. A few agonising minutes later, her mother spoke.

"I heard about what happened." Billie didn't respond. What should she say to that? It wasn't exactly surprising.

"I can't believe he did that to you. Watched you for all that time. I feel like it's all my fault, it's been so hard for me."

Here we go again, thought Billie. This was just like her mum, turning it around so it was all about her.

"The press have been hounding us for information," she continued. "Your sister has had to move out until the fuss dies down. She can't cope."

When Billie didn't reply, she gave her a sharp look.

"I don't suppose you care about your sister, or any of us for that matter. Then again, I should be used to that, it's been years since we last heard from you."

When she still didn't answer, her mum reached out and tucked a lock of Billie's hair behind her ears. It was one of the most annoying things she could have done. She used to do it all the time, despite the evil looks and loud protestations from Billie.

"Why did you abandon us, Billie?" questioned her mum in a gentler voice. This was it. This was the perfect opportunity for Billie to say all those things she wished she had been brave enough to say to her mum years ago. But what difference would it make? She had spent enough years with her to know her inside and out. Billie knew that she could have the best, well-researched, concrete argument against the things her mother had done wrong, but it still wouldn't be enough for her to acknowledge that she'd made a mistake. And she definitely wouldn't apologise. Her whole life, it had been her mum's way or the highway. She was the master of denial and she was clever. She knew how to manipulate Billie so she would end up apologising to her instead of the other way round.

She stared at her mum, and even as she imagined all the things she wanted to say how she had betrayed Billie, how she had shown signs of not believing Billie, how she twisted everything so it was about her, how her sister was the favourite she knew what her mum would say. She would deny it all and twist it around to make herself the victim. There would be no admission of guilt, no apology and no attempt to make amends. So what was the point? With this conclusion in mind, she felt she had achieved some sort of closure.

She had always thought that she needed to have it out with her mum; to wring out the apology she knew she deserved. But, it wasn't up to her to do this. Her mother was who she was, and it would be her loss if she couldn't make right what she had broken. For too long, Billie had lived her life in the shadows of other people, hiding away from the world, scared of what they might do. She would not be scared any more, and that began with her mother. She straightened her back and looked her mum in the eye.

"What are you doing here, Mum? What do you want?"

Her voice was calm and collected and she saw her mum's eyes widen in surprise at her tone. She was obviously expecting the meek and mild Billie of old. Well, this Billie had survived Eric's abuse and come out the other side. "Well, I thought this might be a good time to stop all this daftness of you ignoring us. It's silly and juvenile. We are your family, you can't just shut us out. I mean, I only found you because the newspapers printed that you were still in Worcester." Even though she was expecting this sort of reaction, a swirl of disappointment ran through her at the lack of sympathy and compassion in her mother's voice.

"I'm sorry, Mum, but I've no interest in reconnecting with my family. I've managed five years without you and I will be fine on my own. You don't care that much or you would have reached out before now. I know that you love me, and I love you as well, but I don't want to be around you. I can't forgive what you did. I can't go back to where all the memories are. I want a fresh start."

This was the first time she had ever stood up for herself. The old Billie was such a people-pleaser, but from now on she would make her own decisions even though it hurt to be so cold towards the woman who had given her life. She had to do this.

"What are you talking about, forgive me for what? I gave up my relationship with my mother for you. Yes, we reconnected for a bit, but after you left, I couldn't do it. I couldn't forgive her after all. It wasn't easy for me either, you know. All I've ever done is love you," cried her mum. Tears welled up in her eyes.

This was exactly what Billie was afraid of. She hated to see her mum cry and she knew that. She was trying to emotionally blackmail Billie, but it would not work. Billie was no one's puppet anymore.

"I don't want to talk about it, Mum. I'm sorry, but I think you should leave. I'll give you my forwarding address and number in case of emergencies, but that's it."

Her mum pulled back her shoulders and wiped the tears from her face. She must have seen that she was fighting a losing battle this time.

"Okay, if that's how you feel I'll leave you alone, I won't bother you again. I just thought you might have needed me, but I guess you've got Adam now."

"Adam?"

"Don't look at me like that, I do read. I saw the article he wrote to you. I think the whole world saw it," she scorned.

When Billie didn't respond, and instead blushed and looked sheepishly at the floor, her mum let out a gasp of shock.

"Billie, please tell me you went to see him after he wrote that?"

Billie shook her head, refusing to meet her eye. How had she gone from feeling so strong and in control to being berated like a small child? Her mum knelt on the floor, forcing Billie's head up so she was looking at her.

"Love, I'm going to give you one piece of advice before I leave. If you have ever listened to anything I've told you, you listen to this. I must have read that article twenty times, and each time I read it, the love Adam has for you became more evident. It screamed from each sentence. It takes a very special man to be able to open up like that, make himself vulnerable, and to the world, no less. I know what he did was wrong, but he saved your life. He was the star witness in putting that man in prison. Billie, we might not be getting along right now and be as close as I'd like, but no matter what has happened between us, I want you to be happy.

"Adam can make you happy, Billie. He put his own uncle behind bars. He isn't going to fall under his control again. His writing was so honest, he admitted what he had done. Doesn't that earn him your trust? He loves you, Billie. He loves you in a way that I have never been loved. You have been to hell and back and you deserve to be happy. Don't let that evil bastard take away a man who worships the ground you walk on. Just think, you'd be sticking two fingers up at him by letting yourself be happy. Please, Billie, go and see him. Go and be happy with the man you love. Please," said her mum tenderly.

With that, she kissed Billie on the cheek and stood up to leave. Just as she got to the door, her hand on the handle, she stopped. Without turning around, she spoke.

"It takes a very brave and strong person to admit when they have done something wrong. It takes an even stronger person to apologise. I've done things I'm not proud of," she took a deep breath. "I've let you down, I know that. I've never been able to say it, though. I'm sorry I didn't do the right thing. I love you, Billie, you are my baby girl and I let you down." Billie could hear the sadness and tears in her voice. This was a side of her mum she had never seen. "I should have protected you and I didn't, I was too scared and selfish. I hope one day you can forgive me, and I can have my baby back." She didn't look behind her as she left.

Billie lay down on the floor and sobbed. Bobby came over and she cried into his fur. She cried for the mum she had just seen. The one who cared for her and wanted her to be happy. Why couldn't she be that person all the time? It made her chest hurt. She had finally apologised. She had said everything Billie had been desperate to hear. She knew her mum wasn't a bad person, she was just a scared and stubborn one. She had missed her mum. Even though she was selfish and self-centred, she did love Billie. Deep down she knew she'd done the right thing. Maybe in time she would reconnect with her family, but at the moment she couldn't.

Although her mum loved her, and had made the first move, Billie knew she would not be able to have a fresh start if she stayed in contact right now. She needed to rebuild herself; to find out who she was when she was free from the control of other people.

Billie also cried for Adam. To hear her mum saying his name, begging her to go to him. It had planted a seed of hope in her heart. It was willing her to get up and go to him. But she was so scared. She didn't want to hurt anymore. She didn't want any more drama or upset. She just wanted a normal, happy life. Could Adam really give her that, as her mum believed?

# Chapter Forty-Four

## Adam

Adam answered the knock at his front door and a stranger walked straight into his flat. She appeared to be in her late fifties, with dyed brown hair. She was plainly dressed in blue jeans and a matching jumper, but she walked confidently into his kitchen, and turned to look at him. He knew who she was when he concentrated on her eyes and the shape of her nose. He had studied Billie enough times to recognise her face within her mother's.

"I'll get to the point, Adam. I'm Billie's mum and I need you to go over there now."

Adam was taken aback by her forthright manner. She was the opposite of Billie in every way; the way she held herself was confident and sure. Her voice held none of the sensitivity or compassion that Billie's did. He was prejudiced already because of everything Billie had unwittingly told him in hospital but this visit cemented his opinion of her. The way she'd walked in and expected him to do as she said and listen to what she wanted to say. He wondered if she knew that Billie was a better woman than she'd ever be, and that was why she treated her the way she did.

"Billie doesn't want me to go there," replied Adam quietly.

He had to force down the tirade that was longing to burst from him. He wanted to make her realise what she had done to Billie was despicable. She had known what his uncle was doing and she hadn't done anything about it. She'd let Billie resort to an overdose. He blamed her unequivocally for the fact that Billie might have died. She could have prevented it if she hadn't been so wrapped up in her own life.

"Look, I went to see her today. I talked to her about you I told her to come to you. To forgive you and be happy. I may not have treated her right, or always done the right thing, but I know my daughter and I want what's best for her. I could see the desperate longing in her eyes, just at the mention of your name, but she is petrified that you will hurt her. She won't let herself come to you. You need to go to her."

She walked over to Adam, who hadn't moved from the front door. She came right up to his face, a fierce look had transformed her features, and she was very intimidating.

"I read what you wrote. I've been in this world long enough to know the truth when I read it, so I know that you are what she needs. But, I swear to you, if you ever, ever hurt my little girl, I will come for you. And this time, you won't walk away with a small wound. You won't walk at all."

She moved away. The menacing look replaced with a cool, calm and collected one. She walked towards the door, then looked back and said, "Now, what are you waiting for? Go, be happy. Make *her* happy."

Billie's mum smiled, and Adam could see Billie in it. Maybe she wasn't as awful as he'd thought. After all, he knew better than anyone how easy it was to make a mistake.

The door to Billie's flat was open. She was lying on the floor; Bobby was draped over her. When he registered Adam's presence he walked off, looking at him as if to say: 'it's about time'.

He felt physical pain in his heart at the sight of her curled up on the floor, so small, enveloped in her sadness. She must have heard him enter but she didn't move. He wondered why she hadn't panicked, but then she spoke.

"I told you to leave me alone, Adam."

Ignoring her, he got down on the floor and wrapped his body around hers. He pulled her towards him and breathed in the smell of her. His whole body hummed with pleasure at how right it felt to hold her. His touch broke her defences as she turned over and wrapped her arms around him. He could feel the warmth of her tears through his shirt. He stroked her flaming-red hair and whispered all the things he'd been dying to say to her. She cried herself to sleep and eventually he felt her relax in his embrace. He gently lifted her into his arms. Walking over to her bed, he manoeuvred her so he could pull back the covers and put her in it. He tried not to wake her, but as he placed her down her vivid green eyes locked on his.

"Don't leave me," she pleaded, desperation evident in her quiet voice. He carefully moved her over and got into bed with her.

Pulling her head down, so she was lying on his chest, he answered, "Never, I'll never leave you."

# Epilogue

## Six Years Later

The guard has just delivered my breakfast. Normally I eat with the others but I've been put in solitary confinement as punishment for trashing my room and attacking my cellmate.

The other prisoners and the guards looked surprised when they found out I had pulled my bed off the wall and knocked out cold a thirty-six-year-old motorbike thug. I am old, but they don't seem to understand that I have to stay in shape. Strength is control.

They have taken the picture from me. The picture is the reason I am in here. I wasn't allowed to bring anything with me, but it doesn't matter because it's seared into my brain. It's a family photograph: a mother, a father and two children. They are smiling at the camera, they aren't even trying hard to be happy it exudes from every feature. The mother's love for her children transforms her. She is beautiful and radiant. Her arms are wrapped around the child in front of her, clutching her like a precious stone. The father fills the picture, using his large frame to touch every member of the family. Their protector and provider. He is looking at his wife with pure adoration. They are the epitome of the perfect family and it makes my blood boil. Anger courses through my body like poison. I can't escape the image. When I close my eyes, I see it. When I open my eyes, I see it.

I know why they have sent it to me. I didn't think Billie would have had the guts, but then I barely recognise her in the photograph; joy and love have evolved her into a new woman. I can no longer see the indicators of my control, of the damage I caused. She is a normal, happy woman. This has made me the angriest.

I put so much time and effort into shaping Billie, she was my most successful project. She lived for ten years under my control, whether I was there or not. Just the thought of me followed her around.

There is no sign of that fear in the picture Adam sent it. I am allowed to use the Internet now I've earned enough privileges. I saw Adam's article when I googled his name. I laughed my way through it. I was convinced there was no way Billie would go back to him; my power and hold over her wouldn't allow it. I taught her not to trust anyone, and now I know she has, that thought makes me want to smash things again. But, the bed is nailed down and I have no cellmate. I settle for hitting my head against the wall. The thud of my skull hitting the wall echoes around the empty cell. I won't have it; the pain is clearing my rage. A plan evolves as the blood trickles down the back of my neck. I have nothing but time ahead of me. I must put that time to good use. I will have my revenge.

Yes, I am stuck here until I die; but that doesn't mean I can't get to them. I have honed my skills of deceit and control. I just need to be patient and clever. Adam sent that photograph in a brazen attempt to show they have won and I have lost. But instead he has unleashed his own downfall. I will see to it that all he has is photographs of a happier time. They will be sorry. I'll make them pay. I'll put them both back on their puppet strings where they belong.

## The End

# Acknowledgements

Having this book published by Bloodhound Books is another amazing step on my writing journey and so there are new people to thank who have helped me achieve this dream. Obviously, my first and biggest thanks is to everyone at Bloodhound Books. You have all helped me make this book everything I hoped it could be. Betsy is incredibly supportive and amazing to work with. Everyone at Bloodhound has been incredible, I can't thank you all enough.

It has always been my dream to be traditionally published and there is one person who has been instrumental in that happening. She is an amazing lady with a huge heart and she is the epitome of selflessness. She is one of those people that doesn't realise how amazing she is. Joanne Robertson has only known me for a year and in that time, she has helped to completely change my life and has become one of the closest people to me. Her kindness, positivity and unwavering support have made it possible for my dreams to come true. I only hope I can do the same for her one day. She will always have a special place in my heart.

Another person that helped to make my dreams a reality is Alexina Golding. When I met Alexina, I had absolutely no idea how that one meeting was going to make my life so much better. She met a complete stranger and happily went out of her way to make that person's dream come true.

The 'world of books' as I like to call it has all the best and most supportive people, Kim Nash, Jen Lucas, Linda Hill, Anne Williams, Teresa Nikolic, Neats Wilson, Noelle Holten, Claire Knight, Ellie & Jo Smith and Emma Welton to name a few. You have warmed my heart with all you have done to help me and support me. There are many more book bloggers that I'd love to thank but I'd be writing another novel just with their names. Thank you to all of you who have helped me with my journey as a writer. I'd particularly like to raise a glass to Kim Nash and her book club ladies. The night I went to speak at their book club was the first night I felt like a real author. The confidence it gave me is unquantifiable, I will be forever grateful.

Like possibly every Mum at one stage or another, mine has worried that she hasn't been a good enough. But I'd like to thank you, Mum. Everything you have done has led to this moment. I'm sitting here writing acknowledgements to a book that I have written because of everything that you have done. You gave me my dreams and helped me achieve them. I love you more than anything.

My best friend is not a reader; I've failed each time I've recommended books to her. So, when I finished writing this book, I dismissed seeking her help, assuming she either wouldn't be able to or that she wouldn't even read it. How wrong was I? In fact, she has been instrumental in publishing this book. She has helped with everything and she is amazing at it too. She read it and gave me such confidence and belief in myself. If she hadn't, I'm not sure I would have published it. Elle, my soulmate, you are fantastic and I love you – thank you!

My final, and most important, acknowledgement goes to my husband. I was lucky enough to find the love of my life at twenty-one. Thank you, husband, for always being at my side. For picking me up at my lowest points and for your unshakable belief in me. The only reason I can write a book about love is because you have given me more love than I could ever deserve.

Made in the USA
Lexington, KY
20 September 2018